AFTER YESTERDAY

JADE RIVER SANCTUARY

SAVANNAH KADE

GRIFFYN INK

CHAPTER ONE

D evin James pushed through the coffee shop door, his dog Curie perfectly at his side. He hadn't been in here before, but the place came highly recommended by Ash.

That meant the coffee smelled just right, the sandwiches were great and the seating was outdoors under a pergola. It did not mean they would handle him well, but Devin was willing to try it. He wouldn't get much of anywhere in life if he didn't just jump in and try.

As he opened the door, all eyes turned and looked at him. With a guess, he glanced up and over his shoulder and spotted the little bell still swaying. Apparently, it made noise and he'd alerted the whole shop to his appearance.

They looked down at the dog but quickly spotted the bright yellow service vest and no one made any further issue. Devin headed toward the front counter and pulled one of the laminated menus from the holder. He motioned with a nod to the young woman behind the counter, patiently waiting to take his order. They weren't very busy midafternoon—something that he'd aimed for because it made these first visits go smoother.

When he figured out what he wanted, Devin turned the menu around and pointed to the item, showing it to the woman.

Her mouth moved, and he watched her lips. She seemed to say, "Do you want home guilt?"

"Home guilt" was absolutely *not* what she was asking about. But that's what his brain told him her lips said. Pointing to his ear, he then twisted his open hand back and forth and shook his head, indicating that he couldn't hear her.

She held up one finger for him to wait a minute—a sign he was beyond familiar with. She said something too, probably "Hold on a minute," but he couldn't be sure, because she turned away as she was saying it.

She disappeared through the door behind the counter, as though something would magically appear by her leaving. Devin watched the empty space for a moment before looking to the two other aproned clerks at the other end of the bar. Neither of them looked up and he wasn't willing to speak, not in front of people he didn't know.

Then one of the baristas looked up at him with a smile, touched her ear and turned away. She was handling the drive through. At least no one had yelled overly-enunciated words at him—not what you do to a Deaf person.

With his phone in hand, Devin began tapping out his order. Whatever she needed to ask, she could message back when she returned. He was still typing when a hand waved in front of his face—arm extended, the feminine fingers were together, palm down, motioning in several short bursts. He felt his eyes widen.

That was someone who knew sign or at least knew how to get a Deaf person's attention. Looking up with a smile, he watched her sign with long fingers in fluid motions. "What would you like to order?"

It was normal not to look at a signing person's hand but at their face. The words came in the periphery. Right now, *nothing* came in the periphery.

2

He knew that face.

From where? Why did she look so familiar? Had she come to the Sanctuary? Had he seen her at the hospital? He couldn't place it.

Blinking, Devin shook his head, then signed, "I'm sorry. Again, please?"

"You wanted to order the large Americano?" She was looking at him a little oddly, too, but it could be nothing.

Nodding, he tried to figure out where he knew her from. The signing population wasn't that big—but it was still bigger than most gave it credit for. Sometimes he recognized a person and they were from TV. But no one on TV would be working behind the counter at this coffee shop. So that didn't make sense.

"Do you want whole milk, skim milk, soy milk, or oat milk?"

Whole Milk! he thought. Not "home guilt."

"Whole milk," he signed back then ordered a sandwich to go with it. She finished the order, putting everything in. But then she tilted her head again, as if *she* recognized *him* from somewhere. It was the head tip that got him.

With his hand next to his face in an *L*, he pulled it wide for "Luisa." His eyes had to be as wide as his grin. He hadn't seen her since . . .

Her eyes grew big. Her mouth dropped open.

This was the girl who'd left school when they were in sixth grade, barely eleven years old. He'd showed up in third grade, the only Deaf kid in the public school. His interpreter had followed him everywhere and was the only person who could speak to him. Luisa had learned sign. She'd been the first student who could, or would, talk to him. They'd hit it off like a house on fire.

Then her cousin had learned some too. Gabi had never been as fluent as Luisa, but the three of them had hung out after

3

school, played pranks, dressed in costumes as a unit for Halloween and everything in between.

Then one day, they were gone.

Rumors were that one of the girls had died. Mrs. Montalvo —Gabi's mother, Luisa's aunt—had simply picked up one or both girls and left. People said she wasn't able to deal with the tragedy. No one had even told him goodbye.

Now he looked into her face, relief washing through him at having found her. How many years had it been?

She looked him up and down, surprise washing over her features, too, as her hand went to her shoulder in a D, asking if it was truly him. He watched as her mouth moved: *Devin? Devin James?*

She fingerspelled j-a-m-e-s and he almost flew over the counter in an effort to hug her but just managed to restrain himself. They'd barely been kids the last time he'd seen her. They were adults now. Still, his hands flew. "It's amazing to see you! I heard rumors but . . ."

She held her hand out, stopping him. "I'm not Luisa." She held her fingers in a G at her chin. "I'm *Gabi*."

Devin stopped dead. The girls had always looked a lot alike, but shouldn't he have recognized his best friend? She looked at him again. Her gaze pointed as she signed one more time, "Not Luisa, Gabi."

CHAPTER TWO

"Give me one minute?" Gabi signed, her heart pounding rapidly.

Devin James was here. He recognized her. She had thought from the moment she walked into the room that he sure looked a lot like the boy she had known through elementary and middle school.

Gabi told herself that she was just putting random pieces together: this man was blond with green eyes, and he was Deaf. But *no*, it was actually Devin.

She struggled to breathe normally. She'd had such a crush on him back in the day. Hell, it was more like a torch she'd carried for all these years when one thing after another had gone wrong.

She'd need more than just a moment to compose herself.

Stepping into her office she took off the apron that she donned when Becca came in and said, "There's a Deaf person at the counter. Can you help them?" That had seemed plenty normal, and she'd not been prepared. Putting a hand to her heart made her feel like Mama, but she did it anyway.

She'd been managing this shop for a year now and she

needed to get the hell back out front. No matter who walked in here, she had to be a good example. The employees were already working on his order—she had punched it in like the old pro barista that she was.

Pulling herself together as best she could, Gabi stepped back out front. She was a professional, she could do this.

"I'm sorry about that," she told him. He'd moved slightly further down the counter to wait. "I needed to hang up my apron."

"Oh, you're not the counter person?" he asked.

"No. I'm the manager." She offered it with a level of pride. Even though not everyone would think much of managing a coffee shop, she was proud. There were limits to what she could do without getting caught. This might be as far as she could go, so she was going to shine like the damn sun at her job. "What do you do?"

He was an adult now, surely he did something. He wasn't dressed as though he were homeless or just hanging out, though he wasn't in a business suit either. Maybe she should have been a little less direct, but it didn't seem to bother him. Devin seemed happy to catch up.

"I'm a grant writer."

"Anywhere specific?" Gabi couldn't make her hands stop. She wanted to be polite, but she also wanted to soak up every detail. She'd missed him so much.

"I just moved. I was with a big corporation. But I'm now working with a service dog training sanctuary."

Her lips pulled wide with a smile. "That sounds amazing."

"Why are you here?" he asked as her hands worked of their own accord. She was making herself an iced coffee with about fifteen extra shots. She needed her hands to answer him and thank goodness it stopped her somewhere around four.

"Here at the shop?" She'd considered asking if he would want company, but she didn't know if he was even going to stay.

Though she realized she'd been too stunned to ask him if his order was to go. "Wait," she asked if he needed his food bagged.

Instead, exactly as she'd hoped, he made a motion toward the outside where black iron chairs and pretty tables waited under a wooden canopy of vines. "I'm going to eat here. Can you join me? I would love to catch up."

Her nod was maybe too fast, too eager, but she couldn't help it. Somehow Devin James was standing in her store, on the other side of the country from where she'd left him decades ago without a word. He didn't seem to hate her, and he wanted to "catch up."

She wanted to tell him everything. *She would never be able to.*

Gabi told her employees what she was doing and asked him to wait a moment while she finished making her own coffee/caffeine bomb. Free coffee was one of the perks of the job. Then she grabbed his coffee as well when it came up and made her way around the end of the counter.

"Oh, your dog?" The superbly well-behaved dog had a service vest on.

He smiled and nodded. "Her name is Curie."

She didn't know if she was allowed to pet her, but her hands were full anyway. At the doorway she motioned for Devin to choose a table. The sandwich would get delivered to them. She was, after all, the manager. Becca and September would be happy to bring Devin's sandwich out to him and they wouldn't be able to get the gossip because they didn't know ASL—at least not enough to keep up.

Good.

Gabi sat down and set Devin's drink down in front of him as Curie placed herself by Devin's chair and laid down. She was anxious to hear what had happened in the intervening years and just as anxious about the questions he might ask her.

He smiled and asked again, "Why are you here?"

"It's a good job."

7

He laughed. "Sorry. I mean, why are you *here?*" He moved his hand in a sweep meaning a broader sense, and added, "In Virginia?"

At least he hadn't meant philosophically. Gabi wasn't sure she could answer that one. It was a heavy, heartbreaking story. Virginia had been a surprise to her, too. She'd known Devin in school in Texas.

"The company moved me here," she told him. That was something she could answer. "I worked the counter at the Austin store for two years. Then I was manager for six months. When they opened this one, they asked me to come here and start it."

"That's impressive," he commented.

Gabi didn't want to go any further with it. "Why are you in Virginia?"

"I went to Gallaudet for school," he told her with a grin. He knew she would remember that had always been his plan.

It was the only all Deaf university in the US. Taught entirely in sign, the school was in DC and offered a host of degrees. Devin had one.

Though she was jealous, she smiled. The twist in her heart was a happy one. "I'm glad you got to go. What degree did you get?"

"Information tech and public health."

She felt her eyes go wide, but she'd always known Devin would achieve what he wanted. What she hadn't known back then was how her life would change when her cousin died.

They were still talking even as his sandwich arrived, and Becca gave Gabi a single eyebrow raise as she set the plate down. Gabi tried for a professional smile that said the hot man sitting across from her was just an old friend, but his eyes were blazing, as glad to see her as she was him.

"It was amazing," he told her. "Everyone signed everywhere. Lots of the stores nearby had employees who were Deaf or at least signed. There's a pizza place that only hires Deaf people. I worked there for two summers during school."

"That sounds like exactly what you wanted."

"It was."

"Did you just stay in the area after you graduated?" Though this wasn't exactly the DC area, Charlottesville wasn't that far.

He shook his head, the fire in his eyes fading. "No, my mother got sick about four years after I graduated. We did a number of treatments, then got into an experimental trial in Bethesda."

That didn't sound good.

He continued, his hands as capable as always, talking and eating at the same time. "When the treatments ended, she decided to move somewhere close. She wanted a good view from her windows, so Charlottesville was it."

"Oh, no," Gabi commented. She'd lost her own mother just the year before. It was never easy, but she hoped he didn't have the tangle of feelings that she did. She remembered Ms. James, how the woman had always been so good to her and her cousin. "When did she . . . ?"

"Not yet," he said it with a sad smile and a shrug. "She's still hanging on."

How horrifying to know his mother was dying.

When her own mother died, she'd simply gotten a phone call that the woman she'd expected to meet for dinner on Saturday night was gone. It was honestly part of the reason that she'd moved out here, sight unseen, to open a new store for a company that she liked but didn't love.

It had been time to change her life.

If only she could actually figure out how to change it.

CHAPTER THREE

Devin's thoughts scattered and bounced as he drove up the long gravel driveway to Jade River Sanctuary. Perched at the top of the mountain, it offered spectacular views and a soothing, shaded drive, covered with full, green trees and flanked by the river. But he saw none of that now.

He'd never expected to see one of the Montalvo girls again.

Yet here he was. Gabi was in town, and he was almost surprised how excited he was to find her. They had traded phone numbers and promised to keep in touch and Devin wondered if the underlying reticence that he sensed in her was just his imagination.

As he crested the last hill, he spotted the front of the main building and thought of her. Parking the car, he let Curie out, grabbed his phone, and snapped a picture for Gabi before heading around the side and back to his cabin. The dog stayed right on his heels.

Devin checked the time, almost four. He didn't quite have enough time to change, but he was going to anyway. He jogged along the path and, though he didn't have time to even grab his things and change into good hiking boots, he stopped and snapped a picture of the row of matching kennels that Ash and Brandy had built.

He still had Curie's little wooden nametag from when his dog had been a trainee here. In fact, that was how Devin had found out about the Sanctuary. His mother had made him apply for a companion dog.

Curie had barely left the place and moved in with Devin in Vermont before they turned around and moved back in. Stopping again, he took a picture of his cabin, Curie pausing next to him. He thought about how it might look to Gabi. His was identifiable from the others by the row of hanging pansies on the front. His mother had planted them for him and sent them home with him the last time he'd visited. He needed to call her tonight, he reminded himself.

The weather was finally starting to warm up and he changed into lightweight ripstop pants, for actually working, not just sitting in the sun with a coffee. As soon as he got his boots laced up, he paused on the edge of the bed for a minute. The others would be gathering out in the courtyard. In fact, they were probably already there. But he still took a quick moment to line up the pictures and send them to Gabi with "This is where I work."

He hoped he hadn't sent them to some random number she'd rattled off. But there wasn't time to worry as he pushed out the door, Curie following along until Devin let her into the main room of the lodge where she could take a break and play with Shadow and Astra—Roz's dogs.

Stepping into place in the circle the group had made, he watched as their mouths stopped, and their hands started moving.

"We can start now." Roz, their fearless leader, looked at them one by one, her straight black hair swinging in a short bob. The streaks of pale silver highlighted as it moved. Her movements were a little stiff. "Now that we're all here we can talk about the next step."

Devin kept his eyes aimed at Roz and at Beck standing next to her, as the two of them announced what everyone already knew.

"Today is our last day with just one cohort—" Beck's hands flew smoothly through the motions and Devin appreciated it. The others were novices—with stiffer movements and the occasional missed word or tense. "Tomorrow we'll go to the shelter in Richmond." He spelled out the city. "We will be looking for dogs to become Hearing Ear Dogs. So let's run down the list again of what temperament we'll need and what tests they'll have to pass."

They discussed what the current dogs would need as well. The current four dogs were being trained to assist diabetic patients. They were learning to recognize various glucose levels and how and when to alert. They were being trained to sniff socks from various diabetic patients as well as basic service obedience.

"What kinds of interference can we predict," Beck was asking them, "As we bring in a new cohort of less trained dogs, and as we train the newer dogs for a different type of assistance?"

Devin appreciated that it wasn't a test. Beck was truly hoping for any last-minute thoughts or ideas. Even though they had already hammered out the plan, they'd all been tasked with imagining their way through it and finding trouble points.

Though Devin hadn't been here for round one, and he'd come in after the current round had been chosen from a different shelter, he was still included in the conversation. The team signed all the time when he was around, and they would also do that around the new batch of trainees.

He'd worked at home from a desk for his old job, securing grants for community programs and public health initiatives.

Now, he was only at the desk part time, having already made it to round two for a big grant that would fund this round of service dogs. He knew all the research and had written the grant technically but with passion. He'd always believed in the programs he worked for, but this was personal.

Given his newness, he didn't have much to add as this would be his first shelter visit. Curie had been the only Deaf assistant in the first round of training. Roz had chosen to do this next training with a cohort all immersed in one kind of training. She'd chosen to train the diabetic assistance dogs first, as they paid out the highest from the government funding. Devin suspected she'd chosen to do hearing dogs next because of him.

In his short time as her employee, Devin found out that Roz was a fierce and kind boss. Though she kept some cards close to the vest, Devin had figured out—from the grants she'd asked him to write—that the place wasn't fully in the black yet.

When they asked him how well Curie was trained, and what things he wished his companion was trained in that maybe they had missed, Devin hoped he did it right.

CHAPTER FOUR

Turning the key in the front door of the little house, Devin pushed it open. He knocked in the code he and his mother had set up—twice, then a pause, then twice again. He couldn't hear it, but his mother could.

Curie sat patiently beside him waiting until Devin motioned her forward. They'd been here together a number of times, but it spoke to Curie's solid training that she still waited. Devin always brought the dog to see his mom. His mother had been the one who'd first heard about the Sanctuary and insisted that Devin apply.

Given his income, he'd had to pay for part of it, though he hadn't told his mother that's how it had shaken out. The irony was not lost on him that he was now collecting a paycheck from that very same place.

His mother hadn't said the words, but he knew she wanted him to have the dog so that he would have a companion when she was gone. In his thirties now, he hadn't had a serious relationship in some time. Certainly, hadn't ever married and didn't have any grandkids for her. None loomed on the horizon either. They'd never said it, but he and his mother both knew it was due in large part to the fact that he'd spent much of his time taking care of her.

He'd stayed in school, getting his first degree at Gallaudet then heading out to George Washington for a masters in public health, which he'd done with an interpreter and only a handful around him who only passably spoke his language. He'd worked several jobs before settling in as a grant writer, having finally found the sweet spot—enough pay, enough reward, and enough free time—only to have her diagnosis pop up a year later. Devin had spent his forty hours each week working for a paycheck then operated another full-time job, driving her to and from doctor's appointments, therapies, and treatments.

She came around the corner now, eyes bright but skin pale. It seemed to him she moved a little slower than last time. But he'd been having those same thoughts off and on for eight years. Only now the doctors had basically cut off hope. Each time before when a treatment failed or reached the end of what it could do for her, there had been another option. There had always been a next step with hope . . . until now.

"Mom." He held his hand up to his chin and watched as she smiled.

She ran her fingers along the wall as she walked toward him. She'd been doing that for a while, just as a way of keeping herself oriented when her balance failed, as it was doing more and more frequently now. She lived alone—the way she wanted it—but they couldn't afford for her to fall.

That would be dangerous. Their solution had been constant vigilance and running her fingers along the wall. Looking at her now, he cataloged all the backup systems. She wore warm clothing because she was constantly getting cold. The slippers on her feet came up over her ankles and had non-skid soles. Her pants had big pockets for her cell phone and the phone had a rubber cord that she kept clipped onto her. This had been their life for the past handful of years—backup system after backup system, as her own body failed small piece by small piece. Devin could see now how it added up.

He pasted on a bright smile, trying not to let her see how his heart cracked at the knowledge that whatever time she had left was limited. His throat squeezed even as she settled herself at the table finally, having come around to the realization that she could just let him pour her tea, serve her food, and take care of her while he was here. She hadn't wanted him to move in. This was the compromise.

He pulled the pitcher out of the fridge and made her a tall glass of tea. She'd always loved it, but she'd taken up drinking it like a fiend since she first began chemo. He would get the usual plates of crackers and cheese. She wouldn't eat more than a few, but he would.

Though ASL wasn't her first language, she signed like a native. "Tell me about Gabi Montalvo."

"I was so surprised!" he signed back with one hand, the other reaching into the cupboard getting the food. He pulled jelly out of the fridge and a knife from the drawer.

"She recognized you?"

"I don't know if she did at first, but after a minute, yes." He set everything onto the table.

His mother diligently reached for her glass of tea first. A southern woman to her core, she drank her tea sweet enough to almost stand a spoon in. When he was a kid and had learned about basic health and diabetes in school he'd encouraged her to reduce her sugar. When he learned about the systemic damages of diabetes while getting his public health masters, he'd again urged her off it. But now it was sustenance, and he carefully monitored the level drops so he could pour her another glass.

"It was strange," he took a sip of his own ice water. "It took me a minute to recognize her too, and I could have sworn she was Luisa."

"Interesting," his mother motioned, one hand on the glass,

the other speaking to him, "though the two girls did always look a lot alike. It's been . . . ?"

"Just over twenty years." He'd figured it out after he'd seen Gabi the other day.

"Twenty years is a long time," his mother said, taking another sip of tea. Devin smiled. He'd thought the same thing and she pointed out the same conclusion he'd come to. "Neither of you had yet gone through puberty. So, it's a reasonable mistake."

He had to agree, but he wasn't prepared when she changed the subject.

"So the awful rumors we heard, were they true?" Before he could answer she asked another question. "And it was Luisa who died?"

CHAPTER FIVE

S he woke up in a cold sweat, the nightmare returning after a handful of good months. That wasn't a surprise though, given the events of the week.

The dream had haunted her for several decades. Along the way it had replaced several others that she'd had as a child. Tonight, they all flowed together—one tragedy into the next.

She dreamed of the officers that—to this day—she couldn't identify. She could still see them hauling her father away as they had tried to board the plane. She remembered how mad she was that he had complied with their requests. It was only later when she was older that she realized he had been buying time for her and her mother to escape.

She remembered landing in Miami and going through the checkpoints with her mother. Then flying to Houston and waiting for a father who would never arrive. And finally, her Tia welcoming them. Hugging her tightly, telling her everything would be okay.

Gabi had no idea if any of these memories were true, or real. If they were actual other memories that had been mashed together or simply things her brain had made up to fill in for the stories she had been told.

She had gone to Texas, where she'd attended elementary school. That was true. Gabi knew that. She'd had a cousin her own age.

The part of the dream that she knew was fact was Mama screaming and then yelling, *"Gabi, what did you do!?"*

Everything had changed that day.

They had buried her cousin in a rush, hiding from friends and family—even the one sister-in-law that had lived in the same apartment building. Exactly one week after her cousin died, they'd been in a new apartment in a new city. They'd landed on the north side of Austin and started over. But everything had been different.

The Montalvo girls, Mama had called them.

Gabi remembered how she wished that they could be like Lorelai and Rory on TV but there were no wealthy grandparents to pay for private school. There was no cute little house or friendly job that paid enough. There were no sexy boyfriends who owned their own business. No stability and, some months, no rent money.

Mama traded one job for another, each with extra hours, or under the table work or handsy bosses. That part—Gabi hadn't realized until she was much older—had been a problem. They stayed until the pain of leaving had been less than the pain of staying. But something always drove them out.

Sometimes they'd moved to other apartments and other schools when the job changed. Sometimes the job changed because they'd moved. Nothing had ever fully been explained to her. When she asked, she'd been hushed and told that she had everything now. But as she sat there in the dark of night, her hands twisted into the sheets, she took a deep breath.

She was fine. She was in the apartment that was the nicest

she'd ever lived in. The sheets on her bed matched for once in her life. She looked around the room—separate from the living room/kitchen area. Art that she had painted herself hung on the walls. She favored great splashes of bold color, which she liked to claim were a reference to her Latin heritage. But they were maybe more of a reference to a life that had been built for her on tragedy.

Sucking in a deep breath and trying to steady her nerves, Gabi reminded herself that this wasn't the first night she'd woken up. Though it was only one a.m. she still had to be up at four to open the shop.

Gabi prided herself on being a good manager and leading by example. Though she'd certainly paid dues, she never used that as an excuse to not do the work. Thus she would be the one unlocking the doors at five.

She desperately needed to get back to sleep, but it wouldn't happen without a little intervention. She padded her way out to the kitchen and poured herself a glass of whiskey, drinking it slowly while standing at the sink. This one little window looked out over the small, manufactured pond in the back. The moonlight reflected off the smooth surface of the water—no ducks tonight.

She was confident the apartment building had imported them as a selling point, but mostly they just pooped on the grass. When she'd first seen it, she thought it was whimsical. And that the stacked washer and dryer in the front hall closet were everything she could ever wish for.

She had more wishes now. And no way to achieve them.

Letting her tired eyes drift shut, she made her way back to the bed, grateful to be able to afford the place on her own. She crawled in, her mind still working even as she drifted away, unsure what her next steps should be.

She'd been told all along that all of this was a gift. A strange and wonderful opportunity that had been given to her and that she should make something of. She knew her mama had meant something more than a manager at a coffee shop. But she was petrified of being looked at too closely.

She could still hear Mama's scream. The words, "Gabi, what did you do?" would ring in her ears forever.

She was used to the haunting sound and the accusations.

She fell back asleep into happy teenage dreams in which Devin James was her boyfriend. He slung his arm around her shoulder in the high school hallways. In those dreams, the kisses had been perfunctory pecks and the romance had been mostly performative high school bullshit. Because that was all she had known at the time.

She'd known a hell of a lot more by the end of high school, much to Mama's dismay.

Then the dream morphed. Suddenly it wasn't her imagination but memory of the grown man he was now. Her woozy brain told her he slipped into bed beside her and slowly peeled her clothing.

CHAPTER SIX

B eck headed into the office, wondering how long he would be able to keep this up.

Roz sat at her desk like always, her gaze on the screen in front of her, her face too close, her eyes almost squinting.

He reached into the tiny fridge that held her favorite flavored seltzer—not the off brand she'd drunk for a while when she was afraid the place would fail—and his favorite soda. He grabbed one of each and held hers out to her. "Put your glasses on."

He didn't know when they had become this—talking to each other like they'd been married for fifty years. But he knew every curve of her face, the tilt of her eyes, the particular shade of hazel of her irises, and he told himself it meant nothing.

He could read her like a book. At least tonight she wasn't worried.

She pulled a bottle opener from the drawer before finally acknowledging his existence. They let the fizz of the drinks pop and pass before he said, "They're in for the night. I sat and waited until they settled down."

"Took longer than the last batch," she commented then took

a drink and looked like she hadn't realized she was thirsty. She still hadn't put the glasses on though. The glasses were sexy, but he never said that.

"Well, they were going into kennels near dogs they had only a short time to meet earlier." He'd done his best to integrate them, but daylight burned quicker than dog curiosity did.

They'd built the kennels in a line at one side of a fenced area, based on where the previous owners had their kennels. He knew Roz had planned to use the originals, but they'd been in bad shape. Beck was ultimately glad they'd been torn down, even if the expense had hurt. They'd been more like shelter cages. The beautiful little green and cream houses Brandy had designed looked more like a version of Snoopy's classic doghouse. They were raised, had a bed in each and a door in the back to access it easily.

She'd designed something wonderful, and Roz had outdone herself making it happen. It didn't make dogs not be dogs though. They had barked back and forth for a while. "It's okay, they're in now."

He paused. "How is the Sanctuary faring?"

She would know he meant money. There had been a moment when it looked like they wouldn't make it. When Roz's son had tried to buy the place out rather than bail them out. The thought still made Beck's gut and fists clench.

"Better. You got your check, right?"

He nodded. He'd sold his car to help keep the place afloat. He needed the Sanctuary as badly as she did. Seemed Ash Cooper had needed it, too. The one who had another life to fall back on —Brandy—had been the one who used her life savings to bail them out.

So Roz wasn't in debt to him anymore . . . but she was now in deeper debt to Brandy. Acceptable, but it kept her up late nights like this, squinting at her spreadsheets.

He polished off his soda and said, "Put your glasses on. Can I have the car keys?"

"It's after ten!" At least she put the glasses on. They shouldn't look sexy, but that didn't change anything for him.

"Yes." He wasn't going to elaborate. There were things she didn't know, and he wasn't ready to tell.

Taking his reticence in stride, Roz dug in her purse, producing the keys. She dropped them in his hand and, as he closed his fingers around them, he wondered how long he could get away with this.

When he'd sold the car, she'd promised use of her SUV to him. They all lived up here on the mountaintop, they needed to get down, but it wasn't like he needed a car to commute from the cabin path to the main lodge. Still, she'd paid him back, the deal was over. He was supposed to replace his car.

But every month he didn't have to pay for a car or insurance was another month he could put the money where he most needed it. It was another month he drove a nice, black SUV—the kind nicely-bred ladies like Roz had, not ex-cons like him. It was another month he looked good each time he showed up.

He stood up and said, "Thanks," as though him taking her keys and her nice car and driving down off the mountain after ten at night was perfectly natural. "I'll be back soon. Up and ready on time for morning."

He gave her no reason to doubt him.

"Is Ash or Devin going with you?" She looked as though it were a casual question. She might have pulled it off with someone else, but he saw underneath. She was curious—trying to figure him out.

He shook his head no as he stood up and decided to get out of the room before she asked anything else. Eventually she would figure it out. Or he would tell her.

He wondered what she would do when she knew.

CHAPTER SEVEN

Devin had called his mother via video chat the night before to check in. She'd talked excitedly about the neighbor who'd brought her a casserole.

He'd smiled and said, "That's wonderful," then listened to her describe how it was exactly what she liked. He didn't mention that the neighbor had asked what she could do to help. Or that he'd texted back and forth about what would be most useful. Certainly, taking some basic tasks off his mother's hands was in that category. She could eat the casserole for a handful of meals without much effort.

Devin spent the morning doing the things he'd been procrastinating on. First, he called the maid and set her up to clean his mother's house the following Thursday. His mother wouldn't let him set her up with a standing appointment, so he simply waited until he noticed that she was tempted to do the things herself. Then he would call and tell her Lydia was coming.

His mother loved Lydia. They chatted the whole time the woman worked, mostly because his mother followed her around and organized as Lydia cleaned. Devin hoped the light work was good for her and not over taxing.

Then he spent the morning going back and forth with her pharmacies, explaining once again that his mother was not a drug seeker. Her late stage cancer was why she needed morphine and oxycodone. He'd done this song and dance to get refills the month before and the month before that.

When he and Curie finally left the little cabin, he made sure he showed up at the lodge and headed into Roz's office to discuss the handful of grants he felt the Sanctuary could and should apply for. He didn't want it to appear that he'd spent his entire morning doing personal work—though Roz knew the situation. He was afraid as his mother got more frail, he'd have to move off the mountain, take sick days to care for her, and more. He didn't want to press his luck now.

But Roz only looked up at him with a smile, reviewed his list and then added other grants that she'd found. Three of them he explained to her he'd already crossed off the list because the Sanctuary didn't quite meet the requirements. The fourth he'd decided not to do because it was so widely sought after that the competition made the effort unlikely to pay out. But he added two more from her list and headed out to the main lobby.

There was a desk in the corner, and he often set up there as the alternative was to work in his tiny cabin. With Curie, Shadow and Astra hanging out in the room with him, he managed to get background research done for several of the applications.

The time passed and Roz was beside him, softly rapping her knuckles on the desk to get his attention. When he looked up, she told him, "You need an office."

"I won't be out here once the guests show up."

"I know but there are other rooms upstairs, empty." She formed each sign meticulously, using no slang and very careful diction. "You can choose one and we can move this desk up there."

Interesting, he thought, *his own office.*

"I'll go look tomorrow," he told her. "Thank you." His day was full, and he told himself that what he felt wasn't anticipation.

Leaving Curie in the lodge with Astra and Shadow, the two of them headed out to help train the incoming group—three of whom were younger. It was normal to train service dogs from a very young age. It helped ingrain the methods and the work. There were fewer bad habits to undo. Many service dogs even came from breeders as puppies.

But for training time purposes, they chose dogs between one and three years old. He'd also learned that, regardless of where they came from, a certain percent would flunk out. They just wouldn't be right for the job.

Roz also had a strict policy of rescuing. The Sanctuary was supposed to be exactly that, from all angles. For the people they helped and for the dogs, so some of the dogs were a little older. He had to admit that, so far, the work was very rewarding. And it let him stay close to his mother. A win-win.

He looked at the incoming cohort. Young dogs, only one day out of the gray, dank shelter. It was exactly like herding puppies.

It was difficult to get their attention—definitely something they would have to train in. He recognized Curie's deft focus as even more impressive after seeing it from this side. As he held his hand in form in front of his face, he tried to draw Austen's attention. She did not want to grant it.

These four were named after literary greats—Shelley and Austen were the girls, and Dante and Marquez were the boys. They were all young, and excited. It felt like a lot as Devin tried desperately to work with Austen just to get her to stop playing.

He was glad he hadn't brought Curie out to be un-trained by this rowdy crowd. Still, Beck assured them all it was fine. He watched as first Lynzee then Beck, and finally Brandy and Ash, saw his attempts to get the tiny dog's attention.

Instead of helping, they all mimicked *his* movements, realizing they were relying on sound and noises. Brandy asked him if he'd tried clapping. Devin did, and it worked . . . for a moment.

It was part of why he was here: just to consult on being Deaf.

When the training was over, he rounded up Curie and headed back to his cabin. He showered off the smell of playing with dogs in the open dirt and then left immediately. He was wired. First, he told himself he shouldn't go, then asked why not?

He'd been most tight with Luisa, but he and Gabi had always been friends. They clearly were now, too. Adult Devin very much liked Adult Gabi.

She had texted him in response to his pictures of the Sanctuary with a snapshot of her gray and cream apartment building with black trim.

"It's pretty," he'd messaged back.

"Sure. But generic," she replied. Then, "You win."

She'd made him laugh despite his heart breaking that Luisa was gone. He'd always suspected he'd lost one of them. He was on his way down the mountain now with a lightness in his heart that he'd not expected. She said to meet her at the park across from the coffee shop.

Sure enough, when he arrived, she was walking up to him with a coffee for her and one for him.

"What do I owe you?" he asked, thinking it was easier than saying *hello* with an awkward hug . . . or should it be something more?

"Nothing." She waved him off with one hand in a 'zero.' "That's why I asked earlier. If I make it for myself, it's on the house."

"Thank you." He grinned. Though his pay from the

Sanctuary was fine, it wasn't anything to write home about. A good portion of it came in the form of room and board. A lot of the rest of it went toward his mother's medications and whatever her insurance didn't cover. He paid for the maid, insisting that she let him. He covered repairs to the house, too. Some he could do himself on his days off, some he had to hire out. He managed fine, but there wasn't a lot left over.

One day—probably not too far off . . . he tried not to think about it—he would inherit the tiny house. When his mother passed, it would all come to him. Though it was only partially paid off, the rest should be more than enough to cover what he'd put in over the years.

It didn't matter though. His mother had given up everything for him. He would do whatever he could to make this last step of her journey easier.

So he thanked Gabi for taking one little thing off his shoulders, but now wasn't the time to dump all that on her. He wondered if they would get there or if they would just catch up, get whatever closure they each needed and move on.

"Do you want to take the path around the park? It's about a mile. I usually do it twice."

He looked down at Curie, always on his heels. He had a ball in his pocket so his puppy could run afterward. He'd thought the dog would be someone he worked with, and Curie was. But he hadn't been prepared for all the other benefits. Devin walked more. He talked more—often just to the dog, but it was more. The other night when he'd been sad about learning that Luisa had died at age eleven, it had been Curie who curled up next to him and put her head in Devin's lap as if she understood.

He would hang out with Gabi, then with Curie.

They headed down the wide paved path as she turned her head, then motioned him to step over just as a roller blader passed at a reasonably high speed. She asked about Curie and

29

more about his job. He asked about her apartment and the friends she had here.

"Mostly it's just this one friend who lives on the same floor as me. I've only been here for a year."

Shouldn't she have more friends by now? Then again, he was living with his coworkers. What did he know?

This time he pushed. "What's next? After you graduate from being the manager of the coffee shop?" He was expecting her to say *regional manager* or maybe that she wanted to open her own place. Maybe even that she'd saved enough and wanted to go to college because she hadn't mentioned it already. He remembered they had talked about it when they were kids.

So, he was surprised when she said, "There is no next."

CHAPTER EIGHT

*S*he shouldn't have said that.

Gabi brushed off his surprise by picking up her pace, as though getting ahead of him would mean he couldn't see. But Devin had always observed everything and that's what worried her. For a kid who couldn't hear, Devin had *seen* exceptionally well.

She wanted to get to know him, she was drawn to him—or drawn *back* to him, maybe. They clearly had unfinished business. While she wanted to know everything about him, he couldn't know about her. That was what worried her.

"No college?" he asked. "No promotion? You're so smart."

"Thank you," she replied, trying to pass it off as what she really wanted. "But I'm good here."

"Husband? Kids?" he pushed.

"No, just this. It's a good life." She smiled but she could see he wanted to ask. She tried to sidestep it. "Do you remember where I grew up?"

Devin and the Montalvo girls had both been raised by single mothers. Though Devin's mother—by the time Gabi had met him at least—had managed to rent a nice little condo with a little yard in the back, Mrs. Montalvo had not.

Maybe it was because she had two children to feed and look out for. Maybe it was because she was Hispanic, and people thought she was an easy target. Or maybe her lack of formal education. Gabi would never really know.

She sighed at the thought, finishing her coffee and dumping the cup in the nearest recycling bin. Watching as Devin did the same, she realized she'd freed her hands up for less stilted conversation. Maybe she shouldn't have. Then she wouldn't be able to blame her lack of answer on the coffee.

"It was fine," he protested.

"It was awful," she countered. "Lots of the units had multiple generations of families in one or two bedroom units. There was a murder. Do you remember that?"

Of course, he did. He grinned. The three of them had gone crawling around the apartment building trying to solve the case and outsmart the police. They'd checked behind the wall in the laundry room, ventured into the crawlspace, and gone out the window onto the roofing ledge. Now, when she looked back, it was all horrifyingly unsanitary and unsafe. They'd done it all carrying notepads where they'd written down clues.

"We did find that knife," Devin pointed out. It had been tossed out one of the other windows and gotten stuck at the edge of the roof in the decrepit excuse for a gutter. It was covered in blood, and it turned out it was not associated with the case they were trying to solve.

They had actually helped close a previous case, though. Which Devin pointed out and Gabi turned it around immediately. "That's my point! There was *another* murder in my building before I moved there."

"Your mother did the best she could."

"I know that." She did. Mama did everything she could. "But I look at my life now and I like it. I have a job that's good. My regional manager is a complete asshole, but he doesn't sexually harass me—"

"Did your mom get that?" Devin asked.

"When I was older, I learned that yes, apparently that happened all the time." Mrs. Montalvo was Hispanic. Smart and ambitious but without formal training she could point to, nothing in the US at least. She was a woman alone with two young children. "I think they thought she was easy pickings."

"She never turned them in?"

"Not that I know of." Gabi thought about it for the first time. Mrs. Montalvo never filed any formal complaints.

Gabi's heart felt crushed. Had that been because of *her*? She couldn't let Devin see that, so she pasted on a smile and added, "After we moved away—" That was the simplest, easiest way she could think of to say it, "—We moved a lot. Sometimes Mama just wanted to go to a new place. Sometimes she lost her job."

"That's terrible. She should have been able to have a good job." Devin looked concerned. She didn't want to say that things hadn't gotten any better after her cousin died. Mama was devastated, and she'd given up a lot. She'd made hard choices.

"She should have," Gabi agreed. Mama wasn't here anymore. That should have changed things. Only it hadn't.

She looked up to avoid hard thoughts. She tried to enjoy the trees in the pretty park that she got to see out the window from her job. That beat anything Mama had gotten. They were starting to bloom in the sun of midday, the spring finally starting to warm up. They might get another snow, but today it was nice.

"This is a good place. My job pays well. I have my own apartment—with my own bedroom!"

Devin grinned at her, obviously remembering that she and her cousin had shared the one bedroom while Mrs. Montalvo slept on the pullout couch.

She didn't want to dwell. There was no way to fix it now or

33

pay the woman back for all that she had done. "I have . . ." Gabi told Devin with a grin, "—a washer and dryer *inside* my apartment."

He'd not had that as a kid either. He looked over at her and motioned, "Fancy! I don't even have that now."

She tried to reason that. "Do you have to come down the mountain to wash your clothes?"

"No there are a few washers and dryers at the main lodge for guests, but also for staff."

"You have guests a lot?" It was better when she was asking about him.

"No. Only when we bring the dogs' people in to learn and work with them."

It took her a moment to realize he'd used that term before. The people who got the trained service dogs weren't "owners" but "their humans" or "their people."

"I stayed for almost two weeks when I was matched to Curie."

"It's very beautiful up there," she told him.

Devin looked as if maybe there was more that he wasn't saying, but she didn't call him on it. He asked, "Maybe you'd like to come visit me next time?"

So there would be a next time. Of course, there would. They were talking now like they always had. Despite her reluctance to share everything, it was still easy. *Too easy.*

It was so tempting to tell him everything.

Devin didn't wait for an answer. He simply said, "You should. It's beautiful. We have hiking trails."

They'd hiked sometimes on the weekend as kids. One of the mothers would drop them at a state park and pick them up at the end of the day. They had packed schoolbags full of old soda bottles they'd filled with tap water and cheap rice-crispy-like granola bars. They thought they owned the world back then.

Then he paused. "You didn't like hiking . . ."

Shit. "No, it's okay. I'm an adult now." She said it with another wide grin. "I would love to go."

He and Luisa had been the ones to hike, and she should remember that. Then, without warning, he asked her the question she had been braced for the whole time.

"Can I ask . . .? I hope it doesn't hurt too much to tell me, but I'd really like to know what happened to Luisa."

She owed him an answer. With a deep breath, Gabi steeled herself to tell the story in a way that she never had before.

CHAPTER NINE

Gabi could see that clearly, part of him didn't want to know. And the other part of him needed to understand.

That she understood. Devin had told her that, all these years, he'd wondered what really happened, and all he had were rumors. He'd not even known if it was true that one of the girls had died until she told him the other day.

He stopped and waited for her to turn around. Maybe sensing that she needed a minute. "I wondered if it was the kind of thing that just circulated through the kids and the parents at the school."

It had been a small community. The families didn't have the money to do things like take vacations and buy fancy cars, so they spent a lot of time with each other. And a lot of time talking about each other behind their backs.

"Luisa was the reason I even applied to Gallaudet. She always told me we'd go together." It was a chance to start the story . . .

Gabi remembered. She'd thought about going, but college was only a pipe dream, despite what Mama had told her. Then again . . . maybe now . . .

But Devin had asked, and given that she desperately wanted them to be real friends again and knowing that he deserved to hear what happened, she closed her eyes for a moment then said, "It's a hard story, but I'll do my best."

He'd held the memory close all those years, not knowing if he would ever see them again. Or if so, which one? He'd gone to Gallaudet, maybe even thinking he might run into Luisa there .. . She owed him this.

He tapped her on the shoulder, and she opened her eyes to see his words.

"If it's too hard, you don't have to tell me."

She shook her head. "It is too hard, but you should know."

There was something in his expression that let her know he was sad before she even started. No matter what she told him, Luisa was dead.

Gabi started with, "You know she would sneak out sometimes at night and meet you."

He nodded.

"I always wondered what you were doing."

He burst into a big grin and laughed, "We talked. We looked at stars. Mostly we were excited that we had escaped and not gotten caught. We were too young to realize there was something else we could be doing."

Gabi laughed with him. "She snuck out some other nights, too."

She watched as his head pulled back and only then realized maybe she shouldn't have said it that way. "It's not your fault! Luisa did what she wanted."

His laughter was gone, but it was a crappy story, so she kept going just to get it over with. "Mama slept out in the living room. We could go in and out the window as we pleased as long as we were quiet. If she knew, she never said anything." She sucked in a breath even though she was speaking with her hands.

With a quick glance around the park, she wondered if anyone was watching. She saw a few distant glances of curiosity, but no one looked as if they understood. "So, Luisa snuck out one night . . . in my favorite shirt. I'd been looking for it and when she came in through the window, I saw and I was so mad."

She could see the look on his face, but maybe it was better if she didn't. She turned and they started walking. The sunlight no longer felt warm, and she could see that he'd gone from worrying it was his fault to worrying that it was hers. Somehow all of it and none of it was correct.

"I yelled at her, and so while she was crawling in, she caught my shirt on the edge." Gabi motioned how it had snagged as Luisa had come through. They were old windows, none of it was safe, but they hadn't realized that at the time.

"Did she hurt herself coming back in?"

"No, that's what's so stupid. I was mad at her, and I yelled at her, but she didn't care." All of that was technically true, Gabi thought, it just wasn't *right*. But she continued so that he would have something to hold on to.

"She just pushed past me and into the bathroom and started taking off her makeup and undoing her hair. She put her head in the sink, washing out all the product and getting my favorite top wet! I went through her side of the closet and found *her* favorite shirt. And I put it on."

"In the middle of the night?" he asked almost incredulous.

"Yeah, I was so mad that I just yanked it on to see how she liked it. When she saw me, we started fighting again, and we woke mom." Devin kept pace with her, not needing to motion for her to go on, but waiting as if he knew the rest of the story would have to come out. She would have to finish telling it.

"We yelled louder. She shoved me, and I shoved her back, then Mama was yelling at us. I don't think Luisa meant to do it —I know I didn't—but we told on each other with our fight. So then Mama knew that we'd been sneaking out the window.

Mama was very mad about the fight and the lies and . . . all of it."

This was the hard part. It was painful no matter how she told it, and she could never tell it without guilt. "Luisa came at me. She was reaching for the shirt and trying to tear it off of me. She was so mad, even though it was her favorite, she was trying to destroy it. Like if she couldn't have it then no one could."

Gabi knew the way her eyes looked. She knew how hard it was to tell the story even if Devin didn't know that there was a whole other side to it—one that she hoped to never tell him.

"She shoved me into the wall, and I pushed at her, so hard. Then Mama grabbed her and pulled her off me . . . She stumbled backwards . . . She hit the table and the big new TV that we had just bought." Gabi watched as his eyes widened.

She could see he remembered that TV. Mama had stayed in a job that was good. She'd gotten promoted and gotten a raise and she bought what they thought of as a "huge TV," though it was secondhand. The girls hadn't cared. Devin had come over and watched movies with them several times.

Gabi steeled herself for the next part. "She stumbled back into it, and it tipped over on her. It broke. Maybe because her hair was wet, it was more conductive or something? I still don't know. But it killed her."

"Electrocuted?" He looked incredulous.

She understood. She and Mama had stood there over her cousin's body not believing it had really happened. Her mother had screamed out, "Gabi, what did you do?" but she'd never made an accusation again.

Mama had tried CPR. Gabi had called 9-1-1. The neighbor heard the commotion and knocked on the door, but it had been locked and they'd been too panicked to open it until the paramedics talked them through it.

By then, Mama had understood. She'd looked up and said, "This was not your fault. Here's what we're going to do . . ."

Gabi could still see and hear . . . and even smell all of it. How many nights had she woken up, unable to remember her dreams but confident that she'd watched her cousin die again and again?

Devin tapped her on the shoulder. She slowly opened her eyes knowing there was no response here that she wouldn't feel bad about.

"Oh, Gabi," he said, "I am so, so sorry. I shouldn't have asked."

He reached out and hugged her then. It felt so natural—so good—even though his arms were different from the last time he'd held her so many years ago. So were hers. *They* were different.

They'd been apart almost five times as long as they'd known each other. Yet somehow, they'd found each other and fallen back into the easy rhythm of being together. Even when the talking wasn't easy, he'd always been easy to tell her troubles to.

It was as if a lifetime had passed and not a day.

Only she was still lying to him.

CHAPTER TEN

Devin was already halfway down the mountain when the text came in. He knew better than to text and drive, but the words popped up on his phone and he couldn't help reading them.

He gripped the steering wheel tighter and looked for a spot to pull over.

There wasn't one, he knew. At best he could find a small portion of the shoulder that was wider and put his flashers on. Not being able to hear another car coming from around the curves didn't help, but the phone demanded a response.

— In the ER.

It was from his mother. He didn't even need to read the name on the message. Who else would be in the ER?

They'd managed to go a decent amount of time without an emergency visit. He'd been lulled into thinking she wouldn't need one, instead of realizing one had to be looming.

Luckily, he was already heading into town to meet Gabi. He'd been excited, his heart beating a little harder even as he told himself that it didn't matter. He didn't know if maybe she felt the same way about him. He shouldn't worry about that, he should be glad he'd found his friend after all these years, but he couldn't help the pleasure of the squeeze in his chest each time he thought of her.

Now that happy heart twisted, and his blood pounded. Fear was the main driver as he pulled over. He hit the button for the flashers. Devin knew he'd be in trouble if someone came around the curve too fast, but he quickly texted back — what happened?

Slapping the phone back up onto the dash, he threw the car into gear and drove faster down the mountain.

He'd done this before, so he catalogued everything. *Work?* Taken care of until tomorrow morning. *Curie?* At the lodge with Roz, Shadow and Astra. Roz had smiled knowingly, though he'd just said he was meeting a friend. She'd pushed him to stay out as late as he wanted. Curie would be fed and housed. *What else?*

His mother's text came back immediately. — I fell. Getting stitches. Don't worry.

The last part was stupid and pointless, he thought. *Of course* he was going to worry. He had so many questions. How many stitches? Where? Why had she fallen?

Frantically, looking for another turnout, he pulled over for a second time. Though he was aimed in the right direction, when he got to the bottom and close to town, he'd have to make a decision.

Needing to calm the fuck down, he reminded himself she was already at the ER. Someone was taking care of her. She wasn't messaging from her bathroom floor or worse. Five deep breaths later, he felt only marginally more sane and messaged back — the hospital or urgent care?

Because his mother didn't distinguish the two and they were in very different places.

— Urgent Care I guess. But don't worry.

Right. He was worried.

She was in a precarious state before she'd fallen. She was on a cocktail of medications, one of which could make her bleed out. Another could let her heart rate get too low if she wasn't monitoring it. And . . .

Stop. He shut down the wicked imaginings as best he could.

Devin didn't pull over again, but when he hit the bottom of the mountain, he turned right instead of left. Away from Gabi and another coffee date in the park when she got off her shift. Away from the thing he had been so excited for that he was now canceling on at the absolute last minute to head toward the thing he was so afraid of.

He was parked and slamming the car door behind him, not knowing if it actually shut or not. At the front desk of the urgent care center, he leaned over the desk, grateful there was no line to huff his way through. Sarah was there in her dark blue scrubs, and she looked up to see him. She flashed him three fingers—not an ASL 'three', but it got the job done—to say, *she's in room number three.*

That let him know that they'd been here too many times already. Him recognizing Sarah was one thing, Sarah recognizing him was worse. She didn't speak, just held up her fingers. But she didn't look worried or try to warn him about anything.

Still, he was through the big swinging door and pushing into the back, just trying not to be a complete dick by running headlong into someone.

When they moved his mother into the little house, they'd known that it would likely be for a couple of years at the absolute most. They had talked to her doctor and set up a plan, they'd made a list of when to go to the doctor, when to go to urgent care, and when she required an ER.

Devin had been the one to find this place. He'd dropped off a file on his mother before they'd even come the first time. He'd checked in with the staff, making sure that they could communicate with him if his mother wasn't able to. So many pieces he'd put into place, and more than once they'd played out.

They'd survived all her worst days so far. They would survive this too.

He opened the door to find her lying on the bed, her e-reader that he'd bought her in one hand. A piece of gauze was wrapped around the other hand showing a little bit of red having seeped through. Another, taped across her forehead, was thankfully clean. But the fact that it was there was telling.

She looked up as he came in, a chiding look on her face. "I told you not to worry," she signed, setting the tablet down.

"Why would I listen? Why would I agree?" he asked.

"It's nothing. Just a few stitches."

"In two different places. You hit your head."

She shrugged and signed "I'm fine."

Clearly, you're not. It was a phrase she had used on him more than once. Most notably, she'd said it when he was a teenager, slamming doors and telling her he was fine.

Funny how the situations had reversed.

"Why did you fall?" he asked. "If you're dizzy, you're supposed to go to the ER." Not urgent care. They had his list and he'd talked her through various situations. She knew when it was okay to come here.

She looked at him again. "Not dizzy. I tripped."

"What did you trip over?" She ran her fingers along the wall to stay upright. She had her house arranged to have seats available so she could stop at any point and rest.

His mother looked away. "It was stupid."

Devin waited her out.

"I ran into the end table, and I knocked the books off. That was at noon, right as I was going to go lay down for a nap." She napped most mornings, so that part wasn't concerning. But the fact that she had run into an end table—one that was in the exact same place that it had been since she'd moved in—was concerning.

"So I told myself," she went on, "that I would pick up the

books when I woke up. Only I came out to get a glass of tea and tripped over them."

Not horrifying. It didn't sound like memory loss. But it was definitely a reminder that things could go wrong at any point.

"How is your head?" he asked, knowing that chastising her would do no good.

She was about to tell him when her eyes darted to the side. Following her gaze, he turned to see the doctor come in. While he hadn't seen this doc before, Devin certainly recognized the nurse. She had some rudimentary sign skills, but she was slowly getting better. She finger spelled a lot, but he understood.

Devin sat patiently while they told him his mother would need eight stitches in the back of her hand and seven on her forehead. He waited while the doctor checked her again.

His mother's eyes tracked the little light on the pen, and she'd answered what year it was and told the story of how she tripped again. The doctor nodded. Devin hoped that was a good sign, but he didn't catch all of it to know if she was concussed or not.

There was some shuffling while the nurse went to get the suture tray.

In the cramped room alone again, his mother looked at him. Leaving the one damaged hand laying flat, she signed. "I thought you were going to meet Gabi."

Shit.

"I was," Devin said, trying to stay calm as his brain railed— again. He'd meant to message her as soon as he pulled into the lot, but he'd been frantic and completely forgot.

Pulling out his phone now he started messaging, catching the movement of his mother's hand in the periphery. He looked up.

"Don't cancel. That would be stupid."

"Thanks for that sage advice." The sarcasm came cleanly. Interesting, the relationships they'd had when he was little had turned into adult ones. Sarcasm had been a force she'd always wielded. He learned from the best.

"You should see her. I know she'd like to see you again."

She tried again. "You don't need to be here."

He ignored that. He still didn't know how severe this was. "How did you even get here?"

He still hadn't finished his message to Gabi.

"I used that driver app you told me about."

Lovely. But this time he kept the sarcasm to himself. Not that she should have waited for him to come get her. Honestly, she'd been right: She didn't need an ambulance and she was smart not to drive herself. Could she still?

The day was coming when the answer would definitely be *no.* They were lucky they'd made it this far.

He tapped out his message to Gabi, finishing up with an explanation of why he had stood her up.

— Oh no.

Gabi's text came back almost immediately, and he could picture her sitting on the bench where they'd met, two cups of coffee in her hands. *Damn.* He wanted to be there. He wanted his mother not to need stitches.

— Is she going to be okay?

CHAPTER ELEVEN

D evin's heart was breaking but there was nowhere for it to break into. No chance to fall apart and let it all put itself back together on its own.

He'd left his mother at her house, safely tucked into bed with only a little more than her usual pain meds. That was good.

She wasn't concussed. That was good.

But she'd tripped and fallen and hit her head in her own home. There was no way to spin that to make it okay. The fallen books were a hazard. His mother couldn't just reach down and put them back. She moved slowly and in short bursts. And when she didn't see something, she couldn't just pull her foot back or even reach out and brace her fall. Her arms weren't strong enough.

The disease was a bitch.

She'd kicked him out. Telling him she needed to rest by herself.

He'd seen her into bed before reluctantly getting in the car and driving. Devin only made it a block before stopping, trying not to think about how she'd once again refused his offer to move in, or even just to stay overnight.

"We're not there yet," she'd told him.

Maybe she was right. But it was the first time she'd said *yet*.

Sitting on the side of the road, his hands on the steering wheel, his muscles shaking just a little, Devin realized he'd done an excellent job of feeding his mother, but not himself. He wasn't about to cry because his mother had said "yet," it was just low blood sugar. Surely.

He looked at the phone and hit the video button before he realized what he was doing. The screen popped up bright in the darkness that had settled while he fed his mother and medicated her and checked the house for potential hazards.

Gabi's hair was pulled up into some sort of sloppy ponytail-bun arrangement. She clearly had on an old sweatshirt, the wide neck hanging down one shoulder. He couldn't see, but he suspected there were pajama pants. He felt the tightness in his chest untwist just a little.

For the first time he realized it was going on nine o'clock. His hands flew. "God, I'm so sorry. I'm calling too late after I already stood you up today."

She laughed at him. "You didn't stand me up," she signed back, her hands slightly passing the edges of the screen. But he understood. She reached out to set down some drink in the mug she'd cradled. "You had a genuine emergency. And you messaged me to let me know why."

"Thank you for being understanding."

He wanted to talk, to let it all pour out—he and Luisa had always been that way, and now he felt that same ease of sharing with Gabi. But he didn't know what to say.

She understood. "Do you want to come over?"

It took a moment to realize he could. Curie was fine. He'd checked in with Roz who even sent a picture of the three dogs all sleeping on one bed like dumbasses. That, at least, had made him smile today.

Gabi lived in town, so he couldn't be that far away. He'd

barely made it out of his mother's neighborhood. He'd driven away in case she'd climbed out of bed and was watching to make sure he left. He was more shaken than he wanted to admit.

He hated these things that reminded him his time was limited. Very limited.

"I would like that." He needed it.

"I'll send you my address. We can order a pizza. You look like you need food."

How did he look like he needed food? he wondered, but she was right. Even as he thanked her, he hung up and plugged the address in.

He needed a friend.

He'd had friends. After the Montalvos had left town so abruptly, he'd been heartbroken. That was when he learned what depression felt like. No one at the school could communicate with him like Luisa. Gabi and a few others knew enough to handle the basics, and there was the interpreter, but she was an adult—a professional who just left at the end of each day.

Luisa had talked to him long enough that she'd absorbed *his* language. Eventually, she'd fabricated a few signs of her own, too. She'd learned to describe the thing she wanted or felt or saw, not fingerspelling the English for it. The Montalvos leaving had made it very clear to his mother how cut off he'd been.

She'd soon moved them closer to the state school for the Deaf. But that meant a new job for her, and new house for them —slightly smaller. But she'd given him a whole world of people who could *talk*.

Devin didn't know it until later, but she'd gained a support system of other parents, too. Hearing parents who'd learned because of their children, and Deaf families who helped absorb him into a culture all its own.

But now? This felt like getting thrown back to the good days of junior high, when his world revolved around school and the

Montalvo girls. Maybe they could just watch a movie, like the three of them used to do, though he shuddered now at the thought of the times they'd watched movies on that TV, only to discover that it had been the culprit—the thing that had brought everything crashing down.

As he put his hands back on the steering wheel, he saw that they shook a little less. Good thing Gabi wasn't that far away. He was pulling into the complex and reading the letters on the sides of the buildings before he realized he'd made the drive. He needed to get his head on straight and figure out which staircase to go up.

The place was relatively new and generically pretty on the outside. But the stairwells were metal and cement, utilitarian only. He stood outside her door—black with a white frame, just like all the others—distinguishable only by the number on it. He knocked with no clue how loud he was, until she opened the door, a soft sad smile on her face.

He saw the same sweatshirt from the call, though this time a bra strap peeked over one shoulder. Fair enough. She had invited someone to her place, and it was his first time in her home, but he'd been right about the pajama pants.

"I ordered pizza," she told him, not even saying what kind. Extra pepperoni. No peppers or onions. He just knew that she was banking on him eating the same thing he had when he was eleven.

"It's probably another twenty minutes. Come in." She turned away then signed over her shoulder like a pro. He would have to ask her where she learned. "What do you want to drink?"

He sucked in a breath wondering if he could make a request. She opened the fridge, bending over and flashing the slip of skin at the base of her back before turning and looking at him. She squinted a little as if seeing his need. "I can do Jack and Coke. Gin and Tonic." She seemed to think for a minute then looked back into the fridge. "I have a few hard lemonades but no beer."

They hadn't even been of sneaking-a-drink age when she left. She wouldn't know this one. "Jack and Coke would be wonderful."

He smiled when he saw her pull down two glasses. She filled them and handed one over, clinking hers against his. "Tell me, is she going to be okay?"

CHAPTER TWELVE

Gabi listened as Devin told her about the trip to the ER—no, it was urgent care. The distinction was important apparently. He'd had two Jack and Cokes by the time he set down the crust on his fourth slice. Gabi almost smiled. She remembered he'd never been one for eating the crust. He finally started to really talk.

"She said *yet*."

Gabi nodded, understanding what that meant. It was an admission that the end was close, closer than Devin was willing to admit. Ms. James was pushing the topic with him. "She hadn't said it before?"

"We talked about treatments, we talked about hospice and how she wants it done." His hands moved softly and slowly, the words coming out like molasses. "But there were no dates. It was the way you and I would talk about what we want in our wills. At no point has my mother admitted that this would be over and that she would die." He paused for a long moment before adding, "soon."

"There are no other medicines or treatments?"

He shook his head. "We've tried them all. Some worked for a

while. Her first surgery seemed to get it all, then she did radiation. But a year later, when we were hoping for remission, there was a blip on the scan. So we monitored that for another year, then it started growing, then chemo . . ."

The list was so long, Gabi thought. *What the two of them had been through!* They were each other's only immediate family. She knew what that was like, being tied so closely to one person.

Somehow, Devin became even more somber. "In the end, they all failed or quit or weren't worth the cost."

"Money?" she asked.

"We maxed out her insurance each year, so no. It was about time, side effects."

Gabi could understand that. She had no idea how she would fight or not if it were her. Ms. James seemed to have moved into the tiny house and be doing reasonably well. But knowing it would likely be the last place she lived could not be an easy time for either of them. "You said she was diagnosed after you graduated?"

"Almost four years after."

Gabi was trying to calculate the time. "How long has that been?"

"I was in school for six years." She tried not to react. He had more than just the degree he'd mentioned the other day. "I took a gap year after high school. Got a job. Tried to decide if the money for college and the time was worth it." He calculated for a moment as if he hadn't counted it before. "We've been at this for almost nine years."

She tried to fight the need to react, to let her head pull back, to keep her eyes from snapping wide in surprise. That was *so long.* It had to be killing him almost as much as it was killing his mother. But Gabi didn't say that. Instead, she said, "You're a very good son. I can see that you're taking excellent care of her."

"I'm trying," he said, "but there's only so much that can be done. And I owe her everything."

Another sentiment Gabi understood. She owed Mama her entire life—a life that had been carved out and handed to her from great tragedy and at Mama's own expense. As well as some of hers. Gabi had been thankful and angry for years, not able to stay to one side of it and trying to hold both. Since Mama had died, she'd given them both a little grace. They'd made the best decisions they could with what was in front of them.

"Tell me about her," Gabi prompted him. As kids, they'd both understood that they were the children of single mothers. But how much of her memory was correct, Gabi wondered. "She went to college, right? As an accountant?"

That was what she'd always believed when she was eight and ten and eleven. But what did kids know?

He launched into a story. "She got pregnant with me when she was sixteen and had me when she was seventeen."

"And your father?"

"He was married. I have his blond hair." That matched her memory, Gabi thought.

"She put his full name on my birth certificate so I could find him if I ever felt the need, but that's it." He took another big swallow of the drink, almost to the bottom. Again.

"Do you feel the need?" she asked. She'd been down that road of wondering what had happened to her own father. Though her circumstances had been so very different.

"I don't know. She told him she was pregnant and he called her a liar, said they'd never been together and never spoke to her again." This time he emptied the tumbler but held onto it, cradling the glass as if that gave him the comfort to speak freely.

Gabi didn't say it, but she wanted to add, *That's how she tells it.* Because she knew better than most there were at least two sides to every story and often three or four. Everyone told their side at least a little bit, if not a lot, differently.

"I remember she raised you by herself." She picked up her

own glass only to find it was empty, too. "Do you want another one?"

"Yes, please."

Maybe having Jack and Coke as their drink with pizza had left them guzzling alcohol for thirst, but it was too late for bottled waters now. She felt a small sway as she headed into the kitchen and pulled the Coke back out of the fridge. The conversation had stalled since she couldn't call over her shoulder or talk while her hands were busy and she was almost in a different room. The kitchen had a single wall and a little pass-through bar, so she could see him, but she was looking at her hands, making sure she didn't spill.

Gabi came and sat back down, handing him the glass. She'd waited tables for long enough that she had both glasses balanced on one palm and the bottles by the neck in the other hand. Might as well finish them off. "I didn't realize she was that young."

Devin took the drink and signed with one hand, the movements a little more fluid than maybe they should be. "They kicked her out of high school for it. She had to go to night classes with the adults to get a GED. Her dad kicked her out of the house when she started showing. She got a shitty little apartment and a fast food job until she didn't fit behind the counter anymore. Then she learned how to file for disability."

"Wow," Gabi commented, taking another big slug of the Jack and Coke. If there was one thing she'd learned, working in a coffee shop all these years, it was that good drinks and good food were better than she'd ever given them credit for.

She could have saved money by eating like Mama had fed them: Ramen noodles, box macaroni, microwave hot dogs. Sometimes, when she was sad or angry at the world, she would still peel a slice of cheese and eat it standing over the counter. It was comfort. It brought the past and her cousin back. It put her in a world where she didn't have responsibilities yet. One where she understood she'd been dealt a bad hand, but not that it was hers to play the best she could.

Yet she didn't recall the kinds of things Devin was talking about. Not what Ms. James had gone through. "I thought she had a college degree. She's an accountant."

"Right." Devin grinned, almost like a proud parent. "She got her GED. Since she was only a junior, that actually had her graduating almost a year early. She applied for college, managed to get a scholarship, and got into married student housing because of me."

Gabi laughed the same way he did. She'd seen pictures of baby Devin, and she laughed at him living in a dorm for the first few years of his life. Reaching down to the small glass coffee table—another purchase of which she was proud—she motioned with the bottle of Jack and topped off their half empty glasses. She should have put more Coke in, but she could tell she was already making slightly altered decisions. "She did all of that with a newborn!"

"A newborn that she quickly found out couldn't hear."

He tossed a lot of the drink back, and when he tipped his head up, he was grinning again like a proud parent. "And then, at not even eighteen years old, she wound up telling all the doctors to go to hell."

CHAPTER THIRTEEN

She woke up the next morning, her head pounding and her lips wet. Gabi took a few deep, dry breaths, but none of it got any better. Her pulse pounded in the back of her skull, once, twice . . . then she remembered Devin was asleep on her couch.

What had they done?

She panicked, noting how late it was. Had she missed her shift? She *never* did that. They would be worried about her. She started to roll out of bed before she realized she didn't have work today. That was why she had been sitting on the couch, somehow still contemplating what to have for dinner and what movie to watch, when Devin called.

She'd initially planned to ask Devin to have dinner with her . . . not as bold a move as she would like, but a step she was willing to take. Then he'd not showed, and she'd worried about him. Later when she'd gotten his message, she'd been worried about Ms. James.

Instead, she'd come home, stared at the walls and failed to decide anything. It had worked out because she'd wound up eating pizza with Devin—just like old times—while they ignored the movie they'd picked and just talked . . . and drank. That part was new.

So was the rest of it . . .

Gabi blinked slowly now, listening for movement from the living room. Was he still here? Had he slept as hard as she had? Because it was difficult to move these heavy limbs and more difficult still to admit what they'd done.

She'd always known that Devin admired his mother. Sure, he'd been a typical tween boy in some respects, and he'd snuck out of his house. But he'd made the girls go back with him and teach him how to get in and out quietly so that his mother wouldn't wake up. Not as much because she would catch him, but because she would lose sleep, and worry about him. He didn't want his escapades to affect her job. Such a dichotomy he'd been back then. Somehow, he still was.

He'd grown into a son—a man—who was purely grateful and extremely dedicated. Gabi blinked, looking away from the spot on the ceiling, a tear leaking out of her eye. She had never reached that stage with Mama. Never had been able to get through the anger and the ramifications of the hard decisions.

She'd never yelled back, never said how mad she was about those choices. But she'd been a part of it, and until she was older and looked back with a different perspective, she hadn't been able to forgive either of them.

Still, she wished she could have that conversation, maybe find some peace in it. Because, yes, she had agreed to it, but she'd been eleven, then twelve then fifteen . . . honestly, still just a kid. A child really, broken by the death of her cousin—a child whose nightmares had never stopped. A girl whose Mama had told her these decisions would make her life better.

And they had. But had they been worth it? They had cost so much.

Taking a deep breath, Gabi reminded herself that Mama was gone, and all decisions were hers. All failures were hers, too. She took a deep breath and put it all aside. Anything that might have mattered didn't matter now.

She could destroy Mama's memory and save herself. But Mama wasn't here to fight it, to defend herself or pay for the mistakes. Or Gabi could stay as she was on the same path. She'd been in Charlottesville for a year. She was making a great success out of her store.

Devin was right. If she didn't fuck something up soon, they might very well promote her. That would mean going into regional business, probably at least managing several stores.

That would get her looked at far too closely.

Finding Devin had surprised her. Then she'd been so excited to discover she still liked him as much as she ever had. It seemed he'd brought a shift with him, pushing something into her life, reminding her of the things she'd wanted before. Even though, "before" was when she was eleven. "Before" was so long ago and built on such childish hopes and dreams. Things she'd fully believed before everything had gotten worse.

Still, her dreams weren't stupid. When she thought of them now—*college, maybe owning her own business*— her heart ached for at least the possibility to fail on her own.

But there was another possible failure to deal with right now, or very soon.

She had kissed him.

Or had he kissed her? Had they simply slowly moved toward each other, hearts and mouths aching, his lips soft but demanding . . . had he wanted it as badly as she had? Or had he simply needed the comfort?

She could feel the memories of it pouring through her system like wine. Leeching into every inch, making her feel heady and light. His mouth had been needy, and it had felt so good to be needed.

Had she ever been needed? Had she ever been wanted by someone that she admired? Because there had been men, and sex, and even relationships, but nothing had ever lit her up like a simple kiss from Devin James. Nothing had ever flared like a bonfire, like kindling catching and setting fire to the deepest, densest parts of her. The old wood whose rings had been forged in childhood—a childhood formed by the very man kissing her.

She remembered the kiss, the trace of his fingers along her jaw. She'd not known he would touch her like he was talking to her. Or that she would be able to understand it. And when she thought about it, she wondered what her life would have been like without Devin James in it. And it would never have been as good.

The sweep of his tongue against hers felt as if he were ushering in a new era. Devin had always felt like that—like hope that the world would be better. And she had left him.

Now . . . she sighed. She was reading so much into a kiss that other men had taught her was simply a touching of mouths, a step toward the finish line of their orgasm and maybe hers. They'd been drinking. Who even knew what it meant! If anything.

Had she destroyed her blooming friendship with a man she felt like she'd known forever?

Or did he even remember the moment like she did?

CHAPTER FOURTEEN

Beck walked away from the training area. He was leaving eight dogs with four trainers, and he felt relatively comfortable with that. The area was fenced and the worst that could happen should be that the whole thing went off the rails.

Devin had showed up looking a little rough around the edges and Beck thought he'd heard the grant writer come in early this morning rather than last night. It was only because of the way the Sanctuary worked that he even knew that about his coworkers, and he tried to ignore it. It wasn't his business. But he had watched Devin a little closely as he worked with each command.

Devin was the least trained of the trainers, and Beck figured that was a good enough excuse for extra monitoring. Also, Devin had the most real-world experience with the dogs—not only with a hearing ear dog, but one trained at the Sanctuary. Still, he didn't seem quite on his A-game today.

Roz hadn't come out for this morning's training, either, and Beck admitted he was a little curious about that. He left the four behind him and headed into the main lodge. He wasn't surprised to find her behind her desk, intently gazing at the screen.

She looked up at him, having maybe even heard him clomping down the hallway. He wasn't a quiet man. Prison had taught him to take up space and he still did it a bit, even if it wasn't necessary here.

"How's it going?" she asked as though she didn't expect trouble.

"I left them outside with the dogs for a while." Beck fought the urge to peek out her window and check on the proceedings.

"Devin looked a little green in the gills, didn't he?"

So she'd caught that despite not being outside. Then again, he'd seen Curie in the main lodge, so maybe she'd seen the newest hire when he dropped his companion animal off . . . or maybe Devin hadn't even picked up the dog after dropping her off last night. "Hey, ummm . . ."

Roz looked at him again. "Do you need the keys this evening?"

How did she do that? "Yes. I have an errand to run."

"Okay." For whatever reason, he always expected her to ask where he was going or why he needed her car. She never did. She'd agreed to this arrangement, and she didn't question it.

Had he not sensed a little frisson of something between them, he would have thought she didn't care. Sometimes he stayed out overnight. But she didn't seem to let it faze her. Maybe he wanted it to.

He was opening his mouth when she once again filled in the spaces with exactly what he was going to ask.

"You want to hire another trainer."

"Okay—"

"And you think we can't afford it, even though we interviewed some."

Whatever he might think about anything else, Roz was on her A-game. Maybe she had been the whole time, despite what had happened at the Sanctuary over the last handful of months. Maybe it hadn't been as bad as it seemed, and it was merely the standard aches and pains of starting a new business—in particular the kind that didn't see *any* income for the first six months.

"Don't worry," she said.

But that made him worry.

"Devin's earning his keep grant writing." She motioned him over behind the desk and pointed to an email she'd received. "We got one. Well, *he* got one."

It wasn't huge as grants went, but . . . "That's good."

"Faster than I expected him to land anything." She smiled up at Beck and he nodded.

He knew Roz had applied for grants to open the Sanctuary in the first place. But he had no idea how the system worked, when to expect results, or when to suggest that they weren't getting any and needed to try something different. However it worked, success was good.

Since Roz said she didn't have Devin's skills with grant writing, Beck was willing to grant the success to the new kid.

But then she clicked around and said, "Look at this," pulling up another email.

He leaned over, catching the whiff of shampoo. No . . . that was perfume.

Not for him. Someone raised like Roz probably wore expensive perfume to visit friends or go to the store. Still, he tried to concentrate on the email thanking her for the offer and formally accepting the position. "You've already hired someone."

"You picked the top three candidates, and I chose from there. You approved her."

True, he thought. Though he couldn't remember now what he'd said or why. He often lost snippets of things he should remember when he was around Roz. He would remember that perfume though. "Which one did you go with?"

"Su," she said, then added "Abbott," when he didn't perk up.

He nodded along until Roz pulled up the application and the screenshot she'd snapped from the online interview. He remembered the woman's face and remembered that all the top three were certainly adequate candidates. "Qualified" was always an issue at the Sanctuary.

Roz had built the business on saving strays—carefully chosen dogs that they could train to be service dogs, thus saving their lives. She'd first brought in a veterinarian with more than one sketchy business in his past, though none of them had been businesses he'd run.

"She was the one in medical data, right?" Her current job was running figures on maternal mortality from various locations. When she interviewed, she told them the work was getting to her. As for her qualifications, she had no formal training. She'd had a few family dogs as a child and a friend who trained show dogs that she helped with. Nothing specific to this position.

Looking at the application again and at Roz's pleased face for having picked this one, Beck was beginning to think the dogs weren't the only strays at the Sanctuary.

Then again, who was he to talk? While he actually had a serious background in dog training, most people would never hire him because of where he'd acquired it. But Roz had. He asked, "When does she get here?"

"She gave two weeks notice. She'll arrive three Wednesdays from now." Roz leaned over, looking at the large paper desktop calendar, and put her finger on the date of the month. Grabbing a colored pen, she wrote in Su Abbott's arrival.

For Beck, the two and a half weeks wouldn't go fast enough. They needed more hands. He thanked her and headed back out into the yard as the day grew long, training the dogs, putting them through various paces.

After lunch, the six of them—Roz included this time—went on a four-mile hike with all eight dogs. That was crazy, but he'd expected no less. They fed the dogs, and he showered before going back to Roz for the keys, hating to ask, but knowing that the situation was one he couldn't change for the better. Not yet.

Luckily, she saw him coming, smiled and placed the thick, keyless fob softly into his hand. She was waving him away as though it were no big deal even as he tried not to think about the brush of her trimmed nails against the palm of his hand.

He hadn't had dinner yet, but he would have to drive through somewhere. With this week's schedule, there wasn't going to be time to do this later and he needed to get her a present now. The *best* present—and he had no idea how to do it.

In town, he headed directly to the bar, sat down, and motioned for a pint. Grabbing a napkin and a pen, he started to take notes until Liam came over. Liam may be his only friend who knew the whole score. Beck was playing all of it close to the chest and trying to keep all the parts of his life separate.

He looked up at the bartender and said only, "I need a gift. The perfect gift."

"Oh, yeah." Liam nodded as he wiped down a section of the bar, his hands never stopping moving—something Beck knew helped him stay on the right track. "That's this weekend?"

"It is. I have absolutely no idea what to get."

Liam shrugged. "Did you ask anybody at your job?"

Beck shook his head. "They don't even know."

CHAPTER FIFTEEN

Devin had been nervous when he messaged her, asking if Gabi wanted to come up to the top of the mountain and go for a hike. This time she could meet him at the end of his shift.

Did she remember the other night? If so, how much of it?

They'd always talked about everything as kids. They told each other what he thought were all their secrets. Now as adults he didn't know. But the other night, he'd confessed everything to her—all his fears about his mother, about his life after his mother was gone and he was the only one left in the world.

Then he realized he'd just thrown it out there like a fucking idiot. Of course, Gabi had lost everyone in her family already. Luckily, she hadn't been offended. He could maybe apologize for that shit today.

But he had no idea if she was attracted to him, or if she had just been drinking.

Had all of his breaking down and confessing everything put her off? It hadn't seemed to, but that could have just been the Jack and Coke talking. And if she wasn't attracted to him—or if she was but she simply didn't want anything more between them—could he push everything aside to maintain their friendship?

He had far more questions than answers.

Devin could only hope a hike on the trails might help.

He changed and headed to the front porch that ran the entire length of the main lodge to wait. When the time passed, he had to wonder if she was standing him up. He'd stood her up. It was fair.

Maybe she wasn't excited about a hike—this was Gabi after all—and it just slipped her mind.

Roz came out and stood next to him, watching as far down the long drive as they could see. He'd told everybody his friend was coming, simply because if they saw her, they'd wonder what the two of them were. He'd even explained how they'd run into each other in the coffee shop and he'd recognized her from when they were eleven. If she stood him up, they'd all know.

Roz folded her arms then unfolded them to say, "I assume you're waiting on Gabi?"

Oh, goody, Roz even remembered her name. This would get embarrassing.

But just then her eyes widened and her eyebrow twitched. Turning to him, she said, "I think I hear a car."

He couldn't see anything yet.

Roz seemed to realize the discrepancy. "In my dreams for this place, I'm going to put in an alert system at the bottom of the hill so we know when people are coming up."

They were, after all, the only thing up this entire road. The driveway was miles long and there was no way to know when someone was coming. That could prove a problem.

She looked at him then, thinking. "It should have lights too, right? Not just sound."

He nodded. "It should blink in some particular pattern indicating something at the base of the drive." They already had light alerts for the alarms.

Roz agreed. "We wouldn't use the same sound for every alert."

He was about to sign back when the car appeared. It occurred to him he hadn't seen Gabi's car before. It was compact, a relatively recent model, pale silver and well kept. It handled the slope and the turns like a champ.

Waving, he moved forward but Roz tapped him on the shoulder. "You know everyone wants to meet her right?"

He'd thought he told them enough.

"You can bring her to dinner with the family," Roz offered. She hadn't used that term when he interviewed but he noticed she was using it a lot more for everyone who lived up at the Sanctuary. *Family.*

Roz walked away, so Devin was on the porch alone when Gabi parked, opened her car door and looked around in awe.

"This is beautiful. The drive was amazing." Her face was lit up and he liked it more than he expected to.

"I'm glad you made it." All the questions and nerves disappeared at the sight of her. He was thrilled that she liked the place, even though it was just where he lived right now.

She stepped up close—almost close enough to reach out for a hug—but they stopped just shy of touching. *Maybe she did remember.* "I'm sorry I'm late. I took a wrong turn."

She hadn't stood him up, so he let it go. "I've been told everyone wants to meet you. Are you willing to make the rounds then hike?"

"Yes, definitely." But then she moved her hands to her bare arms, rubbing on them.

He headed into the lodge introducing her to Roz first. At least his boss didn't act overly involved, but she did have a touch of "proud mother" in her and made sure that Gabi knew Devin had already landed them a grant. "He got us into the final rounds on two more."

"You didn't tell me that!" Gabi almost accused him.

"That's my job," he said.

They found Beck and Lynzee outside and said hello to both. Devin mentioned what each of them did and Gabi absolutely adored the dogs. She even asked first if she could pet them or scratch their ears. "I heard we're not supposed to pet service dogs."

Lynzee smiled. "That's right." But then she sent two of the dogs over to Gabi who offered affection like a true dog lover.

She smiled happily as they walked away. For a moment she folded her arms then she turned to Devin, "Wow, Lynzee has a crush on Beck!"

Reaching out, Devin quickly grabbed for her hands, shushing her. "They all sign!"

"What?" She looked almost confused. Beck and Lynzee had spoken to her, in response to her verbal questions.

"You can't just sign anything up here, thinking no one will understand!"

They'd gotten used to it as kids, saying anything they wanted, wherever they wanted. If anyone had understood them, no one had said. Only his interpreter had even seemed to have an idea, and she'd been disinterested in anything but conveying classroom instruction.

"Did they learn for you?" She smiled at the thought.

"No . . . well, kind of?" He shrugged. "I was the first to get a hearing ear dog from the Sanctuary. So they started learning—or attempting to—" that made her smile, "—before I arrived. But after I got hired, they've all been getting a lot better. Meals are signed, any time I'm there, everything is in ASL . . . to the best of their abilities."

Should he ask her to stay for dinner with his new *family*?

"Where do you live?" she changed the subject, and the rest didn't matter.

CHAPTER SIXTEEN

"I started learning when we were kids, you know." Gabi answered his question as to how her ASL was so fluent. Only Luisa had been fluent when they were younger, Gabi had been passable. It had been twenty years, too. He would have expected an unused skill to deteriorate, not improve.

She signed along, the cuffs of the long-sleeved shirt he'd lent her needing to get pushed back off her wrists. The day had dropped temperature, and the mountain top was cooler, too. She looked good in his shirt. Too good. Luckily, her words pulled his attention. "We moved up near the Austin area—"

He didn't catch the rest. Devin stubbed his toe on a root. Her words stunned him.

He'd specifically chosen a hike with a wider path so they could stay side by side and see as they talked. But now he was behind, until she turned.

"The school for the Deaf was nearby. I met some kids who were Deaf. Are you okay?" She asked it about the way he'd stumbled. But that wasn't why he was not okay.

She didn't know that it was a knife through his heart. "How long were you there?"

"We moved to the area right after . . . the accident."

Oh hell. He hated bringing up these memories, but they were standing still, and he couldn't tell her to shut up.

Though she'd stumbled on the words, she didn't seem much phased by the question. "We moved around a lot, but I lived in the area until a year ago. Until I got the assignment at the store here." She said it almost with a shrug.

Then she turned, anxious to continue the hike, not seeming to realize that he still wasn't moving. But then she caught on and turned around again.

Curie sat at his feet, well trained. She stayed out of the conversation, ready to alert him to any cougars or grizzlies coming down the mountainside. But Curie couldn't alert Gabi that she'd almost shattered him.

He looked at her, knowing his face showed the confusion processing through him. He couldn't untangle it, but he tried. "You left in the middle of the school year."

She nodded, "I couldn't help it. Mama didn't want to stay after the accident."

"I understand. I finished that year by myself." He watched as her face fell, maybe only just now realizing what it meant to lose someone who spoke your language when almost no one else did. "We stayed one more year."

She nodded as if knowing the next part was somehow going to be worse.

"My mom saw that I just didn't have any friends anymore. I was reading a lot, escaping into other worlds. The local librarians learned some sign for me." That made Gabi smile. "So my mom started applying for new jobs."

He didn't need to say more. Especially after the other night, he could see that Gabi understood how big that was. His mother had had a good job. It paid well enough for the little house. Her job kept them fed and she received medical insurance to cover his needs. She liked her co-workers, too. He knew.

His mother had given it all up simply because her son needed something. "We moved to Austin for the School for the Deaf for high school."

He let it sit between them and watched as Gabi's face finally mirrored his. He remembered that expression from way back.

"You were in Austin?" She was stunned. He understood. Now she knew what had hit him so hard.

"Just outside it. I was there at the school with the kids you were learning sign from."

"I liked using it. It reminded me of you." She looked wistful. *"And* there were some things that they said that I didn't understand. Like our sign language was just all ours."

He grinned at that. "I think when you live and speak in your own little family unit the signs get insular." Devin wondered if she recognized that he'd referred to her as his family unit. For the first time, he realized that she truly had been—Luisa had been that close of a friend when they were kids. The Montalvos had taken him in, fed him at their table, even let him sleep over occasionally.

Seeing her again made it clear—but difficult to admit—just how devastating the loss of the Montalvo girls had been for him.

They talked more about where they lived specifically. How close had they been and their paths hadn't crossed? It didn't seem fair.

"We were in an apartment for one year," he told her. "Before my mom found a house she really liked. And we stayed all through high school. Mom stayed there when I went to college."

"We moved around a lot. One apartment after another." She paused. "Most were worse than the ones before. I got a job waiting tables as soon as I turned sixteen." Gabi shrugged. "It's not just the school, there's a good Deaf community there."

She stopped and waved one hand absently as if to say, *I guess you already knew that.* He did.

"There were places that I would have regulars because I could communicate."

That explained why her skills were even better than before, but she was still going.

"It helped when I applied for the job at the coffee shop. It actually got me an extra bonus in pay even though I don't have any formal education in ASL. I got to put that I was bilingual on my application."

"Trilingual!" he commented. *Hadn't the Montalvo girls spoken Spanish at home?*

"Only a little," she told him. "Mama desperately wanted us to be American. I know enough to communicate some basics, but that's about it." Gabi stopped and looked right at him. Were there tears forming at the corners of her eyes? "I can't believe we were so close that whole time and never ran into each other."

He couldn't either. "It's crazy."

"I wish I had known that you were there."

He wished the same now. How hard had he tried to find her? But he'd barely been a tween and didn't have any research skills. He'd looked for Luisa a few times on social media and more, but now it made sense why nothing had pinged. It made him wonder if the universe wasn't conspiring to keep them apart.

With a sigh that they couldn't change the past, she changed the topic. "How is your mother holding up after last week?"

"Like it never happened." He was about to explain that he had to keep reminding her to take care of the sutures, but Gabi pointed up into the trees.

"Look!" A raccoon foraged along a branch, looking as if its hands were full. It looked around, then up and headed down the tree quickly. As it came down closer and closer to them, Gabi backed up until she landed against him.

Devin didn't mind.

She looked over her shoulder, signing as she did. "Is it

supposed to be out during the day? I thought they were nocturnal . . . Does it have r-a-b-i-e-s?"

He shook his head no and showed her the sign. "It's spring. She probably has babies. Seeing them out during the day doesn't mean they're rabid."

"I love that you know that." She laughed and he felt the movement.

"I live and work with people full of this info. There's a vet next door and Beck knows way too much."

She turned around, still close enough to be in his space. "Do you remember that time that we saw the wolf out on that one hike?"

He laughed, remembering how scared they were, how the two of them had followed it anyway. "I do. But looking back, I think it was probably just a coyote."

"Probably." She seemed a little more thoughtful then, and changed the subject as she stepped just a heartbeat further away. "Do you like the job?"

"I really do." It wasn't what he wanted to be talking about right now, not with her close enough to let him know she felt at least something. He almost couldn't sign without bumping into her, but he tried.

"It was just another grant writing job. I figured it would be okay being a part time dog trainer. After all, they said they would train me how to train the dogs, and I already had one." He reached down and scratched Curie behind the ears, noting that even though the dog leaned into it, it wasn't the same as when they were at home. Curie was on duty, and she knew it. "I didn't expect to fall in love with the dog quite so much."

"You look like you love it. Like you fit in." He felt her grin all the way down to his toes.

"I like the dogs. It's fun work. It's more—" he paused, "—*physical* work than previous jobs I've had. But there's no gym up here." He waved the hand out to indicate all that wasn't available on top of the mountain.

Gabi replied, "It's all a gym."

"Exactly. It's beautiful. I like my co workers."

"They all sign," Gabi pointed out.

He was used to dealing with interpreters, texting, and being left out of conversations. Though he knew spoken conversations occurred when he wasn't there, it was almost like being back at school to have ASL everywhere . . . or most everywhere.

But that wasn't what he wanted to talk about. In fact, she was still so close, and he didn't want to talk at all. Reaching out, he snagged the front of the shirt he'd lent her. It hung loose and gave him zero control, but it let her know he wanted to pull her closer.

His heart pounded, waiting to see if she would move into him. When she did, one step, that was close enough. Her eyes were wide, waiting, but she leaned closer.

He remembered how she'd tasted of Jack and Coke. What would she taste like now?

His eyes closed as his lips brushed hers and he sank into the feeling. He felt her breath escape, felt her mouth move under his, felt her arms loop up and around his neck. Then he felt the length of her pressed against him.

Given that permission, he wrapped his arms around her, too. One around her back, holding her to him, the other snaking up under the high ponytail that made her look younger, freer, happier. He let the heat seep through him, the touch of her mouth like magic that let him know he was in the right place.

She was tall, maybe just a few inches shorter than him, and they fit together perfectly. He kissed her harder, her mouth opening beneath his, pushing back, making him think of more. He wanted more.

He wanted Curie to stop bumping against his leg.

Holy shit.

He pulled back, irritated as he looked down. *Did they need to train the dogs that kissing was okay and not an attack?* He could not have—

Curie was growling, her lip pulled back, her snout aimed at something beyond the trail.

Devin looked up. Even Gabi was turning to see the large snake that was winding through the brush right at her.

Telling himself it was probably fine, Devin tipped his head for a better look, but the triangular head and the markings told him it absolutely wasn't.

CHAPTER SEVENTEEN

—H—e grabbed it by the tail and just tossed it into the woods!
— He grabbed the SNAKE?

Chandler's incredulity came through the text in the chat room and Gabi was laughing, though her heart still beat a little faster. Not as much as it had when the snake had slithered down near them on the trail.

The chat was blowing up as she told her friends what had happened.

— Did you hear it first?

— No. Her fingers flew. It wasn't a rattlesnake.

— was it coiled to strike? Of course, Helen wanted details. She'd always been like that.

— No. Which Devin pointed out afterwards.

— As if that made it any less heroic!

Helen had to be smirking at her and Jenna managed to chime in right on Helen's heels.

— Did he act all macho?

— No. That crazy he-man stuff didn't seem to be in Devin's

emotional vocabulary. His masculinity came in underlying bedrock and granite faith in himself and the world.

— His eyes got really wide and he acted surprised that he'd done it.

The comments poured in that he was a keeper. As if Gabi didn't already know that. She was maybe just holding back on admitting it to herself. On trying to make sure she didn't jump the gun because she'd been best friends with him when they were younger. Because she'd had teenage fantasies about the boy she'd lost. Because the man appeared in front of her weeks ago, better than even her imagination had conjured.

Helen, who'd tried to learn some sign when they'd worked together, and managed rudimentary communication commented — The ASL only makes him hotter.

This particular group was made up of friends from the coffee shop in Austin. Helen had worked there while she was in college. She'd left the shop mid-summer on her transition to grad school.

Then there was Jenna, who was more of a lifer like Gabi. When Gabi was promoted to the position here in Charlottesville, the Austin Regional asked her who she recommended to take over management. She'd recommended both Jenna and Toby, knowing it wasn't fair to simply recommend her friend. The management had chosen Jenna and since then Gabi and her friend had more than one conversation about running a store and dealing with employees and broken machinery and, of course, customers.

Chandler had only worked at the Austin store for about seven months before finding a job that suited her better. Gabi was grateful her friend had never made it to a review. But Chandler stayed friends with all of them. In fact, she was the one that started the chat so she could stay connected. Gabi loved this little core group and was grateful.

— I saw that picture. Chandler added. — You guys looked so happy together.

— We were drunk. Gabby replied.

Apparently, she had snapped a picture of Devin and her, leaning back on the couch, midway through their pizza and Jack fueled night. Then she'd posted it online long before sobering up. She didn't regret it, it was a great picture, but she hadn't been thinking clearly and a lot of the comments had been about her "boyfriend." If Devin had seen it, he hadn't commented.

— that only makes it better.

Chandler was quick with her reply. Helen chimed in too.

— It means you weren't hiding anything.

The conversation dwindled down with all three of them encouraging Gabi to *go for it*. But almost as if she'd heard Helen's voice, the words repeated: *It means you weren't hiding anything.*

Gabi hated the tight feeling in the center of her chest. She'd lived with it for so long, she hadn't even noticed it for years. Then, when Mama had died, she'd started to feel it again. It had just been easing when Devin showed up, and that had cranked it all back down tight as a vice on her heart.

As a kid they hadn't told her what the problems were, so she hadn't worried about it herself. She'd just felt the tension in her parents—at least, thinking back she didn't think it was between them. Just that they were stuck and had to flee. It was supposed to make everything good. Nothing had gone right.

The worry sure as hell wasn't doing her any good now, but she didn't know how to shake it.

Her phone chimed, and Chandler was back in for the count.

— You know he's going to fall for the Latin hotness of our girl. Look at the way he's looking at her in that picture.

Gabi scrolled back through her feed as if she hadn't looked at it a thousand times already. She grinned at Chandler's positivity.

That got Helen going again.

— You should make him those papas rellenas you made us.

— oh damn that'll get him! Jenna had asked for them more than once.

Gabi grinned. She wasn't much of a cook, but she had taught herself how to make this one dish. It wasn't easy either. There was seasoned ground meat, and she'd had to hunt down the right spices. Then there were mashed potatoes . . . real ones. And more steps to wrap the potatoes around the meat and then fry them before baking.

Looking back, she still didn't know why she'd decided to try it. But even though the recipe was off the web, one bite took her back to her abuela's kitchen in Peru. Gabi had very, very few memories before her time in the US, but that was one of them.

She had snippets of memories of a playground and children whom she believed were her cousins. She remembered the wide porch and the way Abuela would stand at the railing looking out over the mountains or at the garden.

Gabi only remembered in retrospect that the garden hadn't yielded much. The soil was dry and light colored. She remembered a conversation between her mother and father, which she only now realized was about the inability to find work.

Then her mother had gotten a visa to the US . . . and that had changed everything.

Gabi sank into the memories, not needing any Jack and Coke to take her there. It carried her away from the thoughts of kissing Devin on the trail, the heightened fear of the snake, and wondering if that maybe fed into her feelings for him.

She thought about the lies that she told and how somehow it seemed they truly started back in another country.

Later, she'd learned from Mama that they'd not waited for her father's visa to come through. Her mother was granted hers first and the whole family had started moving. There had been nothing to stay for and they wanted to get somewhere safe and plentiful.

Gabi still remembered in sharp relief how they'd made it to the airport and her mother had thought they were safe. Then the strange men stopped them at the gate. She remembered her father turning around and being loud, distracting the men who came for him. She now suspected it was some kind of organized crime ring, the very people her parents had been trying to get away from.

Then she and her mother had come to live with her cousin. The two Mrs. Montalvos had raised their daughters together on American soil. Though not as they had planned, apparently, almost a decade earlier. Neither had her husband with her.

And then, Gabi remembered, her mother had gotten sick.

CHAPTER EIGHTEEN

"I'm so glad that you found her! You've been happier since you saw Luisa again."

Devin was grinning, but at the mistake the corners of his mouth dropped. "It's Gabi, Mom."

"That's right." But she kept talking as though she hadn't said the wrong name.

The error made a cascade of worries tumble through his thoughts. The falling books the other day that she hadn't remembered and had tripped over. Now she was swapping names. *What else?* He didn't want to think about it.

His mother was barely in her mid-fifties but she looked much older. He wasn't sure if it was life or the disease, or the treatments that had aged her—probably a combination of all of them. He saw other women the same age as her who looked much, much younger and it made him sad. The window for miracles was closing.

She'd done a lot with her life, but most of it had been for him.

How long had it been since his mother had even been on a date? Not since the first time she'd been in remission. It certainly didn't seem to be in the cards now. She'd not made a move to even attempt to date for a handful of years.

He remembered she'd dated routinely when he was younger. Only after years of it had he realized that he was the litmus test most men had failed. Only a few of them had even made an effort to learn any ASL. Then there'd been George, who'd been a teacher at the school for the Deaf. Devin had even liked George.

Though Devin had not been a fan of being in George's PE class, he'd always felt that it was not Mr. Fenton's fault that he had to torture the children. But the man had taken an active interest in both his mother and Devin. Searching back through his memory, Devin couldn't find anything untoward or creepy. His mother dated George for several years and Devin had wondered more than once if they would get married.

His mother had always asked him about the men she dated, and he realized now that a lot of other kids hadn't gotten that kind of attention and care. She always asked pointed questions and twice Devin had said, "he just makes me uncomfortable." Neither of those men had ever come around again.

But even George hadn't stuck. When he'd been offered a promotion at another school in a different state, he and Devin's mom had had a tearful goodbye. As far as Devin knew, that had been the end of it. There had been no talk of a long-distance relationship. Despite the three and a half years together, there'd been no ring.

Now Devin looked around at a small house. His mother had the largest bedroom, her queen-size bed in the center with room to walk on either side. The smaller bedroom served as her office and as Devin's room for when he stayed over. Not that she ever used it as an office.

He had painted the walls in various shades of dove grey and pale robin's egg at her request. The sofa was the deep color of a thundercloud with pops of bold blues and greens on the pillows.

The trim around the windows was a bright white, exactly the way she liked it. It was all her.

There was no great love of her life here to share it.

As far as Devin knew, George was the only real long-term boyfriend. His mother hadn't moved with George, because Devin was in his senior year at the school for the Deaf and she didn't want to move her son.

He'd thought maybe his mother would move to be with George when he finished. But she said it was a bad thing to move right when a child graduated high school, that they needed their home to come back to. Then Devin had taken a gap year.

When he'd gone off to Gallaudet, she'd said the same thing about not moving. When Devin looked all the way back to the beginning, she'd made sacrifice after sacrifice for him.

She was seventeen when she told the doctors that she was not going to give him up for adoption to a family who would better be able to deal with his handicap. She'd simply found a new pediatrician who would help her.

In addition to working full time, and paying her own way in the shitty apartment, she began taking lessons in American Sign Language. She made use of the local library and the online lending system. Then she started to spend every spare minute with Devin at the local community center for the Deaf.

Apparently, once she told the locals, "my baby is Deaf and I'm learning to sign," they'd all basically adopted him and given her a crash course. Devin had been far too young to remember, but he remembered other community centers growing up.

She made a point to be there whenever she could, even though he was just a baby and so many people told her it didn't matter. She told him later, that one of the first things she'd learned was that many Deaf children born into hearing families got their earliest language from parents who were just learning that language.

While hearing children were exposed to a variety of high-level, complex conversations around them, Deaf children only got language when they were being directly addressed. And they only got language at the level that the person speaking to them had it. In the case of hearing parents, it was usually absolute beginner. So his mother took him to the Deaf community center where he was exposed to vocabulary and high level conversations and her own learning accelerated.

When the doctor had suggested cochlear implants, she'd asked around at the community center. She'd learned about the headaches they could bring, and how they didn't simulate actual hearing. She told Devin he could decide for himself when he was old enough, and several times he'd considered it but so far he hadn't made the leap. He liked where he was. He appreciated his language and the culture that she had learned and immersed him in.

That was just the first of the ways that she had done everything she was capable of to make sure he had the best life possible. So now, when she needed something, he jumped.

After her fall, it was becoming more of a routine to come down the mountain after work. He might have dinner with Gabi. If he didn't spend the evening with his mom, he would at least stop by and check in on her.

So now, when she said, "You should have her over for dinner. I'll cook!" All Devin said was, "How about you and I cook together?"

"Yes! We could make that dish!" She grinned. "That one that you like. It's called Marry Me Chicken."

Oh, dear lord. His mother wasn't shy about her thoughts. For the first time it occurred to him that maybe she was trying to marry him off before she passed.

CHAPTER NINETEEN

"Is there any way you can stay?" Roz pleaded, but there was an undercurrent of demand too.

Beck didn't like it. She hadn't yet handed over the keys, despite the fact that he had cleared this day with her several weeks ago.

"No," he told her, his own tone as firm as hers. He hated missing the search and rescue people coming to check out the Sanctuary. It figured there would be a last-minute move to switch to the *one day* that he absolutely needed off.

"I need you here." It was a statement of bold importance and Beck was grateful she thought that way.

"I agree."

"Then stay."

"I can't." He was getting more frustrated with each reply, and she still hadn't given him the keys.

At least he'd buffered a lot of time for this. He should have been out the door already, not arguing with his boss about whether or not he could leave when they'd agreed to this some time ago. He wouldn't be late, but it ate at him.

He didn't like Roz being mad at him, but he wasn't budging. He couldn't.

"Plans change." She shrugged at him as though that was the way it was.

"Mine didn't." *Fuck this shit.*

She shook her head back at him. "It's just a tattoo removal appointment!" She gestured almost absently at his hands.

Once upon a time, there had been shaky and somewhat blurred black letters across his knuckles. Now they were mostly faded away. People didn't see them first anymore. Now, they might not even notice, but they weren't gone.

Beck bit his lip. That wasn't the point. Still, he wasn't in any position to tell her otherwise.

"You can move the appointment." She was still demanding. Not budging an inch. He understood—the Sanctuary didn't need the search and rescue team to come in and train here, but it would help. A lot.

"The appointments have to be done in succession," he argued, though she already knew that. And, honestly, that wasn't the real problem today. He wasn't going to tell her what the real problem was. He didn't say it because Roz knew he'd already quit going to removal appointments once.

He'd halted the progress that he'd made, and it had cost him a couple of extra sessions to get back up to speed. It cost money that he didn't really have to spare. *The kicker was,* he thought now, *he'd done it to save the Sanctuary.* To give Roz all the money that he saved so this place wouldn't go under.

Now she was asking him to change his plans because something had suddenly gone awry.

"I'm sure they can get you in tomorrow."

"That won't change anything!" He was getting angry. He rarely got upset with Roz, he understood where she was coming from. Right now he understood, too, but it bothered him deep in his core that his needs couldn't supersede the Sanctuary's just this once. "I can't go tomorrow. Tomorrow is Sunday."

"Go Monday."

"We have training!"

"We can do that without you." She was almost begging.

Beck shook his head. *That wasn't the point.* The point was he had something that he absolutely had to be at today. He spoke with no heat. "I can't change this."

That seemed to end it. "When will you be back? By evening?"

"No. I have plans."

"The appointment can't be that long." She wasn't mad anymore, just trying to make sense of what he wasn't telling her. But he wasn't going to tell her. He just wasn't ready.

"If it's so important that I'm there, then reschedule *them*." The irritation was creeping in again. He didn't realize until she physically leaned back that he had leaned forward against the edge of her desk. Bending at the waist, he was in an aggressive stance, fingers curled under, weight on his knuckles.

He felt the tiny box pulling at the back pocket of his jeans. He had searched so long and hard for it, and he had to deliver it. *On time.* Liam had helped, after Beck had lamented that he needed *the perfect gift.*

He watched now as Roz stayed leaned away. He tried to move slowly, taking himself out of her space. He thought for a moment that the intimidation was something he'd learned in prison. He'd worked hard since he left to get rid of it. Yet here it was, coming right out when he was angry.

He hadn't hit anyone or taken a swing at anything, but that was something he'd learned in prison, too. Every time you moved, every time you let someone goad you into reacting, it added to your time inside. Some guys had come in on petty charges, but they were now in for life because of altercations with other inmates or for anything that was even perceived as an attack against the guards.

Beck had been determined that he would get out in his minimum time. He had learned to bite down on his reactions and choke back his anger, but he'd also learned to use every measure of intimidation. Now, he'd used it on Roz. She was pulling away.

Too many emotions swamped him. He was so excited about today, and he was petrified deep into his bones. *What if he got it wrong?* He was also now angry at Roz. He should have been able to feel those first two dichotomous things without Roz interfering, because it was already too much.

Now he was just frustrated and actually mad at the woman he admired and liked so much. To top it off, he felt bad—guilty even—that he'd leaned into it, tried to intimidate her. He should never have pulled out old prison tactics that he knew weren't appropriate for the real world.

"Please," he said softly, hand out for the keys one more time. "I need to get going. I would love to be here when the SAR people come. I agree that it would look better if we're both here to talk to them." He said it that way on purpose, as though it weren't about his expertise, but about presenting a united front.

He watched as her jaw clenched. "You won't reconsider?"

He threw his hands up, reacting even though he'd told himself he wouldn't. tamping it down, he paced a tight circle and consciously put his wayward hands at his hips for somewhere to keep them so he wasn't waving them around. "It's not about me! *Don't you think I would be here if I could?* I have appointments today that *I can't miss."*

He still wasn't going to tell her what it was, because fuck her.

He'd said *appointments,* though, so she might catch on that it wasn't just merely a tattoo removal. He'd also told her he wouldn't be back until this evening. She wasn't stupid.

Roz didn't look happy. "They said they need to come later today. But I'll see what I can do to get them to move."

Turning around, she opened the bottom drawer of her desk,

89

revealing the purse she kept in there. He'd known that, and he *could* have come in when she wasn't here and stolen the keys. It wasn't like anything was locked.

For all the bullshit this standoff had created, it was still the better way to do it. He hated that he had to stand patiently with his hand held out, waiting for her to drop the heavy key fob into his palm.

It was time to get his own car. He tried not to stomp out of the building. At least the gravel in the parking lot absorbed his ire as he tread heavily toward the big car then headed down the mountain, angry but trying to breathe. His fists gripped the wheel tightly, even as he tried to relax his shoulders.

He still wasn't late, and he had the entire tattoo removal appointment to get himself in gear because he could not show up to her birthday like this.

He glanced down at the passenger seat where his hopes were captured in a small jewelry box, wrapped tightly in a shiny silver bow. In his heart, he imagined that she would be so excited to get it, that her eyes would light up when she saw what it was.

CHAPTER TWENTY

Devin tried to absorb the heat that flashed through his body, embarrassment that felt almost like a physical pain. He reached his right hand out, gently setting it on his mother's wrist. "She's Gabi, Mom."

Next to him, Gabi offered a small smile that seemed to say *don't worry about it*. But it wasn't okay.

Thanks to Gabi's good graces, the dinner had continued on with her praising the food. Then Mom had told Gabi that Devin had helped make it and, of course, she spouted out, "It's called *Marry Me Chicken*."

He was going to have to peel a layer of clothing if the flush kept creeping up his neck. He loved his mother. He'd brought girlfriends home to his mother before but this . . . this was a new level of push.

Was it because she felt an increased drive to pair him off permanently, or was it something else? He didn't like the thought of *something else*.

Then, when she asked Gabi where she'd been in the intervening years, Gabi replied, "After Luisa's death, we moved to Austin."

Devin watched in his own surprise as his mother's eyes flew wide and her mouth dropped open. She turned to Devin, still stunned. "We were in Austin just a year later."

"I know," he said it calmly, adding, "Isn't that crazy?" But what he was thinking was *Oh, hell no.*

He'd told his mother already that Gabi and her mother had moved to the city. He and Gabi had already put together his best recollections from him being in high school and only partly allowed to drive, about the layout of the town. Gabi had lived there much longer, and she had a better sense of where she and he had been. It seemed they'd lived only fifteen miles or so apart.

His mother appeared genuinely surprised by this knowledge.

The lapse in her memory, combined with the very forwardness of her matchmaking, was more than he could handle. He pasted on a smile and tried to push through the evening. Gabi's knee bumped him once and he knew she was asking what was wrong, but there was no way to tell her now.

When the last of the dishes were put away, and Gabi had thanked Ms. James for the meal, Devin saw her out the door. Standing on the front porch, in the dim yellow glow of the porch bulb, he sighed and tried to explain what couldn't possibly be covered in the few moments they were stealing. "I'm so sorry. She was really pushy tonight and I have no idea where it came from."

But he did know, and even the best option made him cringe. The other scared him to the core of his bones.

"It's okay. Don't worry about it." Her soft expression forgave all sins, real and imagined.

Devin couldn't help that his hand reached up, his knuckles gently stroking the soft skin of her cheek. Touching her was easy. And he felt more comfortable doing it now.

She didn't pull away. In fact, she leaned into it, her eyes

falling almost closed as a different kind of heat washed through him. "I hope she didn't hurt you."

Gabi's eyes flew open, and she looked at him, sad but sincere, instantly understanding that he meant when his mother called her by her cousin's name. "It's been twenty years. It's not quite the sharp knife that it used to be just to hear that name."

But there was something in the way she said it, something about the way she reacted at the time that made him think the knife might not still be as sharp but that it did still hurt. She was just trying to minimize it now.

"I'll talk to her," he offered.

"Don't worry about it. It's fine."

They stood awkwardly for a moment. Clearly neither of them wanted to let the conversation end, but neither quite knew how to keep it going.

Gabi took a bold move. "I would invite you back over to my place, but I have work in the morning."

"So do I." He said it as though it didn't matter that her invitation was hypothetical only. Did she mean for a drink or an hour or for the whole night? He couldn't tell.

"When do you get up for your work?" she asked with a bit of a grin sprinkled over her lips.

"Seven?" he said it with a bit of a question on his face, as he tried to think most mornings he was awake before he needed to be. That was something he really liked about this job: the ability to roll out of bed as his body saw fit.

"And your commute?" she pushed, openly laughing at him now.

"Ooh, that's a hard one. I actually have to walk *past* the training grounds and up to the lodge to drop Curie off. Then walk back!"

"So she can play with Shadow and . . . Astra? Why can't she just go to training with you?"

"Beck is clear that we don't want other dogs interfering with the training."

She'd met Roz's two big dogs and seen his cabin when she'd come up the mountain the day of the snake. She'd met Shadow and Astra and then stayed for dinner with the *family*. She'd fit in well, seamlessly moving between sign and English, talking to everyone, integrating smoothly enough to make both Roz and Lynzee smile at him later and tell him that she was a good match.

Devin was calculating. He could easily stay over at Gabi's if that's what she was implying. He would simply get up early and head back up the mountain. But Curie was inside with his mother. He had not brought his dog to Gabi's apartment before. While, technically, she was a service dog and able to go in public spaces that certainly wasn't the case for individual places.

Her words interrupted his plans for a night he hadn't really been invited to. "I have to open the store by five."

He felt his mouth drop open and then he just felt stupid. It was a coffee shop. *Of course she had to open it ridiculously early.* She probably didn't even want him to stay over as she would need what little sleep she could get. Hell, he found himself checking the time. "You should get home and get to bed!"

He and his mother had already kept her out way too late. But he kissed her, and the kiss lingered, Gabi leaning into him, her mouth searching, her arms winding around his neck. For a handful of long, drugging moments, he didn't care that they were standing in the light of the porch where all his mother's neighbors could see them. He didn't care that he didn't know what he was doing. He wondered if they might just take it too far, right here on the front step.

A long moment later she stepped back enough to sign, "I have to get going."

Her breathing faltered and he understood all of it—the hitch in her breath and his, that she had a ridiculously early call time. He didn't want to be the reason that she became a manager the employees resented.

Unable to help himself, he tugged her back for one quick kiss. Though she sank into it again, he ended it almost as soon as it started, enjoying the happiness that seeped down inside him.

Then he watched as she walked down the little stone path, climbed into her car, and waved to him one last time. Devin headed back inside. Definitely time to get his mother into bed.

If he wasn't staying at Gabi's—and clearly that wasn't happening, though the thought made him ache for it—he and Curie would head back to the Sanctuary. Sleep in their own beds. He squashed the fantasies that were starting to swirl.

His mother needed him and his full attention. He'd had hers for decades, he owed her nothing less. Rolling the little jingle ball that she'd gotten for Curie, he watched as his pup romped happily through the small space. Several other dog toys lay around on the floor and it started Devin thinking of the other day and the stitches that would get removed soon. He picked up the toys and stashed them safely in the corner while she went through her regular routine.

He looked around as if child-proofing the place and worried about the corners on the end tables now. About the magazines that still came in the mail. They were stacked on the coffee table. Could she slip on them if they fell?

"I'm ready," she told him cheekily. They'd both laughed that he was now tucking her into bed, the way she had done to him when he was little. The laugh made the reversal of their situation less concerning.

But as he told her goodnight and promised to lock up behind himself, she said, "I just can't believe Gabi and Luisa were in Austin that whole time!"

Smiling, he kissed her forehead, then headed out the front door, but his heart was sinking lower in his chest. She was mixing up facts that she already knew, things that had been repeated to her correctly just this evening.

Like a specter in the dark, *yet* was creeping ever closer.

CHAPTER TWENTY-ONE

Gabi put in her request for time off for Sunday and Monday. She'd put it in to herself, ironically, but insisted on the proper channels. Not giving herself the days off if someone else had requested them before.

She wondered if she'd been subtle, asking Devin when his days off were. His didn't line up to perfect weekends either—like coffee and customers, dogs needed 24/7 attendance. Roz apparently worked to give each of the employees at least one of the weekend days off. But Devin said sometimes their days off were split, and sometimes she gave them an extra day if they hadn't had a weekend. Either way, the two of them hadn't fully lined up yet—not enough for what she wanted to do.

There was every possibility she'd set her own schedule, and give herself the two days together, then find out that he simply wasn't available. If so, she would spend her two days on her own.

Though she had her cadre of friends online, she was mostly alone here. She had one coworker from here that she liked—Maggie. They had gone out several times, once to a bar and even roller skating with Maggie's friends, but it wasn't the same as having a real friend. Gabi knew she was tagging along, and they both also knew that, in the end, she was Maggie's boss. If it came down to it, that would absolutely supersede any friendship they had.

She had Mika, the woman two apartments over in the building. They'd moved in within a week of each other and started new jobs. Mika was a reporter at a local magazine with some nationwide traction, but not enough to break anything huge. Neither of them was making enough money to afford to move upward out of this place. That meant they were well matched.

Gabi enjoyed Mika's company well enough. But even after a year, it wasn't the kind of hardcore friendship that she needed. Mika wasn't someone she could tell her deepest, darkest secrets to. That remained tucked safely in the coffee chat—four friends that Gabi hadn't seen face to face, some of them for years.

And some that she'd never told . . .

If Devin wasn't available this weekend, she wasn't quite sure what she was going to do. When she arrived home from work it was just after noon. Because her shift started so insanely, ridiculously early, she was off when most people were just getting lunch. Pulling out her phone, she took a deep, fortifying breath and messaged him.

— I have Sunday and Monday off. Do you want to spend the weekend with me?

It was a blatant invitation. She hit send then chewed at her lower lip wondering if and when he would message back. There was every possibility he was out in the yard or on a hike with the dogs or maybe in the new office he told her about upstairs in the lodge.

Roz had helped him clear everything off the desk and then haul it up the stairs. Devin had laughed when he told Gabi the story because Shadow and Astra had barked at them. They were *not* trained service dogs—in fact they were the least well-trained of any of the dogs. Gabi had seen that for herself. They weren't bad by any measure, but compared to a service dog? They looked a little unruly.

Still, the two big lugs had followed along, as if to be sure they didn't drop or break anything. Devin said they must have been barking very loudly, because they'd brought Brandy and Lynzee who joined in to help carry all his things upstairs. Then, of course, Brandy had looked around the place and said, "He needs a file cabinet. And isn't there a chair in one of the other empty rooms?"

He'd sent Gabi pictures of a mid-sized room with a desk placed under a window with a view she could only dream of. There was another picture of an old worn leather armchair in the corner, in case he just got tired of writing grant proposals and needed to relax. She laughed at the idea and thought of her own office—basically just a large hall closet. She even had a shelf with supplies on it.

Not only did she not have a stunning view, she didn't even have a window. And the thought of just getting tired and retiring to her leather chair while her employees dealt with the public all day? Not going to fly. She was certainly called in every time it got rough out front. That was the job.

Clutching her phone, she tried to think about taking a nap. It was the only way she wouldn't wind up going to bed at four in the afternoon. She didn't need to grocery shop. Didn't have errands to run today. It would be easy to just crawl into bed and try to shake the urge to look at her phone every five seconds.

But she was hungry. Maybe just a good, hot, well-prepared lunch would do it.

She cooked fresh fish, rice and chopped vegetables and ate in front of the TV. She watched shows that she'd recorded the night before. And she looked at her phone as often as she would let herself.

No reply. *Had he even seen it?*

She hated the tension. She'd basically invited him for sex. What if he didn't want to? But she crawled into bed after doing the dishes and recited every fact that made her think he wanted her too.

The way he'd looked at her in that picture. *But he was drunk, so did that even mean anything?*

He'd saved her from the snake. *But he was just a decent man.*

The way he'd kissed her on the porch the other night. *But that didn't mean he wanted it to go any further. Or maybe he just wanted to stay over and bolt in the morning and she'd invited him for a whole damn weekend like a lovesick fool.*

Oh hell, she was a lovesick fool!

Trying not to look at her phone, she rolled over. Her stomach was thankfully full, and the bed was cool. Her brain churned, wondering if she'd made a huge mistake. But in a bout of hopeful thinking, she made a note to change the sheets on Friday. Then it wouldn't be so damn obvious she'd done it for him.

Damn, she was really doing this. Or she hoped she was.

The answer was up to Devin because she had already thrown caution to the wind and thrown the invitation out to him. He'd have to be dense not to know what it was.

Her eyes pulled closed, and her thoughts broke from reality until she woke up with the sheets tangled around her. Lingering memories of Devin's hands on her bare skin tangled in her brain, warring with a heat between her legs that she needed to take care of.

She groaned into the darkened room. Evening had come and now she was awake, needy, and uncertain.

Then, her phone chimed. Dragging herself, hot and

bothered, to the side table, she clawed for the little rectangle of light.

His name was across the top of the screen along with a picture she'd snapped of him. It made her smile each time she saw it.

But now, she held her breath. Devin had replied.

CHAPTER TWENTY-TWO

"Devin, can you show Su to her cabin?" Roz motioned to him. Her hands were still stiff in her signs, but her language was much improved. She'd relaxed over time, and she was communicating much better.

Devin didn't want to tell her no: He didn't want Su to get the wrong impression, and he didn't want Roz to think he wasn't being a good employee. Maybe he could say something later, but for now, he motioned to Su to follow along. This would likely be rudimentary at best.

Initially, he'd liked this job because it was close to his mother. Also, it allowed him to keep a lot of odd hours, giving him the chance to be with his mother as she needed it. Now he found he truly enjoyed the work. He could see himself staying after . . . he couldn't think about *after*. He now desperately needed this job. As much as Devin hated to admit it, his mother was going downhill.

Where would he find another job that paid well enough and afforded him the flexibility this one did? He was required to show up for trainings and group meetings on time. He was hit and miss on the family dinners, often eating with his mother or

Gabi. But he kept his nights to cook, though those could be flexible, too.

The rest of the time that he needed to be grant writing, he was allowed to do that from anywhere, at about any time as long as he got the job done. He'd already worked from his mother's home and his little cabin in the middle of the night. He'd spent a handful of days already taking his mother to doctors appointments or therapies or even just shopping. He could not afford to dick this up.

Roz seemed to very much believe in supporting her people—and Devin was grateful to be 'her people' now. Even so, putting the new girl with the Deaf guy maybe wasn't Roz's best move.

Su smiled at him, a gesture as generous and sincere as it was nervous. She set down her suitcase and started to move her hands tentatively. "I . . . have . . . been . . ." He saw her mouth move, her facial expression giving away the swear. She looked up, blinked and then added, "learn . . . sign."

"That's. Good!" He tried to be encouraging. He didn't want to make a bad impression on someone he didn't know, and he was dependent on her learning his language. It simply couldn't go the other way. But he asked, "Why say *shit?*"

He made each sign slowly and clearly, separating each gesture as though it were an individual word. It wasn't.

"Because . . . not sign b-e-e-n." She clumsily fingerspelled the last word.

"That's right," he motioned. "It's only for English, not for ASL."

Clearly Su was not going to be the primary point of contact and communication when Deaf people came to the Sanctuary to get their hearing ear dogs. That would be him, most likely, though there were enough competent signers here that Jade River could become the premier place to get these dogs.

Su would need to catch up. Suddenly Roz's reasoning made sense: throw Su into the deep end with him. For him it sucked to be the deep end. Still, he tried to make small talk. Thinking she was mostly an online worker like him, he asked her about her job, curious what exactly she did.

Her answer wasn't tempered by her lack of ASL, but by something deeper. She shut down immediately. Acting as if she didn't understand his question, though it was clear that she had.

He almost asked if she was okay but she looked away and asked about the first "house." He said, "There are ten cabins." *House* was too strong a term for the small spaces.

She shook her head.

He signed cabin again then spelled it for her.

That made her nod. At least she wasn't acting like she understood things she didn't. It was good that she'd put in effort to learn before she came. He had to give Su credit for that. He led her along the trail, pointing to each cabin as they passed.

"One," he said, then fingerspelled *Brandy*. Then he pointed to the next one. "A-S-H."

Su nodded as they kept walking. Her suitcase had wheels, but the wheels were useless once they were out the back of the lodge. Unless they were all terrain versions—and they weren't— the trails meant things had to be carried.

She had a second stuffed bag slung over her shoulder. It all made it difficult for her to talk, but she did okay with the one hand. He'd offered to take the shoulder bag from her, thinking he needed both hands to communicate. He could likely understand her one-handed gestures, but she wouldn't get his. She'd refused, saying "I'm good." He sensed an "I brought it, I can carry it" attitude and he wouldn't disagree.

Her purple hair and blue eyes seemed to go well with her inquisitive nature. Unlike Lynzee's occasional emo sullenness, Su's black t-shirt—with a band name he didn't recogonize slashed across the front—was more about something she liked than something she disliked.

He pointed at the next cabin. "Three is Beck. Four is me."

Her face lit up. "You . . . have . . ." she wound up pointing to the railing and he signed "flowers" for her. She immediately repeated the sign as if to put it into memory.

"Yes, my mother grew them and gave them to me."

He wasn't sure she understood the whole sentence, despite his use of clear and common words. But she pointed again and made the sign for *beautiful*.

He offered a *Thank you*, which he knew she would understand. Then signed, "Cabin number five," pointing to the next cabin on the trail. Then he pointed to Su.

Her eyes lit up despite the fact that every cabin on the trail was basically identical. Roz was getting the next five cleaned out, she'd told him. *More employees,* he thought, wondering how full the place might get.

Su already had her key from Roz. He offered to hold the suitcase for her while she leaned over, fitted it into the lock, and jiggled it a little bit. As clean and nice as the tiny buildings were, he'd seen the ones at the end of the trail. They hadn't started clean and nice. They were aging, too. It wasn't a surprise the old tumbler locks got a bit sticky.

He saw Su's mouth move, claiming her success when the door swung open. When she turned around to him and signed the sign for "yes," he almost laughed. Yeah, he'd gotten that. It was absolutely not the place for the formal sign like one would use in a courtroom.

Su was happy at her success and headed into the stale air. Roz had told him that Su had just left some obscure government agency, doing data collection—not exactly who he would have picked to train dogs. Then again, neither was he. Brandy had an advanced degree in civil engineering. Lynzee was barely a high school grad. Who was to say if Su would be a bad fit?

She'd been friendly, saying hello to everyone earlier and she showed up wearing reasonable shoes—not what he'd expected from someone coming from a work-from-home computer job.

It had taken him a few days to embrace the casualness. Su was primed from moment one. She'd even showed him an entire kit for s'mores for the campfire that night.

So far, everyone liked her. Her odd combo of colored hair, goth band T shirt, and good shoes wouldn't have fit in at any other job he could think of. Here it would all depend on how she handled the dogs. As far as he knew—unlike him, who had another position as the grant writer—she was just here as a trainer. They would see.

Setting her suitcase down, he followed her inside, ready to answer any questions that she could actually form the words to. She opened the one door and signed, "restroom." He almost replied snarkily "Good job," but managed to keep his hands at his sides. The sliding doors were clearly the closet and, aside from the front door, that was it.

The bed was in the middle of the room, made up with one set of sheets that Roz gifted to each employee. They all wound up getting at least a second set. He told Su that, slowly and carefully. Then he pointed out the two burners on the stovetop. "No dishwasher. Half size fridge."

She pointed and signed "question," then fingersspelled F-R-E-E-Z-E-R.

He nodded and signed, "Yes, but small." Again, he tried to keep his words clean and separate as he told her, "Five or six nights a week, the whole group eats together."

Again, he watched as her face lit up. "Dinner?"

He nodded, the easiest and most understandable sign, but he was feeling like a bobble head. Still, he counted it as a win that he hadn't had to pull out his phone and text. She was actually doing really well. Language was just difficult. "We trade cooking."

"Oh no." She looked almost scared. "I can't cook."

"Me either," he said. "But they don't complain."

She shook her head, confused, until he spelled out "complain."

Then she laughed, and said, "They will complain about me." She did a good job of getting the claw at her chest.

Okay, he was more impressed. She'd picked up the sign from seeing him use it once. He laughed at her and said, "You arrived later than we expected."

"A whole day late!" She seemed frustrated by that.

"I mean that it's almost time for dinner. Are you ready?"

She clearly wasn't sure. Signing with the Deaf guy wasn't the only deep end she was getting thrown into. She turned around, looked at her still packed suitcase and bag now sitting on the bed and took a deep breath as if she needed to fortify herself against them. "Okay."

Su made it through dinner, saved by the English speakers. She was awkward with it, but so had they all been. People who weren't used to speaking with their hands didn't quite have the patterns down to eat and talk at the same time. They hadn't learned the benefits. They were busy searching their brains for words rather than focused on the conversation. But they quickly learned they could talk with their mouths full, and they could apparently hear some things while signing others. He'd seen Deaf mothers eating, shushing their child with one hand, and carrying on a full conversation with an adult with the other.

The others were starting to come up in skill. Su might be the beginner but only Lynzee was close to fluent by this point. Beck and Brandy were close behind but still a little stiff sometimes. They communicated very well, though. Devin had grabbed Brandy's hands once and jostled them back and forth, trying to get her to loosen up. She'd laughed and understood, but he hadn't really had the nerve to try it yet with Beck.

Su hung in, looking more interested and curious than disheartened. They'd all lingered around the table until Roz had announced that it was time to hit the bonfire and that Su had provided s'mores fixings.

Ducking back into the kitchen, Roz pulled out a bin she'd filled with ice, beers, hard ciders, lemonade, and sodas. She handed over the marshmallow sticks to Ash almost as a matter of course. Devin had eaten more S'mores and roasted marshmallows here than he had as a scout.

"Ready for a little gathering?"

He was and he hoped to bring Gabi to one soon, but today wasn't going to be that day. She had to be up early to work tomorrow.

Su had said something—something spoken apparently. Devin only caught Brandy motioning to her, shaking her head saying no, "You have to sign."

This time, he read Su's lips clearly. "Crap." Slowly she signed to the group, "Can I make campfire food when it's my turn to cook?"

They all laughed, but then he watched as Ash and Brandy bumped shoulders, seeming to catch on to the idea. Beck, the master chef among them, shrugged.

"I don't see why not," Roz signed, and Su made a motion of wiping her forehead in relief.

The conversation turned to the usual things—trainings, the group meeting the next morning at nine, something Beck was introducing for the diabetic alert dogs—as Devin stuck his marshmallow directly into the flame, watching it catch fire. He blew it out and smashed it between graham crackers and chocolate, before shoving most of it into his mouth at once.

He barely caught Roz's gesture to him. But once he looked up at her, she told him, "I talked with Su earlier. She said the days she works don't matter for her. So yes, you can have Sunday and Monday off."

He tried to be cautious rather than overly excited as he signed *Thank you*. Su wasn't paying attention to him, talking with Brandy and Beck. Maybe he could thank her later, or just not mention it.

It was far too late tonight to message Gabi and let her know he'd gotten the time. But now the question was *what exactly had she meant?*

CHAPTER TWENTY-THREE

Devin showed up to the table at 8:57 the next morning, with Curie following along perfectly at heel. Reaching down, he scratched the dog's head and pulled a few treats from his pocket.

He'd learned from Beck that it was easier just to have treats on hand. Then he'd learned which ones left the least amount of peanut butter or powdered meat dust in his pockets, so that maybe he didn't smell like a puppy snack when he went to see his girlfriend.

He hadn't said the word yet and neither had she, but he was definitely thinking of her that way. Still, Roz and Beck were setting up in their meeting and the others were coming in behind him.

Grabbing a seat, Devin tried to pay attention as Roz moved up to the front of the room, and awkwardly opened an old school, easel type stand. She pulled down a white screen for a little projector Beck was hooking up to her laptop.

Devin looked back and forth at Brandy, Ash, and Lynzee—all seemed as surprised by the move as he was.

"Is this a presentation?" Lynzee asked, her hands moving fluidly.

"Yes," Roz seemed excited at least. Then she left Beck to the set up and looked around. The group was small, but even Su was here and ready to go. "So, last Saturday, you may have seen that we had visitors."

She motioned to Beck who was slowly playing with the buttons, attempting to get the little projector to come on. It wasn't happening.

But Devin was confused. Everyone knew about the visitors, but Roz was presenting it as though it were news. Maybe for Su? She went on. "That team was from Pacific Search and Rescue."

Again, Devin thought, they all already knew that. Hopefully, she would get into the details. Pulling out his phone, he set it on the table. He'd messaged Gabi on the walk over here that he had gotten the time off for their little weekend.

Did she just want to make plans for the days and then send him home to sleep in his own bed at night? Or was there something more that she wanted?

It shouldn't matter, but he wanted to be prepared if she wanted him to stay, and not be pushy or acting like he expected anything if she didn't. *Why was this shit always so complicated?*

He was hoping for option one, but Roz was talking, and he tried to focus.

"They wanted to come and look at the facilities here because they are interested in running their own trainings."

Su was the only one who didn't seem impressed. Probably because this was her very first day on the job and she had no idea this was out of the ordinary.

"What kinds of trainings?" Brandy asked, clearly trying to keep an open mind.

"One—basic search and rescue. They want to use the trails to train the dogs to Appalachian . . ." Roz looked to Devin then and finger spelled "terrain." He offered her the correct sign and she continued almost seamlessly.

"Two—they want to use the old barn on the back of the facility for building searches."

"I'm not sure it's safe." Ash said, his hands moving then stopping then moving again. "Actually, I'm sure it's not safe."

"That's the point." Roz seemed to shrug at it. "Lastly—they're hoping to use the lodge as a place to stay while they are here."

"So not at the same time that we have people meeting their dogs." Ash signed. His movements were small, precise, not bold and colorful like Brandy's. But he got the job done. Devin suspected that was just his voice.

Roz nodded.

"Is there room for all that while we are training? Won't that slow our training down?" Lynzee was asking questions as fast as she thought of them. "Can we afford the lost time?"

"It's likely they won't come until after we graduate the current group of dogs so they can use the entire space."

"Then we aren't starting the next cohort right away . . ." Lynzee was putting pieces together. She didn't seem to like it. Devin was withholding judgment, not sure it was his place as grant-writer to weigh in.

"Will we need to leave?" Beck asked cautiously.

Devin turned quickly to look directly at Beck, surprised by the question. Beck and Ash were Roz's second in commands. Ash the go-to person for all animal health concerns. Beck was the one who's opinion stood for all things training. Devin was startled that Beck was asking questions the same as the rest of them.

Did he not know what Roz had done?

"We're still talking through the details about that," Roz told him. "Right now, it's set so we can all leave if we wish, or we can stay and be part of the training. They need people that the dogs are unfamiliar with to pretend to be victims and get rescued."

That could be fun, Devin thought, but still held his ideas in.

"Is this a done deal?" Beck asked next, his consternation pulling his brows together, once again surprising Devin that he didn't already know the answers. Beck looked down at the small projector again, this time angrily tapping at the buttons.

Whatever hadn't been communicated between them, he didn't like it. And Devin wasn't sure he could handle the tension between them. So far, the major drama had been that Vivaldi wanted to steal the socks when they indicated high glucose levels, rather than alert to them. That Dante responded better to vocal commands than to hand signals. Not this. Devin didn't like this.

"No, it's not signed at all," Roz assured all of them as the projector popped to life, showing a white slide with dull bullet points. "We all need to decide if we want to do this."

Ah, Devin thought. She'd told him when he took the position that it was at least *partly* a democracy. So here it was.

Though the presentation was leaving a little something to be desired, she motioned to Beck to flip through the dull slides she'd already covered. Then she grinned when a picture of a man and a dog popped up. "Here's what I wanted to show you."

Motioning to Beck, she waited until a logo of Pacific Search and Rescue popped up on the screen. Then another of the man and the dog. "This is Caspar and his dog Trixie." Another screen popped up, a woman this time. "And this is Naomi and her dog Raven. They're the owners of PSAR. They have other trainers and handlers as part of their team—"

She motioned again to Beck and this time a full team showed up on screen, all of them looking happy with their dogs in the misty Pacific Northwest air. "Most aren't full time, though."

Devin looked at the picture. They all wore hiking gear of some kind, and most had stuffed pockets and carabiners clipped in various places—as though they'd pulled together for the picture rather than dressing for it. Each had a dog on a leash sitting at perfect attention.

Previously Devin wouldn't have thought much about it but now—between getting Curie as his own and working at the Sanctuary—he saw the differences. The sit position each dog held was perfect. No sway in any hips, where some dogs liked to relax and lean over. These dogs were ready to leap at a moment's notice. He saw their focus was forward, looking at whoever was right behind the camera, ears perked.

To his eyes now, it was clearly not the same as the family pet staying in one place for a holiday photo. Maybe his eyes weren't trained like Beck's were, but they were certainly enough for him to start spotting the differences.

"Would they all come?" Ash asked.

"We don't know." Another non-answer from Roz. *Interesting.* "Once we get dates decided, they can tell their freelance people and they can each decide if they'll make it. So at least two, probably six, maybe as many as twelve or fourteen."

There weren't that many rooms at the lodge, Devin knew.

"I assume we're charging them for this?" Beck clarified, an edge to his signs, and a tension in his jaw.

There was something in Roz's manner that made Devin wonder not just that Beck was asking questions, but something a little tight in the way that she responded. He did not want to be curious. Whatever waves were bouncing between those two, they changed from casual to concerned more than once. Enough to make him wonder if something more than business was going on between them.

It wasn't the first time he'd wondered that. But he still didn't have any answers and he wasn't sure he wanted them.

Roz explained more, but Devin caught the light and slight buzz in the table surface as his phone lit up. His head turned to read it, unable to hide the clench in his chest.

Just as fast, all eyes turned to look at *him* as he spotted Gabi's name and message brightly splashed across his screen. "Sorry!" he signed with one hand, smacking his other over the face of the phone lest anyone else be able to read it before he did.

He pulled it closer before he even read the message. "I thought that was on silent," he motioned. He *always* had it on silent. *It was just supposed to vibrate! What had happened?*

Lynzee grinned at him. "We heard it vibrate against the table."

So he hadn't dicked up the settings, he'd just been monumentally stupid. He knew they could hear the vibrations sometimes.

It was filed under "things Deaf kids learned about hearing." People could hear farts. They heard doors closing—bedroom doors, cabinets, car doors, you name it. And they could hear that you were mad when you closed it. They heard doorbells and fire alarms—though at least there were usually lights with the alarms. And they heard his phone buzz even though the screen literally said "Silent."

Hopefully, they hadn't seen the message that Gabi had sent.

CHAPTER TWENTY-FOUR

hy was this so difficult? Gabi sat in her office not doing her job. Instead, she was staring at her phone screen where she had tapped out a message to Devin . . . but not sent it.

Honestly, it was probably already too late for him to change anything. But she stared at it anyway, still debating if she should ask or not.

The problem was that she actually did know why it was so difficult. It was awful because neither of them had called the other *boyfriend* or *girlfriend*. Because she'd asked him to join her for the weekend and he'd agreed—but neither had said "for sex." There was no way to know if he'd picked up what she'd implied, if she was reading him correctly and . . . *what a mess.*

If she simply threw herself out there, and put it in plain English, and then he didn't want her? That would hurt so bad. If she just let it ride, and nothing happened, she could say it was because, *well, neither of them had really figured things out yet.* She could lie to herself that maybe he was holding back. But once she flat out asked, it would have to be directly answered. *Wouldn't it?*

The anxiety that grabbed her ribcage and pulled her

shoulders up to her ears stopped her from hitting the button immediately.

"Gabi!" The voice came from behind her. *When had her office door opened?* Gabi whirled around to see September standing in her doorway.

The young college student didn't look like anything was wrong. She just said, "There's a guy out here who wants to see you."

All the anxiety lifted instantly. *Devin. But didn't they all know Devin?* Maybe September didn't. Maybe the others really didn't. Gabi often fixed two coffees and headed out the door to meet him in the park. So they knew he existed but they'd only seen him a few times.

She followed the young redhead out to the front of the store, excited to see him and then . . . *Ugh.* Gabi tried to hide the disappointment coursing through her. This man couldn't be any further from Devin if he were actually trying. "Hi, Fred."

They all knew Fred. Except maybe for September.

It had been a while since he'd last come in. After the second time he'd started coming around, Gabi had learned from an employee who'd worked at a different chain that Fred made the rounds to all the local shops. His MO was to order his coffee, then complain about it. He would try to get a free one by getting his "bad" coffee fixed. Then he would come back the next day and do it all over again. As if they wouldn't recognize him. He did this until he had absolutely worn out his welcome, then he moved to the next shop.

Apparently, he'd been through everything within striking distance and was back to her shop. "What can I do for you, Fred?"

Gabi tried to keep a sincere smile on her face, hoping that maybe today was the day that Fred just wanted to say *thank you.* Today was not that day.

"This isn't right!" He held the cup out, sloshing some over

the edge and near the computer register. Gabi was proud of herself, she didn't flinch. But September closed her eyes and tried not to audibly sigh.

Apparently, she had been dealing with it for a little while before she came to get Gabi. With a wave of her hand down below the counter level, where hopefully Fred wouldn't see, Gabi shooed the young woman away. Hopefully she understood it was not her fault. Then Gabi made a mental note to tell her exactly that later.

People thought management was being in charge of people and bossing them around, but mostly it was being in charge of all the crap that regular employees couldn't handle. Fred definitely fell into that category.

It took almost thirty minutes and three whole cups of coffee for Gabi to get Fred to agree that it was right. But the issue was finally resolved. There were still a few people in the shop, a few more sitting outside under the portico and the flowers, so she couldn't raise a cheer when he left, or high five any of the others. She couldn't even visibly deflate.

What she wouldn't give to be out on the patio in the sunshine. Maybe she could take her work outside today. That would be okay. Except for the fact that she had been worrying over her texts rather than ordering supplies.

"Why didn't you give the bad coffee to him? We can't serve it to anyone." September asked.

Ridley was up beside her, agreeing. "I thought we were supposed to let them keep it. A gesture of goodwill or something."

"Not the frequent fliers," Gabi told them. "It wasn't a mistake. He's actively trying to get free things. He says it doesn't taste right. We can in good faith get rid of it for him. So yes, normally we do that, but not with someone who's been around as often as Fred has."

"So he can complain all he wants, and run us around, but he's not actually getting any free coffee out of it." September caught on.

"Exactly. And if he comes in here again, you can start off with what I did at the end." Gabi had quit trying and decided to make a very small portion of coffee in the bottom of his cup. She handed it to him and asked him if it tasted right. Once he agreed, she told him she was going to make him a whole cup just like that. So it would be exactly what he wanted.

By getting him to agree before she made it, he had basically agreed to take it as it was and leave the store.

"That was smart," Ridley told her.

"Thank you." Feeling better, Gabi curtsied to her team, holding her apron out at both sides as she did.

She was turning to head into the back to send her stupid text and order supplies, when she realized she needed fortification for all of it. Turning down the long run behind the counter, she headed to the espresso machine and grabbed a small cup. Filling it almost to the top, she carefully raised it toward her employees in a toast, then shot it.

Damn. It was the good stuff and she blinked, feeling the caffeine surge behind her eyeballs. She might regret that in a bit. Back in her office she flipped the phone over, startled to see that the message had already sent. She must have bumped something when September startled her.

Well, hell. It was not her decision anymore. It was out there.

She stared at the words. — Do you want to stay over?

She supposed she could be offering him her couch. But yeah, it was pretty much a straight up invitation to sin. She dwelled on it all afternoon, constantly checking for a reply that never came. Each time she looked and it wasn't there, her heart sank a little lower.

He was probably finding a polite way to let her down easy.

There still was no return message by the time her shift

ended and, Marietta, her assistant manager hadn't shown up. *Today of all days!*

At least there were several frantic texts explaining that there had been an accident. That it wasn't her, but she was stuck and running late. Gabi was tied up in knots and she still had to do the job until Marietta showed up!

She had given herself a bit of extra time, in the hopes that she didn't have to run around frantically before Devin got there. But that time was rapidly disappearing.

Closing her eyes for a second, Gabi reminded herself that she had changed the sheets already. She'd straightened the bedroom and taken out the trash, but she desperately wanted to shower—she did not want to open the door to him with her hair pulled back in a ponytail smelling of three different grinds. And she needed to shave her legs!

At last, when her assistant showed up, Gabi was already standing at the door, apron flung into the laundry bin in the back. She was out the door and bolting toward the parking lot, praying she didn't hit the same traffic on the way home.

But then she was home and sprinting into her shower, shaving as fast as she could and then realizing she'd missed a spot or two. Forcing a deep breath, she reminded herself that she was fine, and it was way better than showing up having nicked herself because she was a hot mess.

She shut the water off the fastest she ever had, pulled down a towel and checked her phone again—like a fiend. Only this time there was a message. In the few minutes she'd been in the shower, Devin had replied. — I would love to.

She almost had to scroll back up to be sure what her question was. It had been so long. But it was as simple and straightforward as the answer could be.

Oh hell yes! Gabi thought and then immediately, *Oh hell no.*

She pawed her way through her underwear drawer. There was nothing too fancy in it. She couldn't afford the high-end stuff, just the usual variety mall lingerie. And she just threw it in the drawer, not pairing the colors or folding it neatly. Right now she regretted her choices.

She pulled out a bra and undie that weren't really a set. They were different shades of pink. *Good. It wouldn't look like she was trying too hard.* Though she could tell she was definitely trying—or at least worrying.

Stepping into the underwear, she felt the odd sensation and squeezed her eyes shut. *Fuck,* she hadn't been fully dry. She needed to calm down! She needed another towel.

After racing around frantically, she got dried off, and into a second—dry—set of pink undies and hopped back and forth through the apartment in her underwear picking up random items out of the living room, chucking them into the laundry bin for later decisions. Then she dried her hair, put on makeup, and wiped a spot where she touched the side of her face with the mascara wand like a complete dumbass.

She was in the living room moving the pillows from side to side on the couch when she heard a car door down below. Stepping to the large glass window that led to her balcony, she looked out and saw that Devin had pulled up.

Oh shit. He was here. She hadn't even gotten dressed yet. Then she realized she was standing in the window in nothing but her nice mall lingerie.

CHAPTER TWENTY-FIVE

They were going for dinner and a movie, something they'd only done once so far. Gabi felt the odd formality of it, the way people chose that when they didn't know each other. The problem was that she knew him . . . maybe too well.

Adding sex into the mix was too much and it made her nervous at dinner. But she didn't want to go back. She'd just have to get through it.

She sat at the table in the middle of the restaurant—nice enough, but just a high-end chain, nothing too fancy—and thought about her nice lace underwear. Was it maybe too much? It was too late to change now. And it was stupid to let her mind race this way.

It must have been obvious because Devin had finally reached out, putting his hand over hers. With the other he told her, "You don't need to be nervous. There's nothing that has to happen tonight. You can send me home at the end of the night if you want."

Great. It was obvious that she was nervous.

Gabi looked around the restaurant, checking and hoping that no one else nearby understood the conversation they were having. He saw her again. His hand over hers didn't move. "No one is watching."

It was always a risk. So few people did understand ASL—and certainly not fluently enough to really eavesdrop—that it was tempting to have all kinds of conversations out in the open. They would get complacent and every once in a while there would be someone . . . Someone they didn't expect. Maybe a little old lady sitting in the corner booth whose eyes would grow wide, because Devin had brought up *sex* at the dinner table.

Not that he'd said that exactly. And the old lady wasn't even looking. Gabi forced yet another deep breath. "Do you remember when we were at the mall and we were following that one couple of girls around because they were making fun of everyone?" in ASL, of course.

Devin laughed. He did remember. "They had no idea."

Not until one of the girls had said something so outrageous that the two of them had doubled over with laughter loud enough to draw attention from passers by. Only then had the girls' eyes grown wide as they realized they were being actively eavesdropped on. Devin had assured them they were funny, at least, but they'd been embarrassed.

Gabi never wanted to be in that situation.

She pulled her hands in close and told him, "It's been a while for me. I don't want to mess anything up between us."

He nodded. "I don't think it will. But I agree that I don't want to. So let's just go along and see what happens. No pressure."

She couldn't turn down an offer like that . . . "But I want it to happen. I want it to be wonderful."

He laughed, and this time when he looked at her, he said, "Great. No pressure. *Thanks*."

They'd done better after that. Her rattled nerves had finally settled. However it went, she knew the two of them would be okay.

They'd seen the movie, a horror flick they both wanted to watch—like the old days. And they'd driven past three theaters to get to the best one. She liked the full recliners, but mostly it was because Devin knew they always had their closed captioning working. A lot of places claimed to have it, but it was constantly broken—something Gabi hadn't learned until he'd come back into her life.

The seats were huge, but he still reached over and grabbed her hand, almost as if they'd made it to being high school sweethearts. Then, when the movie was over, they almost didn't speak at all, climbing back into his car as he drove them to her apartment. As if they both wanted this and didn't want to jinx it.

He parked below the balcony again, never having told her if he'd seen her standing there in her underwear. She hadn't asked. Only this time, as she made a move to climb out, he stopped and looked at her. "Do you want me to come up? Or do you want me to go home?"

She felt her tongue slide along her lower lip. Gabi knew exactly what she wanted. It shouldn't be hard to say that he was offering her either option.

She said, "I want you to come up. I want everything."

CHAPTER TWENTY-SIX

They danced awkwardly around each other up the stairs as he trailed her. *Was he looking at her ass?* It was the only place that would be appropriate.

Gabi fumbled with the key, her nerves showing again. But his hand settled at the small of her back and the flush in her skin no longer felt like steeling herself for future embarrassment. Inside, she set her purse down and looked around the room. He'd stepped in when he picked her up, but what had she missed?

When she finished a sweep of the place and turned back to him, she found he'd simply dropped the small bag he brought from the car and was only looking at her. Whatever might be in the room that was incriminating . . . He wasn't going to see it at least until tomorrow.

With a smile growing slyly on her lips, she asked, "Do you want something to drink?"

It didn't strike her as odd, the quiet tenor of their conversations. There wasn't the usual noise and static of words. There was just a softness that settled in, their thoughts and conversations were plenty big. Sometimes signs had hands slap or things touch—as a hearing person this was the sound of ASL.

But right now, his words were filling up her vision. "No. I just want you."

For a split second, her brain flashed back to her eight-year-old friend. Then ten, then eleven. Her heart seized at the memory of how she'd disappeared on him. She'd wanted to sneak out one last time and see him, but Mama had never gone to bed. They'd never slept in that horrible apartment again.

Now, here he was, this man in front of her.

A man who didn't know—

He was leaning in slowly, giving her every chance to back away. But his fingers found her hair and held on. They were nearly the same height. She just fit with him. She didn't have to stretch or mold herself to him, she naturally belonged. Each curve of her body molded to each plane of his as her own mouth sought his.

They'd kissed before. But as her mouth finally closed on his, she felt it. The understanding that this kiss wasn't the end but the beginning.

He pressed into her, his breathing deep and heavy, as if he were finally where he wanted to be—the same way she felt. He kissed her lazily, as if they had all the time in the world, but Gabi needed something . . . everything.

Her tongue swept his and it was like igniting him. His hand gripped her hair while the other slid down her back, leaving a trail of sweet shivers along her spine until he gripped her ass and pulled her close enough to feel just how much he wanted her.

Hands tracing each other, feeling the curves and muscle under skin for the first time, they pressed into every touch, both of them begging for more. It quickly changed to plucking at buttons and tugging at zippers, then to frantic peeling of their own clothing and each other's.

Devin quickly stripped to nothing, standing before her as if waiting for her okay. Fully erect, he seemed heated, not embarrassed. She waited, somehow having stopped touching him, in her own slightly mismatched underwear. He looked her up and down, need flaring in his eyes and stealing all her worry.

"May I?" he asked, one hand the only thing that moved.

She nodded.

She was in his arms, leaned back as he kissed her. His fingers traced her skin, seeming as if he were randomly trying to touch every part of her, but her bra flicked open in the back and his finger slid under one lace cup, pulling it down as his mouth found her nipple and she cried out to a man who couldn't hear her. She did not care, because hell—what he could do with his hands.

She was naked, laid back over the arm of her couch, and getting played by a man who could clearly make his own music. Gabi couldn't catch her breath, the pleasure of his fingers stroking her rolled through her, then rolled again. Her fingers dug into his forearm where he braced himself against the back of the couch.

Was she upside down? Did she care? No, she did not. She just needed him.

"Now." One free hand, one motion, one smile on his face, and he was inside her.

It shouldn't have felt better than being touched, but it did. She should have touched him more. She should . . . her breath and her thoughts escaped as she felt like a firework rocketing into the sky and ready to explode.

CHAPTER TWENTY-SEVEN

He'd come until he felt as if his brains had turned to mush. Then it took a good few minutes to gather any single thought from where they'd melted out of his ears.

"Are you okay?" He was still breathing heavily, still draped over her where she was draped over the arm of the couch. It had seemed like a good idea at the time.

Devin started to move, he didn't want to crush her, or hurt her, or basically have her think that his brains had melted out of his ears. He'd had great sex before and he'd been in love before, but he wasn't confident he'd done both until now.

Gabi tugged him back down. "I'm good." The words were slurred, her motions not clear like usual. She spoke with one hand, the other still digging her nails into his arm. It would leave a mark, but he didn't mind at all.

Still he stood up, wondering if he would be dizzy, if it was true that all the blood had rushed to his cock. But once he was upright, he found he was remarkably clear-headed. He knew what he wanted. He'd known for a while, but tonight—not just the sex, but the whole thing—had brought it into sharp focus.

He'd lost years when he'd been right near her. He wasn't going to lose any more.

Reaching out, he took her hand and peeled her up off the couch. Only then did he look over her shoulder and realize the curtains on the sliding door to the balcony were wide open.

"What?" She'd seen the look on his face.

"I think we gave them a show." *Shit.*

But Gabi just smiled. "I find that right now I don't care."

Well, then. The thought had barely moved into his brain when she asked, "Did you see the show I was giving right when you pulled up?"

"What?" *What show?*

She explained about how she'd seen him from the window before realizing she was standing there in just her lingerie. "I will make sure to look next time."

He was being presumptuous that there would be a next time. He turned to look for Curie as he had done several times throughout the evening. The first time Gabi had asked what he was looking for and he'd explained he was used to having his dog at his side.

This time she said, "She's welcome here. You should just bring her next time."

So there could be a *next time.* Both the thought and her invitation for Curie warmed him.

Skirting the edge of the room, she pulled the curtains shut without posing naked in the window. Then she went to the kitchen and poured a large glass of water which she shared with him. It shouldn't have felt intimate, but they'd not quite turned on more than the entry light, and the feel of the space was as if the whole world belonged to just the two of them. Some modern day Adam and Eve, naked and drinking water, with nothing to do for the whole weekend but have sex and explore whatever gardens they could find.

He guzzled the water, thirstier than he expected. But she took the glass back, set it on the table and took his hand. He let her lead him into her bedroom, the space colorful and inviting. He'd only seen in through the slightly open door in passing before now and it felt like being welcomed into the heart of her space.

Still holding his fingers in hers, she opened the bedside drawer and set a condom on the comforter next to where she pushed him to sit. *Oh hell yeah.* He'd been at attention since she'd asked if he'd seen her in the window and he was having fantasies about being greeted that way from now on, but this? He was rock hard.

Then her mouth was on him, and his eyes rolled backward.

She stroked him and he took as much as he could without coming. Then he pushed her onto her back on the bed and returned the favor until she bucked against the covers. Her breath came hard and heavy, moving her breasts with each gasp. God, she was beautiful. They belonged to each other now.

He'd expected none of this. And he was going to revel in every moment of it.

Rolling the condom on, he found her demanding him inside her again. It was a heady feeling to have her need him like that, but it only lasted a moment before he felt the build up. Slowing down as much as he could, he worked to drive her desire up. Her hands reached for him, grabbing first his arms then his ass, as if she could make him move faster.

But then she was coming apart in his arms again, the change in her as she seemed to simultaneously arch and melt for him drove him to his own edge. The soft heat of her pulsed around him as he finally let go.

Eventually they collapsed together, then curled up, before admitting defeat and crawling under the covers. He'd burned every calorie he'd eaten, and he didn't want to move.

One arm was under her shoulders, wrapped around her, the other he used to speak softly in the dim light. "I'm glad you asked me to come up."

"Me too," she replied before settling her hand back across his chest.

It was stupid, he thought, but they fit together perfectly. He leaned his head over a bit to feel her hair against his face. Devin wasn't one much for believing in soulmates or destiny, but something felt ridiculously right about this. They'd been apart for decades and only found each other now.

But now seemed like exactly the right time.

"Do you want to go hiking tomorrow?" he asked, thinking they could hit a state park, but she didn't respond.

He was getting ready to ask again when he felt the shift, the heaviness settling over her, and he almost laughed to himself. What an idiot he was. Gabi had granted him her entire weekend. But she'd gone to work this morning just like he had. Only with it being a Saturday, he hadn't shown up until ten. She'd been in at six.

No wonder she'd fallen dead asleep in his arms.

If he was smart, he would follow because chances were, she'd be up before dawn. And he was hoping he could be right there beside her.

Though he wanted to, he didn't fall asleep immediately. Gabi seemed peaceful, content, and satisfied, but he always wondered when he was with a hearing woman. Had he made any strange noises he didn't know about?

He'd learned as a kid—like many Deaf kids—what he could and couldn't control. Sounds, slamming doors, phones on vibrate . . . adults and teachers had told them that hearing people could tell those things. No one had coached him about sex. One of these days he'd have to ask her because, God forbid, he did something horribly unsexy.

She shifted slightly, rolling in a little closer. But the move pinched his arm, shifted the blood flow until he felt the hot ripples all the way down to his fingertips. There had to be a way to make this work, he wanted her in his arms but he needed to feel his fingers.

As he tried to shift, Gabi moved with him, her eyelids fluttering though she didn't come awake. Rolling away, she still trapped his hand but it didn't cut off the circulation anymore.

The covers had shifted, pulling down and leaving her half bare and he took the moment to savor the view. With his free hand, he lightly traced the curve of her spine. Even in the dim light, he loved the rich color of her skin. It made him think of the coffee she served and of days in the sun.

He didn't want to wake her. She clearly needed her sleep. But he trailed his fingers softly along her arm, the dim light blurring the edges. He told himself if she woke up, he'd make it worth her while, but she didn't. Dead to the world, she reacted to his touch by rolling further, then sliding back up close into him. She nestled her naked ass into his hip and made his body react. She might be dead asleep, but he wasn't.

Her hair rolled in whatever curl she'd done to it for their evening, gathering itself and its voluminous waves in his face. He reached up brushing it up further on the pillow, before he tucked himself around her, telling himself he would sleep.

Devin buried his nose into her neck and inhaled the scent of whatever soft perfume she'd worn. There was just an undercurrent of espresso. He smiled to himself in the dark.

It was everything he wanted. Whether it was random, or a stroke of good luck, or some kind of destiny, he could settle in here. He reached up, softly sliding his fingertips along her shoulder as he moved around to hold her tight. When his fingers brushed along a slight ridge.

She had a scar.

His eyes flew open, straining in the faint light that came from around the edge of the curtains. Wide awake now, he traced it again with his finger. *He knew that scar.* He had a matching one.

Devin felt his blood start to boil.

CHAPTER TWENTY-EIGHT

Gabi woke to faint sunlight, tender muscles, and the soft gooey feeling inside her that things were finally headed in the right direction. Smiling, she realized this was not just the usual dedication to get up and face another day. To go to her job and try to simply enjoy the little things along the way. *There were big things now.*

When she stretched, she reached her arms up high over her head, moving carefully so as not to bother the man beside her. She didn't want to shake this wonderful, liquid feeling of happiness. The light coming through the window told her she'd slept later than usual for her. It was still plenty early, and she didn't want to wake Devin. She rolled over to look, to smile at the warm naked man in her bed.

Only the bed was empty.

Frowning, Gabi paused, listening for movement from the bathroom, but she didn't hear anything. Devin almost couldn't be quiet if he tried. She remembered the two Montalvo girls taking so long to teach him how to sneak out of his house. She almost laughed thinking how he'd wondered why his mother kept catching him.

Kitchen, she thought and held the covers to her chest in some kind of misplaced modesty. As she sat up, she pushed her hair out of her face and blinked the sleep away. But she heard nothing from the kitchen either. The apartment wasn't that big.

She almost opened her mouth to call out for him, a ridiculous impulse and she squashed it almost before she had it. She'd learned decades ago that she only actually spoke the name *Devin* when she was talking *about* him, not *to* him. She could call out until she roused the neighbors but it wouldn't do any good.

Looking around for her clothing, she swam through her still foggy brain until she remembered they'd left it all on the living room floor. Climbing out of bed, she let the covers fall away and rummaged through her drawers for a large T shirt. She even stepped into underwear, though why? She had no idea.

She still heard nothing from the apartment, only one singular creak from someone upstairs. She didn't have to see in the mirror to know that her features were pulled into a frown.

Down the hallway she saw the bathroom door wasn't even closed, so she pushed it open and found it empty. That shouldn't be a surprise, though. She would have heard the shower running or something.

He was probably sitting on the couch eating cereal.

But Devin wasn't there, and when she glanced through the opening she saw the kitchen was empty too. *Where was he?*

Her brain only registered it a moment later: There was still clothing on the floor but only hers. His bag that he'd dropped just inside the door—gone.

Breathing quickly and trying not to panic, she raced to the balcony window and threw the heavy curtains wide. The T shirt barely covered the tops of her thighs, but this wasn't a show, not like she'd given last night, and right now she didn't care. She looked down into the lot and found his parking space was empty.

Devin was gone.

Unlike a lot of others, she didn't spend her time watching murder mysteries and true-crime stories about missing people. But she had to admit it certainly looked as if he had left of his own accord. *Why would he go?*

Her breath stopped. She stood with her hands still on the curtains, holding them wide, unable to process what she was seeing. *Why would he?*

Then it hit her. *His mother.* Something must have happened with his mother.

Panicked but relieved, Gabi ran to the bedroom and nearly yanked her phone off the charger as she checked it for messages. *Nothing.*

It must be bad, she thought, if he'd left without waking her, without telling her where he was going, or even asking her to come along. Phone clutched in her hand, she thought for a moment, then tapped out a frantic message.

— woke up and you were gone. Is your mother okay?

Gabi couldn't quite put her finger on it, but a nerve struck and once again she didn't hit send. Much like she'd felt the other day when she was asking him did he want to come for the weekend? Did he want to stay over?

Letting her thoughts wander, she tried to put together pieces that fit. She thought back through last night. It had been amazing. They'd both fallen asleep with smiles on their faces. Devin had wanted to stay with her . . . she'd asked, and he'd said yes.

That wasn't the problem.

Once again, she checked the phone. Nothing had come in. Still, she hated that she wasn't willing to send such a simple message. Not yet.

Could he be one of those men who fucked and left? Was he only in it for the chase?

She supposed it was possible, but she struggled to believe it. Nothing leading up to last night had made it seem like that was the case. Though she hadn't known him in the interim, she had known him twenty years ago. That wasn't Devin.

Fuck it. She hit the button, sending the message.

He just wasn't that shitty of a person. She knew it.

She considered putting on real clothes and driving by Ms. James's house, but what would that do? Whether or not the car was there wouldn't tell her anything. Knocking on the door would only wake the woman up, likely. Most people didn't rise as early as she did, and Gabi would feel like shit for bothering her.

Now fully awake, she wandered the apartment with her T shirt covering her confused and bruised heart as she waited for Devin to reply.

CHAPTER TWENTY-NINE

He'd stayed until four a.m. . . . until he couldn't stand it any longer. Devin thought Gabi might wake up and he could yell at her, but she didn't.

He considered just leaving. But what was he going to do at one in the morning? Drive aimlessly around Charlottesville? Go back up the mountain?

He wanted to go home, and he was just a bit surprised to find that home was the tiny cabin with the spectacular view. Home was where he could see the front door and the kitchen and the closet all from his pillows and where Curie curled up on the nice squishy bed Devin had bought her.

He wanted to go back, to curl into a ball and pretend he didn't feel this deep betrayal. But he knew motion made noise. If he pulled into the parking lot, the dogs would likely go off, waking up Roz. He didn't want to do that. He didn't want anyone to see him doing a real walk of shame.

He'd been had.

He waited there in the bed that had been so warm but suddenly felt so cold and at four, he'd given up. On the one hand, he hated himself for sneaking away and on the other he didn't think it was a bad idea at all. *She deserved it.* And he deserved to be able to leave and take his horrible thoughts with him.

He told himself that he would get away and stay away until his anger settled, but now he didn't think it ever would.

How could she?

Trying to talk himself down, he'd let his inner voices suggest that he should stay and hear her out, that she must have her reasons. The more he thought about it though, he couldn't fathom a single reason for her to do this. Nothing that should have come between *them*. Other people, maybe but not between her and him.

Lord knew, they'd just put themselves in a position to have absolutely nothing between them. Only there was, something big and ugly and he hadn't even known it was there.

The whole thing was twisted and awful and he couldn't put his finger on any way that it might work out, anything that she could say that would make it okay.

So, rather than staying, he left. At four a.m., he was willing to just drive around Charlottesville. It was still way too early to go up the mountain and wake the people he lived with. Though he did have his own cabin and they had theirs, it was a commune as much as anything. Roz often said the word "family" and he'd thought of it as a descriptor, until now. He would have to sneak past the people who knew him and—he was figuring out—cared about him.

Instead, he drove by his mother's house, checking on the car in the driveway. That everything was neat and tidy and locked down made him feel better, but it didn't give him a place to stop. He drove past a closed grocery store, a hair salon, and an emergency vet all tucked into a strip mall.

Eventually he passed an open coffee shop and turned around. Not Gabi's, of course. He parked and headed in, trying to be an actual human and not a hot ball of rage. He ordered using his phone because no one there seemed to sign, and he placed the simplest request for a tall cup of dark black coffee.

The bitterness hit his tongue in tune with his morning and the caffeine was beyond necessary. Had he even slept at all? He didn't know.

It was still early, and the dogs would go off, but it was no longer the dead middle of the night. He'd burned some time driving around the city and the sun was coming up. Even with the coffee in his system he felt the shakes start to settle in and the exhaustion creeping in at the borders.

The caffeine kept him awake as he headed out of town and down the old country roads then up the mountain, and finally to the gravel drive. The dogs would wake Roz if she was still asleep, but if she came out to check on him, he would collect Curie. Otherwise, he would try to be as quiet as a Deaf man could and just head back to his cabin.

He pulled into the lot, parking next to Brandy's car. Getting out, he had no idea if he had succeeded in staying quiet, quiet enough to fool the dogs. But he looked up at the lodge and no lights came on.

He missed Curie. He shouldn't have left the dog behind. He could have had a companion right now—which was the whole point of having her! Devin had thrown over his faithful friend so he could go have sex with a woman. He hadn't even thought anything of it. He'd just left Curie with the babysitter and headed out.

Stuffing his hands down in his pockets against the cold air of the morning, Devin berated himself for a series of bad decisions. Putting his head down, he trudged around the side of the lodge, then crept past the kennels, hoping not to wake any of the training dogs.

If they barked, hopefully, it was just the usual noise the dogs made and everyone slept through it. Instead of heading to the left, and along the trail, he moved to the right, passing alongside the veterinary office to a small path that led between cabins five and six. He'd have to pass by Su's new place, but he wouldn't have to walk by Brandy and Ash and Beck.

For some reason it seemed worse to wake the ones who'd been here before. Maybe Su would just buy that people came and went at all hours. It was the lesser of the two evils, he thought, and told himself it was just a matter of fewer people for him to wake at six in the morning.

But he didn't even wake Su. She was already on her porch in full running gear ready to head down a trail. He tried for a friendly wave as if everything was normal. But what even was normal? He was so messed up.

If Su caught it, she didn't stop. She waved him on and when he turned to check, all he saw was the bright pink running gear and the purple ponytail bobbing down the path.

It wasn't a bad idea. He could use a hike this morning. A good one with steep hills and hard climbs. But right now he was too tired. He would need to collect Curie before he headed out. There had already been one snake incident. Maybe he should have told Su ...

Too late. But that was the whole point of having a companion dog: To make up for the things he couldn't hear. Still, right now, he could barely see straight. He fit the key into the cabin door, and headed in. The heat was on, the place was exactly as he left it, yet somehow he felt the cold down into his bones.

CHAPTER THIRTY

His good hiking boots ate up the trail, his breath soughed in and out. Devin pushed them both hard.

At his side, Curie trotted along, not seeming to mind the hard work. Though Devin was trying to keep his eyes open and stay alert for dangers on the trail, he was still too mad to be attentive. So far Curie hadn't alerted to anything.

As a Deaf man, he'd learned other things to watch out for to make up for the noises and sounds he didn't hear. He paid more attention to lights, signals, movement in the periphery that others ignored because they didn't hear a noise to go with it. But right now, he was mad enough to have tunnel vision.

He'd crawled into bed without Curie, without Gabi, and with his sense of rightness and happiness ripped completely away. It wasn't surprising he'd slept for only three hours before he woke up. He'd dreamed of climbing through the window at the Montalvo girls' house, of having the sharp piece of metal on the bottom sash slice into his shoulder.

They'd been kids. They hadn't known it at the time, but it never should have been there. It had to be some kind of building code violation. But he had that same scar on his left shoulder blade from climbing through that window. The same one that had snagged Luisa wearing Gabi's shirt on the night she died. Or so she said.

Devin questioned everything now. Had she really lived in Austin all that time? Why was she so fluent in ASL? Had she come here because of the store? Or was she stalking him?

The last one bothered him. He shouldn't even think it. It was that ridiculous. Still, he considered getting on social media and checking out her accounts. He'd seen her post the picture of the two of them. She was just out there as Gabi Montalvo so she would be easy enough to find. He was only on a few social networks a little bit himself. But he should be able to see pretty easily if she had actually come to Charlottesville before he had. Was it some sick cruel joke?

His toe snagged on a root, and he almost went down, but he was too mad to fall. Ignoring the pain radiating up his foot was easy. It didn't touch the pain radiating out from his heart.

When he'd woken up and realized he wasn't going back to sleep, he'd thrown off the covers, gotten dressed and headed up to the lodge. Ten a.m. on a Sunday morning—Roz was always awake by now.

As a new dog owner, he finally understood that there was overlap between having a dog and having a child. Sleeping in wasn't an option, the dog had to have a chance to go outside. Not unless Devin wanted to clean a mess off his floor and deal with the fact that Curie felt bad about doing something she'd been given no other option for. He wouldn't do that.

At the lodge, Devin had entered through the back door and smiled for the first time in hours as Curie had come running over to him. Devin could swear the dog had a smile on her face, too. He didn't sign it—Roz would see—but he silently promised never to leave his companion behind again.

Devin was standing to find Roz and let her know he was back when she strode into the room. Tall and stately—always—her dark, dark hair swung in a bob that spoke of money she didn't have anymore. Her manners were an interesting mix of high society and sincere caring. Devin was grateful that she seemed to see and didn't say, "I wasn't expecting you until Monday night."

She'd just smiled until he shrugged and said, "Plans changed."

He motioned to Curie, and they headed toward the back door before he even realized how rude he was being. Turning around, Devin stomped his foot to get Roz's attention. She turned back, a soft question on her face, having learned it wasn't a rude gesture at all. Just something for people who didn't hear.

Devin mustered as politely as he could, "Thank you so much for watching her."

"She's never a bother," she told him, and he believed her. "In fact, I think she makes these two behave better."

That Devin could easily believe. Curie had been happy to be back with him, hard hike or not. And Devin was grateful that the dog was on the slightly large size of medium and had no issues keeping up with him on the trail.

He was at the clearing before he realized how far he'd come. A heavy piece of granite jutted out from the trail, forming its own edge. The cliff below dropped for hundreds of feet—if not thousands. Devin didn't know.

He wasn't tempted to step off, he had his mother, his friends, his job here, and his anger to nurse. But he didn't get close to the edge either. He wasn't in the right head space to be careful. Still, he stopped for a moment, the view majestic before him. It calmed him. Dips and valleys, mountains in the distance, all older than time, suggested this would pass.

Devin wondered if he could see into another state if not for the smoke-like fog that clung in patches. Below him, the Jade River wound through the deep crevasse it had cut for centuries before him, dark and mysterious this morning as it carried memories along. Yet he saw none of it.

The red haze of his own fury gripped him and narrowed his vision, stealing his happiness and his sanity and even the ability to see what was directly in front of him. Devin hated her for it.

In his jacket pocket, his phone began to vibrate. First once, then twice, until the notifications came fast enough that they were basically indistinguishable. Pulling it out of his pocket he saw multiple messages from Gabi. He saw a message from his mother telling him she hoped he was having a good weekend. Just the standard fare.

He messaged his mother back. — out for a hike. enjoying the view. How are you doing?

He would go visit her this afternoon. Even though he had intended to spend his whole weekend in bed or hiking with his new lover and basically enjoying a honeymoon phase, he would instead go check on his mother. Maybe see if he could cook her dinner and leave her leftovers in the freezer.

This was his first day off for his special request weekend that had seriously gone to hell before it even started. He couldn't miss the fact that he had other messages. Previews popped up and he couldn't ignore Gabi's blazing trail of questions.

— Is your mother okay?

That's what she thought this was about?

— Are you okay?

While he stood there, another one came in.

— Will you please talk to me?

What for? Why would he talk to someone he couldn't trust?

He was so mad just looking at the name that he had saved the contact under and he saw those four little letters G A B I and the image of her smiling face. His eyes narrowed.

Shoving the phone back into his pocket, he turned around immediately, motioning for Curie to stay to his side, as if the dog wasn't going to do that anyway.

He headed back across the mountain trails plagued by a new thought: *What if he was wrong?*

CHAPTER THIRTY-ONE

Devin raced down the hill faster than he should. Curie was in her harness, buckled into the passenger seat beside him.

Devin was proud of himself, as much as he'd spent the last ten hours blinded by fury, he was taking good care of his dog. They'd raced home from the hike, Devin suddenly having a burning need to go and check. Hope had unfurled in his chest, though he had immediately squashed it back down.

What if he was wrong? Would he be able to crawl back and apologize? How would he be able to tell her what he believed?

But he didn't think he was wrong. There was every possibility that all he was doing was finding damning proof . . . assuming it was there to be found.

Near the end of the hike, when Devin was running full steam ahead, Curie had looked like she was slowing down. Devin had simply scooped up the dog. Service dogs didn't tend to be small. They often needed to be able to reach things like light switches and door handles, to be large enough to warn people.

Curie wasn't a huge breed—some kind of mix of beagle and something else. But anger and adrenaline gave Devin strength and he'd carried the dog for maybe the last mile, letting her rest on the bed and giving her extra water once they got to the cabin.

Curie snacked on food and treats while Devin jumped in the small shower for the quickest wash of his life. Now they were practically racing toward his mother's home. Virginia police were not known for their politeness with speeders, and they didn't give a crap if it was an untraveled mountain road. But the dog hadn't alerted him to sirens and Devin pushed the limit a bit.

He tried to slow down and be a good citizen in his mother's neighborhood. Parking carefully rather than arriving like he was sliding into home base. He knocked on the door—two knocks, a pause, and another two knocks—letting her know that it was him.

He found her in the living room curled up in the corner of the sofa, one of her many magazines open on her lap. Her face lit up. "I wasn't expecting you!"

She looked so perfectly normal that, for a moment, Devin completely dismissed the drama and the anger and all things Gabi Montalvo.

His mother looked *good*. Her color was strong. The sutures had come out, leaving only a small pink scar on the back of her hand. The line would fade over time, the nurses assured him. But he hated the pressure at the back of his eyes because he wondered if there would be enough time for the scar to fade.

Right now, he believed it. His mother had her feet pulled up under her on the couch, looking comfortable and snuggled in her flannel pajamas and thick socks. She was often cold, he knew, but she looked like she'd put on weight, and she was clearly moving relatively well.

As she uncurled herself and she left the magazine on the couch cushions, easily moving across the room, her hands were saying, "You look upset. I thought you were with Gabi this weekend."

At least she got the name right. All the anger that had kept him rigid like steel somehow disintegrated. His shoulders slumped, his spine lost the fury that held it straight, he almost couldn't tell her. But he did.

"I think she lied to me, Mom." He'd planned to come here and make his mother a late breakfast and then casually look through the photo albums. But he cracked in under a minute.

His Mom looked at him through slitted eyes as if she could see everything if she just checked close enough. But Devin didn't want her to see that he'd made love to his new girlfriend for the first time. That he'd had a few glorious hours when he'd believed the road he was on was going to be vastly different, and infinitely better, because of Gabi Montalvo.

Instead, he said, "Let me make you breakfast."

"You don't have to cook for me," she countered. "I can still make my own breakfast."

There it was: *still*. Much like *yet*. Like his concern over whether the scars would actually have time to fade. *Still* reminded them both that whatever this was, it was temporary.

"What happened?" His mother wasn't going to let him get away with just making a fritatta or something.

He wasn't willing to share. "She lied."

"Why do you think she lied?" His mother was still standing there in the living room, five feet between them. Curie waited through the conversation, sitting at Devin's feet. Three different times, he tried to answer. *How much was he willing to tell his mother? When he wasn't even positive he was right. Not yet.*

Eventually he shook his head. "What if I'm wrong?"

Jacinda James, always logical, looked at him and asked, "Can you answer that question yourself?"

"I think so. Let me make you breakfast and then I can look through the old photo albums."

For a moment, it looked as if she was going to refuse, but then she relented. He headed to the kitchen, still stiff and awkward, controlled by his anger and now his worry. What if he'd left Gabi there, asleep in her bed, worried for him and his mother . . . and the worry was all his fault. *What if he'd read it all wrong?*

But he didn't think he had.

He pulled out grated cheese and the carton of eggs. He turned on the oven and laid out the bacon on a pan, sliding it in before the oven was heated—as if he could make his anger pass and the bacon cook faster.

When everything was diced and in the pan and he had scrambled up the eggs and cheese, his mother returned to the kitchen. She stood next to him at the counter, solid on her feet, carrying several thick photo albums. He motioned for her to wait, there were eggshells to clean and a few escaped pepper seeds. But she tucked the books up awkwardly under one arm and grabbed the disinfectant spray and a paper towel.

Devin smiled, reminding himself that—despite all their concerns and shitty diagnoses—there might be several more good years ahead because no matter what the doctors had told him, she handled herself quite well.

When the space was clean, she set down the stack of albums and began flipping through the first one. Seeming to know what he wanted, she turned to pictures of him and Luisa from when they were eight. Old pictures waited under clear plastic protection pages.

Some were professionally printed, some were clearly taken on a lower quality digital camera and printed out for herself. Those images were more blurry than sharp, emotion caught in smiling faces, if not the details he needed.

But he hadn't told his mother what he was looking for. Hell, he wasn't quite sure what the proof would be himself.

She turned page after page. While he wished the pictures

would get better in quality as the time passed in them, he knew they only had a handful of years before Gabi and Luisa would disappear from the photos entirely.

Then the next page revealed a series taken of the three of them sitting on the couch watching a movie on a weekend night. His house. It was different when his mother hosted them. He hadn't seen it then, but he did now. The soda was name brand. There was a huge bowl of popcorn in front of them and a handful of candy bars.

Neither of the moms had been wealthy enough to simply send the kids to the theaters to buy their own tickets and expensive movie snacks. But even so, there'd been a difference in the level between the two homes. Though he saw it now, it wasn't what he was looking for.

His mother started to turn to the next page, but Devin motioned for her to stop. Then, as if he was getting any level of privacy out of it, he asked her to check the bacon and to serve herself some of the eggs while they were still hot. She was kind enough not to call him on it.

He looked more closely. The whole page was full of pictures of the exact same scene. The level of popcorn in the bowl didn't even change. His mother must have snapped a series of pictures quickly as the kids giggled and laughed.

She must have printed up every single version, because there it was: Gabi with her head turned to the left.

This one was taken with a real camera and clear, sharp edges gave him all the proof that he needed.

He looked up at his mother then. She'd already stilled, her movements seeming to understand that he'd found what he needed. Softly, she asked him, "Were you wrong?"

Devin felt the wicked heat rush through him again as he replied, "No."

CHAPTER THIRTY-TWO

"Are you okay, Gabi?"

"I'm fine." The words came out automatically despite the fact that she knew September wouldn't believe her. Clearly, from the way everyone was tiptoeing around her at the shop, she was not fine.

Last night, Mika in her apartment building had seen her putting her key in the lock, her hand shaking, silent tears running down her face. Being a good friend, Mika had asked her what was wrong then taken her out for drinks. That had been the only decent night's sleep Gabi had gotten.

"Fred's here again," September told her, and Gabi felt the irritation wash through her.

It was the only emotion she'd felt in close to forty-eight hours. She'd messaged multiple times before quitting. If only she could call and irritate him with a ringing phone. But no.

She still thought it looked like he'd left her apartment of his own accord. But why wouldn't he say anything? . . . *And then he had.*

Without getting up she asked September, "Didn't you do the taste test coffee for Fred?"

"We've used it successfully three times on him. And yes, that's how I built his coffee today. But when he was handed the entire cup, he went outside, talked to someone and then came back. Now he wants to talk to 'the management.'" She used air quotes and Gabi nodded. There was no way out of this.

"I just don't understand why he's still here," Gabi hadn't meant to say it out loud. He hadn't gotten a single free coffee out of them this round.

"Maybe he's lonely, and he just argues with people for something to say," her employee suggested as Gabi dragged herself upright and looped her apron over her head.

That was sad as hell, Gabi thought. And then she wondered if she was going to become a Fred herself. Who did she even have?

Mika down the hall in her apartment building was the best friend she had here in town. She didn't really know anyone else. The best friend spot had belonged to Devin for a brief shining moment of time but clearly that was not the case now. Gabi didn't even know what she'd done.

She was grateful for her chat group. She'd poured her heart out the other night, crying as her thumbs moved over the phone, telling them what had happened. They'd consoled her, told her she was better off and more. Things she needed to hear. But she read them, she didn't *hear* them. There had been no hugs other than the *virtual* ones that had come in.

Maybe she should put in for a transfer to somewhere she knew people. But where would that even be? Her friends were scattered.

Mika had helped, but Gabi needed a real friend. Someone here, in person, a shoulder she could cry on. Someone that she could be a rock for, too. Someone whose advice she trusted and someone she could help through their worries.

Or else she would end up like Fred.

She headed out front, wanting to say, *Listen, Fred, we've done*

153

everything we can for you. If you don't like our coffee, you need to go somewhere else, because coffee is literally exactly what we do. Instead, she sucked in a deep breath and pasted on a smile—that wasn't any different from any of her other smiles these days—and she mustered up a good, "What can I do for you today, Fred?"

Another man stood beside him. Like Fred, he was older. He was clean. Both men were, but they look disheveled. The first few times she'd seen him, Gabi had wondered if, Fred was homeless. But it seemed that wasn't the case.

"Hi. This is my friend Paul. We noticed there was some trash out on the sidewalk out front, and sometimes it blows out into your sitting area outside."

Gabi was opening her mouth to say she would add that to her List of Employee Chores, when Fred surprised her.

"Paul wanted to know if he picks it up and keeps it clean, could you give him a free coffee in exchange?"

Was Paul on a fixed income? Maybe one of those people barely keeping a home he already owned as local property values kept rising. She had to think about it for a moment. There could be legal ramifications. For example, she couldn't let anyone volunteer behind the counter because, if they got hurt, insurance would have to cover it, or the person could sue. But outside . . . the sidewalk was a public area, and the seating area was accessible from the sidewalk. Sometimes people just sat there and ate their own lunch because it was pretty and shaded.

"I think so," she offered. Technically the man would be picking up trash in public spaces. September looked at her, but Gabi didn't say it out loud. The fact of the matter was, they discarded a certain number of cups of coffee every day. Doing it for something that kept the store more welcoming to customers . . . ? Well the cost of what she was giving away would be well under the cost of the service. Clearly, she and her team hadn't been doing enough.

"Let's try it," she said. Even as the words came out she found herself wondering if Paul would even show up. At least if he didn't, she wasn't out anything. Then she would add the tasks to the employee list, which had been her first inclination. Honestly, everyone would be happy to have Paul do it. No one liked picking up trash.

Fred turned to Paul and smiled. Then he made the letters with his hand. "O K," before signing, "She agreed."

Startled, Gabi waved her hand at Paul, getting his attention. "Are you Deaf?" she signed, and the man's face lit up.

It explained everything. The way he'd walked in following Fred, not interacting and letting Fred speak for him. She just assumed that because they all knew Fred, he'd let Fred do the talking.

"You sign?" he asked.

She nodded and barely refrained from saying "My best friend taught me when I was little." It was yet another wonderful thing that she'd gotten from Devin James.

Seeing the look on Paul's face perked her up though, and she found he was far more than expected. He asked her for specific work times and who he should ask for if she wasn't there. How should he show that the task was completed?

Those were the questions a solid employee would ask. She began to have faith that he'd be here every day. She gave him a cup on the house right then and looked forward to seeing him the next morning. Someone to sign with even if it wasn't Devin.

It was time to teach the employees ASL, she thought—more than just a few signs. There was a thriving Deaf community in Charlottesville and this could be the go-to place.

Grateful to have another task, even if she was sad that it was one that reminded her of Devin, Gabi waited until Fred and Paul were down the street, and the three other customers had been moved through the line, before she announced, "We are all learning ASL to communicate with our customers."

She had to face something new, because she'd asked Devin if

he was hurt or in danger, and he had replied, "I'm safe. But I'm livid. Don't speak to me again."

CHAPTER THIRTY-THREE

He'd felt like an empty box for a while now. The weekend he'd been excited for was now several days in the rearview mirror. He'd filled it with random tasks, visited with his mother, cooked maybe a little too much. But he couldn't fault himself; Mom had individual servings of several of her favorite foods in her freezer that she could thaw, microwave, and eat. She hadn't commented much more, only to nudge him to speak to Gabi.

And that right there was the problem. He couldn't speak to Gabi.

He'd not eaten much and it was suddenly his night to cook for the group. He'd added his requests to the grocery list, but it hadn't all come back. Eating his feelings might be good and he had a cheeseburger in mind. His sudden craving for food was probably a good sign, and he wanted to feed it . . . but not alone.

He would have asked Lynzee to come with him, but she'd recently decided she was going to try being vegetarian. Beck had turned him down. Ash wasn't available. He had veterinary checkups for the afternoon, but he'd begged Devin to bring him back a burger and said he'd text his order.

Devin wandered through the Sanctuary and found Su and Brandy out in the training yard with Vivaldi and Brahms.

"Did you say hamburger?" Su asked excitedly, her signs not fluent but already improving. Immersion did that to a person, but part of the problem was that she was immersed with people who were also learning. Devin was the only native signer. But, he thought, she could use the practice and he could use a friend. He liked the new girl fine, he just didn't really know her.

Then Su's face fell. "Brandy and I are taking Vivaldi and Brahms into town for training." She slowed down a little bit fingerspelling the names and Devin was reaching up to do it, but Brandy quickly pointed out the dog's sign names.

Su, being on her A game, motioned her way through them rather than just nodding and accepting it. Repetition and practice made it all come faster. But Devin noticed Brandy looked a little uncomfortable for a moment.

"What?" he asked.

"Why not—instead of Su and me taking the dogs into town —you and Su take the dogs into town and get your groceries and burgers?"

It took him a minute to realize she was hesitant because she was handing him one of her tasks. But Su's face lit up. "I would love that!"

"Should I also bring Curie?" He liked the idea but was planning for his own pup to come along, and maybe get a few bites of burger. There was always a question about bringing in extra dogs for training.

"Ask Beck?" Brandy suggested.

It figured that would need to go up the line.

He told Su, "I'm making dinner tonight and I need a few things."

It wasn't surprising given the state he'd been in over the weekend. If they knew what they were making, they could simply request things on their list and Roz would get it. But sometimes things weren't there, or Roz didn't find some odd ingredient Beck wanted or she got the wrong thing. Still, for the most part, the food was covered.

Su motioned to Brandy, "I'll go ask Beck?" Then she looked to Devin and ran off like a kid.

Good, he needed a friend who was excited about just getting a damn burger.

Within a few minutes Su was back. "He said we can take Curie, that Curie should . . ." she paused again. "Be good by herself and we do our attention to other dogs."

Devin nodded. She missed a few words, but she was communicating a reasonably complex thought pretty well in a language she hadn't even attempted before a few weeks ago.

"Then let's go get burgers," he signed, wondering if she was actually excited for burgers or if the Sanctuary wasn't a good fit and she was needing to escape for a bit. For Roz's sake he hoped it wasn't the second.

A few minutes later he was pulling the seat cover off the passenger seat of his car for Su to sit on. The trainers—all of them—were all covered in dog hair all the time, but he tried to keep the car relatively clean.

He placed Curie in the middle of the back seat and Vivaldi and Brahms on either side of her. Curie held court and the other two seemed to understand they were to mimic her.

"They're doing really well," he told Su as they headed down the mountain. He was impressed with how well the dogs stepped into their car harnesses, leapt into the back of the car without needing to be lifted or prodded, and sat still while getting hooked into the seat belts.

Su looked a little petrified and Devin realized he needed to indoctrinate another hearing person . . .

"I don't have any ticket or accidents on my record." She frowned for a moment then he added, "Deaf people sign while driving. It freaks the hearing out but it's not unsafe. You shouldn't do it until you're fluent though."

Her eyes widened as she seemed to think about that then realize that maybe she was comparing his signing-and-driving to hers. Nodding, she returned to the original conversation. "They improve a lot," she said.

"That's their job, good for them." He'd heard the first set of dogs had a washout, but they'd all stuck this time. "Burgers first, then groceries?"

When Su agreed, he turned toward his favorite burger joint —a local place where he'd read the info on the back of the menu and found out the owner worked behind the counter. They headed in with three dogs along.

A kid sitting at one of the tables turned and their mouth moved, from the way the kid responded their mom was explaining about the yellow service vests and how that allowed them inside. Curie had the only actual service vest though. Viv and Brahms were still in their starter vests which said *Service Dog in Training* across the side in large letters and under that, *please don't pet me.*

They placed their orders with Viv and Brahms doing great. Though Su offered to translate for him, Devin preferred to place his own order and he also put Ash's order in to go. Then they sat at one of the open tables rather than a booth, wanting each dog to have their own space to the side.

It would be unusual for there to be more service dogs than people in a standard situation, so stacking them up three deep at the end of a booth wouldn't have made sense. It was the middle of the afternoon, so it wasn't horribly busy—an excellent early training run. People came through though, and he watched to make sure the dogs didn't get distracted. He was pleased when Su did, too.

Though he was in a position senior to her, it wasn't by much.

And since he was grant writing, too, her training hours and knowledge would surpass his pretty quickly. *If she stayed.*

They would head out to other public places for more trainings later, maybe even back here, when it was busier. In their later stages the dogs had to handle crowds, interruptions, loud noises, everything. Even though these guys were mostly being trained to alert when their owner had a precariously high or low glucose level, they still had to qualify as service dogs and be trained well enough to be allowed in public spaces.

When the food came out, they unwrapped the burgers and dipped their fries in garlic aioli and black truffle ketchup. Su bit in and her eyes about rolled back. Then, with a full mouth and one hand, said, "Oh my god, that's amazing."

She knew those signs pretty well. He laughed.

"Please don't tell Beck I said this, because the tofu masala the other night was great, and Roz made chicken and green beans, but . . . I have been craving a cheeseburger."

She grinned and asked, "How did you find this place?"

"I was in the hospital one day with my mother. She was having inpatient surgery—" From the look on Su's face, he waited for a moment and then finger spelled *inpatient* and signed it again. "So when she finally got out she said she wanted a burger. Then she pointed here and said, 'Let's try it.'"

"Good job, Mom!" Su commented. "I will definitely come back here."

"I've been back more than once." He wasn't sure Su was getting every nuance of the conversation, but he wasn't going to hold back.

Mostly, he was grateful that he fully tasted the food. He'd been concerned about what he was going to cook for a meal tonight, afraid he would serve everyone dry macaroni or some bland casserole given the way he was feeling. But he had more confidence after finishing the burger and handing the last corner of one patty down to Curie.

"Do we need to do the same for . . ." She signed Viv and Brahms' names.

Devin shook his head. "They have to learn to see other dogs get treats and not react."

They headed to the grocery store next, where, once again, people tried to pet the dogs and interact with them despite the clear signs. When they were out in town, they wound up training people as much as puppies. He could easily read Su's lips: "No, you shouldn't pet them. They're working."

He found the block of cotija cheese that Roz said she hadn't been able to locate. Then he asked, "We have garlic, right?"

Su shook her head, "You are asking the wrong person. I made campfire hotdogs!"

He laughed and grabbed some, then just as they were checking out, his phone buzzed. He shouldn't have looked at it but it was communication. For Deaf people, communication was at the heart of so many things.

He shouldn't have checked. Once again the screen said, *Gabi.*

This time, her text said — Will you please talk to me? What did I do?

Instantly back at full anger, he let Su talk up the cashier.

— you know what it was.

Her reply came back quickly.

— No, I don't.

He ripped off another text and sent it without thinking through the haze that clouded his every thought. — Then how many things did you lie about?

CHAPTER THIRTY-FOUR

Devin sat on the bench waiting. He'd sat here before, relaxed, waiting for Gabi to bring his coffee. Then, he would sit across the walkway and look into the windows of the coffee shop as if he could see her working. Now, his back was straight, his feet planted firmly on the little cement pad the bench rested on.

This time his back was to the street. He didn't want to sit and watch. Curie waited patiently at his feet, until the dog perked up. For all that Curie was here to be his companion, the dog hadn't seemed to have gotten the message that *we hate her now.*

Immediately on his feet, Devin faced her. He needed to be moving, needed something to vent this restless energy that coursed through him. He wasn't even sure if it was still anger, maybe just resignation. God forbid he wanted her again.

She'd pushed and pushed, seeming to need to know what it was he was mad about. And he needed to know how she didn't already understand. As the days had passed, and his anger had faded just a little, he'd discovered he needed to see her too, so he could ask her how she could have lied to him so much.

He needed answers, though he didn't have high hopes of getting them.

"Devin, it's good to see you." But even as she signed the words her emotions faded. As if it wasn't actually good to see him or as if she knew she shouldn't say it.

Devin countered with stiff signs. "It's good to see you too, Luisa."

Suddenly frozen, she stood there in the park, eyes wide.

He hadn't been wrong.

She faltered twice before protesting. "No. I'm Gabi."

"Stop lying!" His motions got sharper as her words made the anger flare inside him again when he thought he didn't have any more to give. Like a fool, he argued back with what came immediately to mind. "I went to my mother's house. I looked at the old pictures. Gabi never had that mole."

He pointed at the beauty mark just at the edge of her eyebrow. The one Luisa always had.

She looked away. "Moles can grow."

Devin wasn't having any of it and there was no conviction behind her words, anyway.

Luisa's eyes turned slightly up at the edges. He'd seen again in the pictures that his memory had been right all along: Gabi's slightly—ever so slightly—turned down.

He'd known! He'd been right about who she was the moment he first saw her.

And she had lied to him. The whole time.

It hit him like bricks as she looked away again, ashamed of the lie—he'd stupidly held out hope that he was wrong. That there was something she could say that would make it okay. But she didn't say it.

In fact, she didn't seem to know what to say. Devin did. He found the questions pouring out. "Why did you lie to me? Why are you pretending to be Gabi?"

Then another wave crashed over him. How had he not

thought of this—demanded answers—before? In all these days of stewing in her lies, it hadn't occurred to him that there might be even more lies at the heart of it. "Is Gabi dead or is no one dead?"

Reaching out harshly before he even finished the sentence, Luisa grabbed his hands, crushing his fingers into fists beneath her own. Then she took one back and reached up in front of her face, eyes flaring with her own angry fire as she signed, "Shut up!"

Yanking his hands back, he stayed where he was, feet planted, leaning forward angrily, gesturing loudly. "You *lied*. You don't get to tell me to shut up."

But she said it again. *"Shut up!"* Her eyes darted from side to side like a fugitive. "You don't know who can understand you!"

That took him aback. His view widened from the narrow glare he'd leveled straight at her. Around the park he saw only one couple in the distance seem to look on interested. But the woman glanced away as if embarrassed to be caught.

"No one's watching," he told her his tone still harsh, the knife through his heart still stinging.

"It doesn't matter!" Her fingers smacked together, making him wonder if she was hurting herself. "It's dangerous for me."

She signed the last bit in tight little motions held close in front of her chest as if keeping someone else from seeing her words.

"How?" he asked. "You're the liar."

She squeezed her eyes shut and turned her head away. An odd thing to do to a Deaf man. She could literally not listen. He should have walked away but, like the fool he was, he waited.

When she looked at him again, he saw the tears squeezed in at the edge of her eyes.

"Please," she said, and he realized she was no longer confused, no longer mad that he had not been speaking to her. *She was afraid.*

CHAPTER THIRTY-FIVE

This was it. It felt as if every bone in her body were cracking.

She felt truly alone, though the truth was she'd been alone for a long time. Mama had done this with her, for her, and in many ways *to* her. But Mama was gone. There was no one left to share the carrying of this load.

"I will tell you everything," she told Devin. "But not here." *Not where people could see.*

He didn't respond for a moment, just stood there looking at her as if she spoke a foreign language. Or worse, as if everything she said was lies and he couldn't trust any of it.

She tried again. "Follow me back to my apartment. I promise, I'll answer all your questions."

She found in that moment that she wanted to tell him everything. As mad as he was—and as much as he could cut her, and as much as getting cut might kill her—she knew she was still ready to be rid of this weight. It was too much. She had carried it for far too long.

But Devin still looked at her oddly, clearly not wanting to go to her apartment. She understood; it wasn't neutral ground. "I can't go up the mountain with you," she offered, "because everyone there knows sign."

He sighed heavily, still not saying anything. It was like begging a brick wall to love her. "Where can we go? Where no one can see? Just tell me somewhere."

If someone found out, it could be the end of her and she was willing to take her chances with Devin, but not with random people in the park. Not with someone who might report her . . . to her job, the police . . . anyone.

If Devin turned her in, she would consider it fate. She would deal with the consequences. But she was not going to put it in the hands of random people. She tried again. "Devin, where can we go? Somewhere alone, where no one can see."

He shook his head a few times as if he couldn't think of anything either. "My mother's house?" At least he was speaking to her. She wanted to say yes.

But . . . "As long as she's not home."

Ms. James was far more fluent than she was. Gabi used her language mostly in the coffee shop, and with Devin and for random conversations. His mother had learned when he was an infant and used it daily. There was no way to get anything past her.

Devin shook his head and said, "No. It won't work, she's always home."

"Then follow me to my apartment. I promise I'll tell you everything."

Though what was there to even tell? It sounded like he'd figured out most of it, the big parts anyway. She could fill him in on the details, maybe tell him what it was like and why they'd done it. Maybe he would understand enough to not make her life a living hell. Maybe, just maybe, he would understand enough to love her again because they hadn't even said they were boyfriend and girlfriend, and she didn't know what they really were or could become. But she loved him.

And she'd felt loved when she was with him.

He still didn't answer. When, at last, he said, "Fine," it was clearly grudgingly. The lone sign thrown off sharply as if she had left him no other options.

She imagined her life if she didn't tell him now—if she kept going the same way—what would it be like? Most probably like the last year . . . after mama had died, when she truly carried it alone, when there was no one she could even open her mouth to and say, "This is what hurts. This is what's hard."

She didn't want to keep going anymore. Turning away, she left him standing there. He knew where her apartment was. If he wanted his answers, he would show up.

As she climbed into her car, she realized she had no idea where he'd parked. She couldn't see his car. So she pulled out of the little lot next to the coffee shop and looked back to the bench where he'd been sitting when she first walked up. It was empty.

He might even beat her to her place. Though she drove quickly, the same old demons now out of the closet and chasing after her, when she arrived, his car wasn't there.

Forcing herself to get out and climb the stairs, she unlocked the door, and walked in like a zombie.

She should get a cat. It was something she'd thought so many times when she walked in. She would love another live creature here, something to greet her when she got home from work. Hell, maybe even two. What difference would a second one make? But if something happened, if someone found out, if she were caught: what would happen to her cats?

She'd never adopted any because forever was a promise she couldn't make.

She stood in her empty living room, her purse still over her shoulder, the smell of coffee still clinging to her shirt and her hair. The longer she waited for Devin to show up, the more she began to regret her decision to tell him.

CHAPTER THIRTY-SIX

She felt more than heard him behind her. When he entered the small apartment she was still standing in the same spot in her living room. Though she had set her things down, there was no frantic race this time to attempt to clean the apartment or be sure that she didn't smell like her job. She'd just stared coldly at the wall.

Her jacket lay across the arm of the couch. Her purse sitting next to it because there was no end table to put her things on when she came in the door. She kept meaning to get one, but now it felt pointless.

There were no deep, soul-searching kisses either. Though she suspected that no one but Devin could see it, she was cold and broken and trying to stitch any part of her life back together.

Slowly, she turned around to face him, watching as he closed the door behind him.

"I'm here," he said, pointing out that he had held up his end of the bargain.

She nodded. There was no time like the present. "You're right," she admitted. It was the first thing that needed to be said.

She meant to go on, but he burst out with angry indignation. "I know I am! But why did you lie to me?"

"Because I lied to everyone. I *am* Gabi now. It's what people call me. It's on all my records. I have been Gabi more than twice as long as I was Luisa."

"But *why?*"

With a deep breath, Luisa—she had not thought of herself that way in decades, at least not often—said, "Let me start at the beginning."

The beginning was way way back, but the rest only made sense if he understood the start. "We lived in Peru with my grandmother."

"I know," he said again, only this time he was at least less angry. "Outside of Lima. You got visas."

"No." She held up her hand carefully. "That's the first lie. My mother got *a* work visa."

"Wait. Your mother? Mrs. Montalvo who is Gabi's mother?"

She shook her head. "No, my real mother. The woman who gave birth to me."

Begrudgingly he motioned her to go on. Despite the anger that still seeped out from him, she was grateful he was being patient. "My mother was the only one who got approved. She was pregnant with my little brother, so we left right then, still waiting on a visa for my father. They were hoping my little brother would be born on American soil."

Devin nodded, but she saw his face as he put the pieces together. There was no little brother. He was trying to figure out how that happened.

"My mother's paperwork got me into the country legally, but my father didn't make it. My mother didn't think they should try to sneak my father in, but in the end that didn't matter. He didn't make it out of Peru."

Something about Devin's expression told her that he remembered they had come from Peru, but he hadn't known the extent of the story. And that, as a young child, it occupied a very large portion of her memory.

She paused, wondering if Devin would ask, and he did.

"What happened to your father?"

"I never saw him again. He died soon after my mother and I left . . . under mysterious circumstances." Or at least that was what she had found out in her early twenties from Mama. "My mother and I managed to make our way to her sister in law's house—my father's sister. She and her daughter were waiting for us, but she only got two instead of three."

"Her daughter was Gabi?"

Luisa nodded. "Three weeks later, my brother was born very premature, probably from the stress of all of it."

"He didn't make it," Devin guessed.

She shook her head *no*. She'd never known the baby. She'd been young, only a few years before she'd met Devin. But she missed that little brother more than ever now that she was the only Montalvo left.

"Go on," he motioned.

"Then my mother got sick about a year later. And she died, too." Luisa could see it on his face, and she hated the pity there.

It was a tragic story. And it did define her. It changed everything and every decision she'd ever made. It changed how people treated her. And it changed her status here in the US. But she did not want to be pitied for it. Not even by Devin.

Her parents had literally given up everything for her and she wanted to make the best of it.

"So you stayed with your cousin Gabi and her mother, your aunt." He had the same pieces he'd always had.

She nodded, hoping she'd made the point that despite the things he might not have known, that she'd not told him when they were ten what had happened to her mother or about the brother she'd never met, the things he did know about her were true.

"But with my mother gone, her work visa was no longer valid. I was likely undocumented then." She saw something flicker in his eyes then. "Mrs. Montalvo took very good care of me, took me in like her own daughter. But there were things she couldn't do. I could go to school, but she couldn't get me on her health insurance. One year we lied and said I was Gabi so I could go to the doctor for a checkup."

For a moment his eyes fell closed and she felt it sink in. They'd been kids and they'd been best friends.

"You never said anything."

"Of course not! When we met, I was barely eight years old. I barely understood it myself. What would you have done if I had told you? You had a very strong sense of right and wrong, which I appreciated, and I still do." But even as she forced him to think about that—that maybe it was fair that an eight-year-old hadn't told another eight-year-old something that could maybe get her deported—she saw the other information sinking in.

He now felt as if she had lied to him every single day she'd known him.

It seemed like forever that they stood there with her watching him, Devin with his eyes closed, opting out of the conversation, while he tried to process it. Shy of reaching out and tapping him and forcing him to open his eyes, all she could do was wait. Eventually when he did open those green eyes that she knew so well, they were almost a different color.

He asked, "What really happened the night Luisa supposedly died?"

She shrugged and said, "In a way, she did."

CHAPTER THIRTY-SEVEN

His heart hurt. His chest felt as if it had caved in. It was difficult to process all of it through the haze of knowing that she'd lied to him . . . for so long. It was difficult to trust and grab onto the things she said now.

Gabi . . . no Luisa . . . started carefully. He was mad at himself too, because he knew who she was the moment he'd first seen her, and he'd let her convince him he was wrong. *But why?*

"That night . . ." She took a deep breath. Her tongue darted out to lick her lips as if she were talking with her mouth and not her hands. Then stopped before she started and added, "Most of what I told you is true. Just reversed."

Most wasn't good enough. But she had to already know that. He was here for the truth, nothing more, so he stared at her until she started again.

"Gabi snuck out."

That made more sense to him. The idea that Luisa had been sneaking out without him didn't. Who would she have met? Why wouldn't she have told him?

"She took my favorite shirt." He remembered that part of the story. "She was even wearing my jeans. Do you remember those wine colored ones I loved so much?"

He nodded. That made more sense, too. Gabi was far less concerned about her possessions, whereas Luisa believed that her things were hers and shouldn't be touched without permission. Luisa treated objects as if they were precious, Gabi always wondered why anyone even cared.

"She crawled in through the window, wearing all of my favorite things."

He could see it on her face, even now—all the irritation of an eleven-year-old girl catching her cousin, basically her sister, having stolen her prized things.

"She caught her shirt—my *favorite* shirt—on that sharp edge on the window. She ripped it."

The anger made sense, too. The Montalvo girls didn't have a lot. He knew they'd shopped at the local consignment and resale more often than not. Though they'd cost pennies or just a few dollars to get, Luisa's favorite things were not replaceable.

"She just washed her hair and didn't care. I was so mad. I yelled. *I* started the fight."

He almost asked her. *Did you though?* Hadn't Gabi started the fight by stealing her things? Then he reminded himself that he didn't trust Luisa and he wasn't really on her side. So he didn't say anything.

"I was so mad that I pulled her things out of the closet and put her favorite shirt on. So when she got out she could see me ruin it. The problem was she didn't care, not like I did. It didn't matter when I ripped it. She would just get something different. She laughed and that made me even more angry."

Devin stood there, barely breathing, unsure what to think and which parts of the story to trust. But he had to admit, knowing the Montalvo girls like he did, this version made more sense.

"And then we woke Mama up—"

He interrupted. "Your aunt, right?"

"Yes, technically. She was my mother for most of my life though."

It was fair, he thought, but he didn't say so. All of it was just excuse after excuse. She made it sound as if the stories weren't so bad, as if they maybe weren't really *lies*. He didn't comfort her, didn't say anything soothing, just waited for the next piece. He was still trying to filter it, still deciding what he believed and what he couldn't.

"Mama got mad at us, but the fight was physical by then. I had shoved Gabi. She shoved me and I hit the wall. She fell back onto the couch. We were in the living room then, and Gabi fell onto the pull-out couch, where Mama had been sleeping." She paused, then added. "I reached out and grabbed Gabi and tried to shake her.

"She laughed at me and that made me even more mad."

Despite the fact that the story was crushing him, that part made him flinch. Gabi was wonderful, and she and Luisa were like sisters. Like real sisters, they fought sometimes. Gabi had known that would hurt Luisa most.

He wanted to feel so much sympathy for this young girl who had pushed her cousin into the television set and killed her. But then he reminded himself, *was that even true?* And he didn't want to feel the sympathy anyway.

"Mama got in between us and tried to pull us apart. But I was holding on too tight. She yelled at me to let go and when I did, Gabi stumbled backwards." Her eyes were glazed at the memory—as they had been when she'd told him it was Luisa who'd died, too.

He didn't know what to feel. And, sweet Jesus, he thought, *it was everybody's fault.* Maybe it was better that Luisa hadn't pushed her cousin herself. Mrs. Montalvo had had a hand in it too. And so had Gabi.

With her hands showing what had happened, the description

was clear enough to see how Gabi had stumbled backwards and smacked into the TV until it had toppled first backwards, then forwards, then onto her. He knew that living room and he could almost see the glass breaking and shattering onto the floor around her.

He wondered if all TVs were capable of electrocuting someone like that? Or if the Montalvos simply had the bad luck to get unsafe systems. Most everything they had was secondhand. It was entirely possible the TV had been defective in some way.

But Devin said nothing. He just watched, listening, and judging. There wasn't room for speaking.

"Mama reached for her," Luisa said mixing up the story lines. Mrs. Montalvo had still been her aunt then, or had she lied for so long that she no longer knew the difference? "Her body arched. In my memory I can see sparks and electricity, but I don't know if that's real. I remember what we learned in school, and I yelled at Mama not to touch her. I was so afraid both of them would get electrocuted. So I ran around and unplugged the TV. I remember grabbing it quickly and fire shooting up through my hand. But again, I have no idea if that's true or just what my mind filled in from a horrible situation."

Devin reminded himself that she had been eleven. However shitty it had been, she'd been young. Those decisions and those traumas shouldn't be laid at her feet. But she wasn't eleven anymore. She'd had decades to fix the error. She'd had decades to choose not to lie to him.

"We moved the TV and it was clear she wasn't breathing." Luisa looked at him, her eyes wide, tears running down her high brown cheeks.

He steeled himself again. He had loved this woman for so much of his life, but he couldn't afford to sacrifice himself on this altar of her lies.

"Mama tried CPR. She tried mouth to mouth. She was

screaming. I think I was screaming. The neighbor was pounding on the door, but Mama couldn't get up and I couldn't move to let him in. Mama yelled for him to call 9-1-1. I think I just stood there in shock while she worked, and I don't know how long it was. It felt like forever. My brain kept telling me that Gabi wasn't dead. That Mama could save her. Or the hospital could bring her back if Mama couldn't.

"I know she kept working all the way through until the EMTs busted through the door, but when they asked her name, Mama said 'Luisa.' Then she looked up at me, that sharp look that told you not to argue." He watched as she gulped.

It was a terrible story. He assumed it was true, but he hated that he had to question it.

"When they left, they told us we could follow the ambulance to the hospital. The neighbor had a car and said he would drive us. But when he ran to get his keys, Mama said, 'I don't think this is going to work. We can fix it if it does. But if she doesn't make it, we have to be ready.' She cried and she told me, 'That was Luisa. If I only have one daughter left, it will be a daughter who can have everything that we fought so hard to get.' She grabbed her purse, and looked around for the neighbor, then she put her hands on either side of my face and looked me square in the eyes. She said, 'You are Gabi now.'"

CHAPTER THIRTY-EIGHT

Devin couldn't do anything but stare at her. This story at least made sense but . . . "That sounds like a woman who was very determined. Wasn't she already an American?"

"Yes, she was an immigrant," Luisa said. It was surprising how easily he'd switched to thinking of her that way.

"She and my uncle came about eight years before my family did. I never met my uncle, but he knew someone who knew someone. They got their visas first. They came to Texas and settled in, and Gabi was born here."

That was the point, Devin thought. But he still found it odd that a mother would trade her own child.

He hadn't realized that he'd signed it until Luisa moved her head, catching his eyes and said, "Yes, I thought of that so often, but I also think that by making me Gabi, she could pretend that it was Luisa who had died and not her own daughter."

A harsh indictment, but the woman was gone. That also meant she wouldn't be able to answer any of Devin's questions. She wouldn't be able to support or deny Luisa's strange and almost fantastical tale—except this time, the pieces all fit together with what he knew of that family.

Mrs. Montalvo would have done anything for either of the girls. Devin had never met Luisa's real mother, and she'd called her aunt 'Tia' most of the time. But the woman was fiercely protective of both of them. Devin had faced her more than once when she'd thought he might be the bad influence.

There was a long pause that hung between them in the room. Neither said anything until Luisa said, "We left the next morning. We just moved and started over. She wouldn't even let me tell you goodbye. I tried, Devin. I tried to climb out the window and come find you, but she caught me. By the time we were in Austin she was calling me Gabi all the time. When we were asked, we told people she was my mother, and that the other Mrs. Montalvo and then her daughter had died."

She looked away, as if it hurt her as much as it was hurting him. He didn't think it possibly could.

"It was just the two of us. She was very good to me. I went to the doctor regularly. I went to school with papers. I got this job with papers!"

Devin felt the anger flare. "None of which are actually yours!"

"I know that!" She was mad now, too. As if she had the right to be. "That's the problem. Now you know, and if you tell anyone, I—Luisa—will get deported back to Peru."

"So what? You have family there."

"They are all dead! There are no jobs. I don't speak the language. Mama wanted us to be Americans. So I know very little Portuguese."

He blinked. He'd always thought they would speak Spanish. But now that he thought about it, that sounded right. He knew Portuguese was the main language in Peru, but it hadn't ever occurred to him before that her native tongue wasn't Spanish. This woman that he'd fallen in love with didn't even exist. He spiraled downward into anger and frustration again.

But Luisa waved her hand in front of him. "It makes sense

that you were the only one who actually recognized me as me. And I know the first day you saw me, you saw Luisa. You saw me as I was. But then you believed I was Gabi, right?"

He nodded, his jaw tight, his teeth clenched. *Yes, he had believed her lies.*

"So how did you figure it out?"

She wanted to know now? A bitter laugh welled up inside of him. "The last thing was that I saw the scar on your shoulder. I remember the night we both climbed through your window, and I went first and cut my shoulder. You called me a fool, you made fun of me, then you climbed through and did the exact same thing."

She closed her eyes for a moment, tears leaking as the corners of her mouth pulled up in a little laugh. When she opened her eyes at him, the laugh faded. "It would make sense though, for Gabi to have the same scar. Obviously, it was easy to do. That window wasn't safe."

"But that was the last thing. When I saw that, then all the rest of it made sense. You look like Luisa to me."

Her mama had banked on it for decades: The two Montalvo girls looked nearly identical. Lots of people couldn't tell them apart. They were constantly getting called by each other's names at school. The night of the accident, Mrs. Montalvo likely hadn't had some grand idea or scheme, she'd just played into something that everyone else already struggled with.

But Devin had always been able to tell them apart. "Gabi never liked hiking and you were eager to go. You and I were always the ones who hiked. Gabi only came a couple of times and even then she was grumpy about it." He took a breath, mad that he hadn't caught it at the time. "You remembered things about hiking, things that happened when Gabi wasn't there. And we talked about the day at the mall when we followed those two girls who were signing and making fun of everyone."

Devin watched as it dawned on her. She'd shared those

memories with him, but they had been Luisa's memories. The hiking things, he might have mis-remembered, because Gabi had come along a few times, but that day it had been just the two of them.

She nodded, as if admitting that it was her mistake. A mistake to let him know the truth.

Her next words seemed to say the same thing. "It's good to be able to tell you all the real things, to share memories that truly belong to Luisa. To *me*."

His chest was going to crack if expanded and contracted again, because hope had swelled with this idea that she was Luisa and it made sense. But he'd fallen so hard for Luisa Montalvo not Gabi. For a woman who had lied to him for every second of it.

But he wasn't going to let himself fall this time. It was anger or frustration, or both, but his good sense clamped down on everything. "No. We won't be sharing our memories. I'm finished."

He watched as the warmth fled her face for despair.

Too bad. He thought: *I didn't do this. You did.* What he said was, "You've lied to me for months now."

"I didn't lie to *you*." She pointed straight at him for emphasis, as if singling him out. "I have lied to *everyone*. It is the only way that I am still alive."

He shook his head. "There are things you could do! You could fix it. You don't have to lie."

"No!" The sign was sharp and angry now, as if she had the right to be angry at him. "I kept trying to find ways out! But every move I could have made would have killed me or hurt Mama."

He wasn't sure he believed it. But it didn't matter, he was done. Whatever his capacity was for being slung back and forth like a rag doll and dropped onto the ground repeatedly, he'd reached it.

"No," he told her even though it wasn't a reasonable answer to what she said. He said it again. "I'm finished." Some level of sheer politeness made him say, "Thank you for telling me the truth," even though he wasn't confident that she was capable of telling the truth at this point.

He didn't say anything more, just turned around and let himself out of the apartment. Walking away down the stairs, he climbed in his car and closed the door.

There was no more work with the dogs today. He obviously wasn't in any shape to do any kind of grant proposal work. He started the engine and headed toward his mother's house. Once there, he parked the car just beyond the bushes so she couldn't see him if she looked out. But then he realized he couldn't even go inside.

This horrible secret that Luisa had been carrying had been put on him. He was now responsible for keeping her safe. And he hated it.

CHAPTER THIRTY-NINE

It was dark by the time she felt she could breathe again. Her face was swollen, her eyes and nose red. She'd cried enough to drink liters of water to replace what she lost.

She hated herself more than she ever thought possible.

He was so mad at her, and it was fair. Everything he said was right. He wasn't the one who'd lied. That was all her. The lies she had told were so big, but they had gotten somewhat comfortable over the years, at least on the surface. Underneath, she'd always had that little kernel—of pain, of fear, of guilt—knowing that she wasn't Gabi Montalvo.

She was afraid to get promoted any further than manager at her job. Though "Gabi's" bloodwork and fingerprints and records were hers after age eleven, as far back as anyone would look, there was still a possibility someone could find out.

What could they do? But even that didn't matter. It was just an issue of *if* they found out. They would start the wheels rolling. Because once someone knew—like Devin—they would either have to lie for her or turn her in to save themselves.

What was he going to do now that he knew?

Realizing she should eat something, she headed into the

kitchen and found she hated all food. She wasn't ready, but she did manage to make herself drink soda just for the sugar.

Still sniffling she tried to stop, but her body couldn't, even though her brain had finally shut down. She looked at her phone as it pinged, the chat coming in. — You okay, Gabi?

Chandler, of course. She was likely just checking up, knowing that Devin had walked away a few days ago. Gabi had told them last night that Devin had agreed to talk to her though she hadn't told them what it was about. She hadn't known for sure herself until he called her Luisa at the park today. Until her entire body reacted to that name and it felt right for the first time in over two decades.

She wrote back — I think so.

When she was ready to cry and rage, and be mad at the world, she would call Chandler. Chandler would tell her she was right. Chandler had her back, no matter what. When she needed a wild and crazy idea to move forward, the impetus and cheerleader to get her going, she would call Jenna. Jenna would push her out of the nest when she was truly done with Devin and ready to take those steps.

Right now, she needed Helen's logic and stability. Honestly, she could kill two birds with one stone. She decided to just call, but it took so much effort to steel herself to scroll through and find her friend's face in the contacts. The picture made her smile, though it was from years ago and she'd never updated it. Still, it took her three tries to make herself push the button. Clearly, she wasn't bad with ideas, but actually moving on them was not her forte.

When it went through, the line rang and rang and rang and at last the click came, but her throat closed up. It didn't matter, she only got Helen's voicemail. She hadn't been prepared and she didn't even know why she wasn't ready to leave a message.

Obviously, she wasn't functioning well. So maybe it was good that she wasn't trying to tell her friend everything right now. She wasn't even capable of forming real sentences. But she gave it her best.

"Hey, Helen. It's Gabi." It felt wrong now. Even though it had seemed okay until even yesterday to have *Gabriela* on her driver's license, *Gabi* on her name tag at work, the same name called out when anyone needed her.

"Can we talk? Whenever you get a chance, call me back. Please . . . Thank you . . . Goodbye."

She sounded stupid and her voice was scratchy. She hoped Helen wouldn't worry. She should have just messaged her friend, but this was one of those cases when talking would be easier. Luisa needed to hear the sound of Helen's voice. It would steady her, she knew.

She turned on the TV and didn't watch it. Time passed as she stared into space, her thoughts flying everywhere. They raced from Mama and the decision she had forced on Luisa at age eleven to today. She was both angry about it and sad.

It hadn't really been her own choice, and she'd had to keep it, or Mama would become a criminal for having done it. Also, it changed her whole life. The lie afforded her so, so much. It had to have been so difficult for Mama to call another child by her daughter's name for twenty years. While she may have done some of it for herself, so much of it had been to benefit Luisa as Gabi.

When the phone finally rang, Luisa jolted, her arm hot and heavy where her head had laid on it. She'd fallen dead asleep and now when she moved it tingled. She blinked herself awake —not that it worked.

Thank God she had gotten some sleep, though. The ring cut through the sound of the TV making her scramble to get the phone. She blinked again, to read that it was Helen and then frantically push at the screen making sure she had the correct button.

"Helen?" But when she got no reply, she realized she didn't have it on speaker, and she tried again. "Helen?"

"Hey, it's good to hear your voice. Your message sounded rough. Still upset over Devin?"

Gabi couldn't help it. She burst into tears again. "That and so much more." She sniffed, hating that her body was betraying her, but she couldn't just turn it off. "Do you have a little while?"

This time her voice was breathless as she was completely unable to regulate herself.

"Whatever you need," Helen assured her, and it sounded like she was settling in on the other end.

Looking at the phone Luisa saw that it was after ten here but at least it was earlier where Helen was. Still, she sniffed two more times as Helen waited patiently. Then Luisa asked, "Can I hire you as my lawyer?"

"*What?*" Helen sounded beyond surprised. "Do you want to sue Devin?"

"No." The thought of that almost made Luisa laugh. "It's just all this stuff with Devin? It brought up something that I never told any of you and I need to tell someone, and I need to figure out what to do."

She could practically hear Helen trying to think through this horrible secret that Gabi might tell her.

"Is it bad?" Helen asked cautiously.

"Maybe, probably." Her throat scratched and she sniffed again. She hadn't killed anyone like in a teenage horror movie. But legally, what had she done? She knew enough to know it wasn't okay.

"Okay. I'm not a criminal attorney."

"No, it's not about that. I'm sure you're not the lawyer that I'll eventually need. I just have to start somewhere and I'm hoping you can point me in the right direction." The tears were coming freely again. There was nothing she could do to stop them.

There was another pause then a determined voice. "Send me ten dollars."

Luisa nodded then realized no one could see her. She said, "I'm doing it now." This time she didn't hesitate to push the buttons. The money was sent.

Then Luisa Montalvo took a deep breath and told her friend everything.

CHAPTER FORTY

"I don't like it!" Beck stood in Roz's office, jaw clenched, leaning over her desk and her yet again. He felt he had to make his opinion known before she did something that could hurt them all.

It was his own fault. He was mad and he shouldn't be. He was mad that he was attracted to Roz when he knew he shouldn't be. He was mad that he shouldn't be, but she was his boss, and he was clearly not the equal she had been treating him as. Or she had been until this shit with the search and rescue guys came up.

Maybe he'd never been her equal. Maybe she'd just needed him to fill in the gaps for her on dog training. Now that she had what she needed—or maybe now that the money situation had balanced itself out, at least for a while—she didn't need him anymore.

It didn't matter, he never should have thought it in the first place. He wasn't an equal in this and it was his fault for thinking maybe he was. He still didn't like this, and he had to say so. "You're seriously going to clear everything out of here and rent the whole place to them?"

"It's good money," Roz told him, still sitting calmly.

It might have bothered him that she wasn't bothered by him. Though he never wanted to admit it to himself, he was bothered by her more often than he wanted. "It's good money *if* more than five of them show up."

"More than five of them *should*," she argued.

"But you don't *know* that. What if they don't come?"

She shook her head at him as if he didn't understand.

He moved back a little but stayed on his feet, arms crossed. He might not be her partner, but he'd put his own money and future on the line when she'd needed it. He should be able to have some say in this. "What are they guaranteeing?"

"Just the two leaders."

He felt his mouth drop open. Only two payouts would cripple the Sanctuary if not kill it. The vote had been to do it if they could make money. *What was she doing?*

"I get it."

Clearly she didn't.

But Roz kept going as if she did. "It's a gamble, but they don't think there's any way they're going to have less than six."

He shook his head at her. "Come on, the best case scenario is that they know their people really well. And they actually *believe* that their searchers are going to show up. That these freelancers are going to take the time out of their own schedules to come cross country for this training?"

"It's not like a group vacation," Roz defended her position. "It's part of their professional development."

"It's my understanding that a lot of them are part time." He might not have been here for the walk through, but he'd done his homework. "Is there a certificate associated with this?"

"Maybe."

Why was she doing this? "People always think their own people are going to show up and then they *don't*."

As the words came out of his mouth, Roz leaned back in her

office chair, raising one eyebrow at him. Yeah, she'd counted on him and then it had all gotten fucked up.

She still didn't want to acknowledge that she'd known he was going to be out that day. "Exactly. *If you had been here when they came*, you might have a better understanding of how it's running. And why they are confident their people will come."

"I told you I needed that day off and that it was immovable." He fought not to wave his hands around. He didn't like to let people see when he was angry. He didn't like to let people see when he was anything—it could always be used against him. "But fine, that's an excellent example. You—in your own decision—counted on me to be here for something that I had specifically said I would *not* be here for."

He hoped he was making sense, but he was mad enough not to repeat himself. "And yet you were wrong. And now you're believing someone else telling you about their employees. It's a whole other step removed."

"You're right," she conceded. "It's a gamble. It's one I'm willing to take."

"Well, I wouldn't! We have to finish all the dog training prior to them getting here. Which means we need to finish a good week prior in case anyone has to come back." They could start the next training group immediately after the last group left, but not with the search and rescue people coming in. "And we can't start again until they leave."

"I'm aware," she told him, her tone not changing. "If four of them come we break even, five we start turning a profit."

"Too small to count."

"True, we start making money at six people, but it could be twelve or fourteen!"

"I get that having twelve or more of them here will change the solvency of the Sanctuary. But so will two or three!" He fought not to yell it. *Did she not see what she was playing with?*

190

He hated the idea of gambling with the Sanctuary's ability to fund itself.

Roz did seem to catch on to his concerned irritation. Or maybe it was flat-out fear. "We're doing better than you think," she said. "Devin's grant writing has gotten us into the final round of a handful of grants."

"I know he got us one, which is great." Beck had been very happy to hear about that. In part because he had seen the books on this place, and it wasn't in the black. "But that grant covers how much of his own salary?"

Roz looked away. He knew, it didn't even cover Devin's salary for a year. Hiring Devin hadn't been a bad choice. Beck had been in on that decision—at least on the decision that they needed another person. Roz had picked Devin as their candidate and Beck had never had an issue with the people Roz chose. Well, not once they got their feet under them. She'd hired Su, and Beck liked her, and she was doing great, but he would never have hired a burnt out data analyst to train dogs.

"Getting into the final round of grants isn't the same as getting the grants," Beck reminded her, just like having six people expected to sign up wasn't money in the bank. "I'm confident that that means he's a great grant writer—"

"He believes in the Sanctuary," Roz said.

Beck wished that love got the grants funded. There was no way for Devin to have proven himself more in the time he had. That he'd already put one grant into their pockets was fantastic, but one wasn't enough.

He forcibly leaned himself back, realizing that he was once again getting into one of his intimidation poses. He was a big guy, thick muscled and heavily tattooed. He was often intimidating before he even moved. He'd even started to grow his hair out since coming to the Sanctuary, and it was honestly almost time to get it cut. When he'd initially interviewed with Roz, he'd been completely bald. But now he didn't worry about someone grabbing him or holding him by his hair. And he didn't mean to intimidate his coworkers.

Plopping down into the chair and leaning back, he tried not to chew on one fingernail out of worry. But he reminded himself this was the main office. He didn't have a chair here. In fact, neither did Ash. The only one really in charge was Roz.

The issue was he understood Roz's gamble, it could be really great money. But he wondered if Roz understood what she was gambling with. Then she pulled the world out from under him.

"I already signed the contract."

He'd come in here, thinking they'd maybe have a discussion, he could talk her out of it. But if it was done . . .

He pushed up on the arms of the chair and stood. Saying only, "Okay then," as he walked out of the room trying not to stomp like a toddler.

His teeth ground and his muscles tightened. Roz was gambling with more than her own livelihood. Ash and Brandy certainly had other marketable skills, they would find another place if the Sanctuary folded. Beck had marketable skills, but he also had a prison record that would hold him back when he applied most everywhere. He knew that from trying to get out of his halfway house and getting a full-time job before he landed here.

Lynzee had only a high school diploma. Though she had been at the Sanctuary for almost a year, which was good experience, it wouldn't be enough to get her to the next good job. At least Beck didn't think so. What about Su? Where else would take her and let her get un-burnt?

Roz may have signed the contract, she might think it was worthwhile, but she was gambling with all their lives.

And she was doing it when he'd just met Hallie.

CHAPTER FORTY-ONE

L uisa called in sick the next day and curled up in a little
ball in her pajamas on the couch.

She'd been concerned the night before about going into
work with her eyes puffy and her nose red. When she didn't
look any better in the morning, she left a message for her
assistant manager. Luckily, Marietta was already set to open the
store and get it up and running.

They'd be fine without her. Luisa had developed a clear
philosophy as a manager, which was that they should be able to
lose anyone and keep running smoothly. It had paid off a
number of times. She didn't have to yell at her employees to
cover shifts or spout bullshit about how they needed to be team
players. Instead, she insisted that every job was understood by
at least two other people. Marietta could do inventory today,
Craig could stock everything and make sure Paul got his coffee.
The books—which only she was allowed to handle—could wait.

She had solid faith that they could work a man down, even if
that man was her.

There was also the issue that she didn't want to go in
because she just wasn't ready to deal with things. When Devin

had disappeared on her she'd been worried. But she'd had two days off. Her employees hadn't seen her go from worried to scared to angry. Though she was heartbroken that things between them weren't what she'd thought they were, she hadn't sat down and simply cried at the loss of him.

Only when he faced her and said he was finished, had it hit her. All the walls she'd built crumbled down, not just around her but *onto* her. Looking back, she was impressed she'd managed to call Helen and make any sense at all.

She could still hear Helen's voice, "Oh, wow, Gabi. *Shit.* Luisa then."

"Yes." She'd said it like a confession, but it was true.

Mama was gone—still Luisa had held the secret for a year. But within moments of Devin figuring her out she'd also spilled it to Helen. Helen did corporate law, not immigration, but it was a good first step. Helen had solid advice and was the kind of friend who understood. Right now, Luisa trusted Helen with her secret more than she trusted Devin.

"You need a criminal immigration lawyer," Helen had told her.

"Is there anyone you can recommend?" Helen hadn't had a name off the top of her head last night. Who would she have called after ten p.m. anyway?

Helen was still looking into it. Luisa was still afraid of the consequences of telling the lawyer everything and she'd confessed that to Helen. "Can the lawyer turn me in? What if something in the process trips a wire?"

"Lawyers don't turn in their clients. We aren't allowed to. And your crime isn't a threat to harm anyone. Please don't worry."

But it was the first time Luisa truly took stock of the fact that she'd committed a crime. She'd thought of it as a lie for so long, that for Helen to use that word was a shock.

"There are no immigration lawyers trying to turn in their

clients. It's not only a shitty business model, but it's not why any of them went into the work." Helen paused and Luisa could just about see her taking a sip of a glass of wine. "Immigration lawyers exist because good people believe that there should be a better process and they understand that people need help. *Good* immigration lawyers exist because people know that this country was founded by immigrants."

"Thank you," Luisa had breathed it out, grateful she had such a good friend, and that the information would help her sleep better . . . once she got past Devin walking out.

Helen added, "My grandparents came over during World War Two, so I'm only second generation myself. You're generation zero here. You're a pioneer."

Sitting on her couch after she and Helen hung up, Luisa cried again. Just when she'd thought she was all cried out, great wracking sobs overtook her each time she thought about Helen calling her a pioneer.

She hadn't thought about the journey here much—not until recently, not until she'd been telling Devin. She'd heard what people like her were called. She'd been told to "go back where she came from" though mostly from people who had no clue about her story, they were just judging by her skin tone.

Jenna's skin was a rich mahogany, and she had gotten the same words sometimes. Though she liked to point out that her ancestors had been in the country as slaves long before McMuffin Irish Dude's family immigrated due to the potato famine. She should be telling him to go back where he came from.

Luisa laughed a little through the tears, thinking about Jenna calling the one man "McMuffin" to his face. When Luisa had asked how Jenna knew he was Irish, Jenna just shrugged. "He had red hair. The odds were in my favor."

Then the laughter changed back to tears as Luisa's thoughts turned again. She remembered the journey here in sharper relief now. It had been buried for a long time, but all this turmoil made it bubble to the surface. She remembered the times her mother had sheltered her as a child while they traveled.

She hadn't understood, then, but now she remembered the size of the group they traveled with. Some of the women, and even some of the girls, had been assaulted, though Luisa hadn't understood at the time, she could put the pieces together now.

But there was no one left to ask the hard questions. Her mother had died before Luisa was old enough to understand what she'd given up in the attempt to get her family a safe life.

They had sacrificed her little brother in the process. Though she hadn't known it at the time, she could see now that her mother had died just a year after her brother was born. There had been lingering complications from the difficult birth. She'd always thought it was random bad luck, but it wasn't. It was all tied to her parents' understanding that there was no life for them where they were.

By the time her Tia had died a year ago, the conversation had been shut down. Each time Luisa had a chance to ask her about it, her Tia shut her down. "It's done. It's a good thing. Don't worry about it."

Luisa had to worry about it now.

She'd been a child. It had not been her choice to come. It had not been her choice to stay. And it had not really been her choice to live as her cousin Gabi for all these years, though she had to admit she'd played a part in that.

Still, hearing Helen call her a *pioneer* had just about broken her. When she finished crying, it made her feel strong enough to do this. Because as Helen said, "you did the impossible when you were six. Imagine what you can do now."

So she sat on her couch and ate microwave popcorn and let the Hallmark Channel run in the background. She cried for everything that she'd lost: A brother she'd never known, her mother that she hadn't had long enough, a father who'd sacrificed himself, and an aunt who had poured everything into the one child who was left.

Helen had said, "When we're ready, when all the legal pieces are in play and it's safe for you, you should tell the rest of the group."

"What if they don't understand? I lied to everyone." Luisa had sniffled once again.

"I understand. I'm still here. I'm sure they will be, too. Honestly, come on. Chandler is going to tell you to go for it. Jenna is going to start an online fundraising account for your legal fees and they're going to tell you the same things that I am now."

Helen told her about DACA. Luisa knew about it, and she knew the recipients were known as *dreamers*. Kids like her, here because their parents dreamed of a better life for them. But it didn't apply to her. She'd entered legally, then lost that status—probably—when her mother died. Then she'd committed the crime. She hated that she now knew it might not have been necessary!

Still, Helen had assured her, "No matter what else goes down, you still have me. My money says that you have Chandler and Jenna. I know them, you know them. I think there's a real good possibility you'll have Devin, too."

She disagreed with Helen on that count. She hadn't heard a peep from him. So she ate her popcorn and waited for Helen to call back.

She dreamed of one day stepping out the door as Luisa Montalvo.

CHAPTER FORTY-TWO

"You should talk to her."

His mother was at it again. Devin gave her the side eye as he sat in the hard waiting room chair at the doctor's office. A few people watched as they signed, most tried to look politely away—or seemed embarrassed—when he looked at them, even if he smiled.

It was fine, they obviously didn't understand the language.

One little kid stared and he could see the mother explaining that they were talking with their hands. Smiling, Devin had waved at the little boy. Dark skinned, the kid also had caramel colored hair and green eyes. Devin was taken aback at the thought that the kid looked like a child he and Luisa might have produced.

It wasn't the first time he'd seen a kid and had that thought. In the intervening years, he'd thought of her often, wondering if the rumors were true, if one of the girls had died. He'd wondered if it had been his Luisa and he'd always hoped that both Montalvo girls were alive and well.

For two decades, he'd wondered what Luisa might be like now that she was older. In those phases where he didn't have an actual crush on someone in the hallways or on campus with him, he could insert Luisa Montalvo.

That was easy, because she was whatever he dreamed up. While that version was definitely imagined, he also knew she was a real person, and he knew a lot of her likes and dislikes from what he remembered. He knew what she looked like, and this kid could have been theirs.

Still smiling, Devin signed "hi" and watched as the mother said "Oh, he said hello."

She showed the son how to wave back until the little boy wasn't interested. His mother's attention however lasted longer than the kid's did. She signed an awkward "thank you."

"Why don't you speak to her?" His mother was always stubborn. He had a lot of good in his life that he owed to that. But right now, he could use a little less of it.

"It's over, Mom."

"Well, you obviously miss her."

"I know and it will take a while, but I will get over it."

"You were so excited to find her." He could see the disappointment in the slope of her shoulders, in the downward turn of her mouth.

How could he even tell his mother that Gabi wasn't who she thought she was? But he didn't say anything. He'd not promised Luisa he wouldn't tell her secret, but he sure as hell wasn't going to. He wasn't that kind of an asshole. It bothered him though, being saddled with it.

What if ICE questioned him? What if they asked if he knew what she was doing? Then again, why would they?

The longer he went without speaking to her and the further away he got from any connection to her, the less likely it was anyone was going to give him any shit about what he knew. He sure as hell couldn't afford to be tied up in any of her kind of legal issues though. He had his job, he had his mother to care for, and now he had Curie.

As always, the dog was sitting at his feet, paying rapt attention in her little yellow jacket that she always seemed so proud to put on.

Devin now knew the training behind that. He'd seen the little graduation ceremonies, how the jackets were always spoken of as a big deal. Even Beck insisted that they should point out that other dogs didn't have jackets. That they weren't as smart or as dedicated as working dogs.

Devin often wondered if the dogs understood any of that, but he tried not to question Beck or his methods, and he did notice that each time he put the jacket on Curie, the dog sat up a little straighter and looked pleased to be wearing it. Maybe Beck had the right of it.

"All I'm saying," his mother continued even though he'd told her before not to, "Is that you were happy when you were with her and now you're not."

"I'll get over it," he repeated. He held his thoughts close about his mother giving him relationship advice. Not that he'd had any really great ones, but coming from a woman who'd never had a long term relationship except George, Devin wasn't really thinking she had it all figured out either.

After all, when George had gotten another job, she'd simply let the man walk away. Devin didn't know now if she'd ever really truly loved him or if he'd just been a placeholder. But she'd never seemed to find *the one*.

Most of the time, Devin thought maybe he should find her someone. But, in the early years, he never met the right person to introduce to his mother. In these recent years, there had been so many other things going on, that both their attempts at romantic relationships had been easily put on the back burner.

Instead of complaining, he offered a concession that was mostly a lie. "Maybe later, Mom."

"Okay, fine if you want to be mad for longer."

He was grateful she was called in to see the doctor just then.

An hour later, he'd learned that her checkup looked okay. The doctor was concerned about her blood counts and wanted to add more Vitamin D and Iron to her regimen, but overall he was pleased that she felt so good and that the memory lapses had been temporary.

They waited a while longer for an injection of vitamin B— another concern—but that was the extent of it. It was enough to make Devin breathe deeply.

Good. She was doing well.

He drove her home and made her dinner because it wasn't his night to cook at the Sanctuary. He told himself he would never regret the time he spent with her. Though she might be doing well, he couldn't become less vigilant.

Later, when he headed back up the mountain, he thought about what she'd said— *that he was choosing to be mad for longer.* And maybe he was.

But Luisa had cut him too deep. She knew that she had lied to him from the first moment she'd seen him. While Devin did understand that she had lied to everyone else and that maybe she hadn't known him when he walked in, even if she recognized his face. She didn't know what he'd been doing for the past twenty years, or how he would react.

But he had called her Luisa.

The door was open for her to tell him the truth at any point. And, after all that time together, she still hadn't. She had made the choice not to tell him.

Only then did he recognize that he was hurt as much as he was mad. Despite everything, despite how they'd made love, how she'd let him into her life, she hadn't trusted him enough to tell him the truth. It didn't matter that he missed her with a pain that felt like losing part of himself, that she hadn't trusted him at all felt as sharp as the lies did.

So, like his mother said, he was going to make the choice to hold on to his anger a little longer. *If he could.*

CHAPTER FORTY-THREE

A knock came at her office door and Luisa almost jumped.
"Can I come in, boss?" The door cracked open, and a head peeked through with a smile.

Just September. Totally fine. The young woman was angling to become management, not to turn her boss in.

But it felt like everywhere she looked, Luisa could see a path straight to jail or deportment and she wasn't sure which would be worse. In just a few days, she'd become almost obsessively paranoid about it.

Maybe because of how quickly it happened. Devin had signed her old name, and everything had snapped right back into place. The comfortable mantle of Gabi had slipped instantly away.

She felt a roll in her stomach when she thought about that moment. It was certainly the butterflies of seeing Devin James again, but it was also the concern that he had immediately recognized *her,* and she'd had to talk him out of it.

She understood why he was so damn mad. He had every right to be. He'd been right, then she'd blatantly and openly sold him the lie.

"Boss?"

"Sorry." Luisa shook off the thoughts that tried to pull her under. "Come on in."

"You said you'd teach me about the inventory when it got slow."

"Of course." The intrusive thoughts came again, and she wondered if she wasn't training her own replacement. It had been two days since she'd told Helen. Four since Devin left.

She hadn't heard back from either of them, but at least Helen had said she'd let Luisa know what she found. Still, every hour that her phone didn't ding was another hour that Helen hadn't found someone.

With a pasted-on smile and yet another attempt to focus on something in front of her, Luisa reminded herself that she still had to be Gabi here. Helen had been very clear not to change anything until she heard from a lawyer.

So she showed September the stacks of inventory the store held on the shelves in her "office." She was going through the various sizes of cups and how to read the lettering on the sides of the boxes when her phone finally pinged.

"Do you want to get that?" September asked.

Luisa boldly lied. "No, I'm sure it'll be fine."

She wasn't even sure it was Helen, or that it would say what she needed. Now that she had a message—any message—it was easier to believe that it was what she'd waited for than to look and see that it wasn't.

September deserved her attention. She'd promised to show the barista the ropes of management. She was also planning, if everything went well, to recommend her into a management training position as soon as one opened up.

Hell, she might even get fired for her inattentiveness long before anyone found out the truth if she kept going like this.

"You can see the tag here," she pointed and waited for September to step over and read it. "It shows the item name, the code the box should have, how many we need to have on hand and where they are ordered from."

September asked about the abbreviation at the bottom and Luisa explained. Then she had her new trainee read the sides of the boxes to be sure they all matched and were in the right place, then she made her count and asked, "How many do we need?"

"One more box."

"Should we order that?" Luisa pushed, wondering if she should move a box and see if the barista caught it.

"I don't think so," September seemed unsure though. "It seems like we should wait until we have more than one box to order."

"Excellent." Luisa smiled a real smile. Then she explained how many she liked to have on hand, which was higher than the required amount. "They'll all eventually get used, so it's only a problem if they become unusable."

"How would that happen?" September looked confused.

"Fire, flood, other damage." She thought about it then . . . She was the same. Sitting on a metaphorical shelf, not to be counted, fine as long as nothing went wrong. But she reined those thoughts in. "I like to have extras because there are two other stores in town, and I always have a spare box when someone needs it. It's just nice to do it and also, it doesn't hurt to make nice with the neighbors. It's an easy way to earn undying gratitude."

She watched September's face change as she caught on. "Smart."

"Thank you." She could do this. She just had to remind herself of that every five minutes or so.

"We order all this from the company the store is franchised from? They are making bank off us."

"Oh yeah. And Greg, our regional manager, has five stores he oversees. But I think there are four regions the Godfrey family owns. So yes, the central office is making bank, but so are the franchisees."

Her brain felt split in half. One part of her was carrying on a fully rational conversation with September, pulling up the ordering system, and demonstrating how to put in a request. Today was a good day because there were two things they actually needed to order.

"We can save a little if we order more items at once, but as a manager, it's your job to watch that and coordinate it," she explained, making the girl sit at the computer and actually input the information so she'd remember it better. "But with the marathon that went through here last week, we had a massive run on medium and tall cups. So nothing we can do about this one."

"I guess be grateful for the profit." September shrugged but kept her eyes on the screen.

The other side of Luisa's brain was itching to pull her phone out of her purse, to check and see if it was Helen. A person couldn't live under this kind of constant stress. But she had to admit she was doing all right. She'd been living under some level of stress since she was eleven, afraid that someone would find her and find out that she was undocumented. Afraid that someone would find that she wasn't Gabi.

Devin James had done exactly as she predicted: Completely changed her life. Even if he wasn't still going to be in it.

And that was something Helen couldn't help her with, not really.

Was there any way to get Devin back? It would make all the difference as she went through this, but he hadn't reached out either.

Again, she steeled herself to hear from Helen first. She'd thought it would happen yesterday and now here she was thinking that her insides couldn't twist any tighter than they were now, but tomorrow they would.

Another knock came on the door, though it was open. Craig leaned in, "September, we're getting busier out front."

"Okay, cool." She stood up and gave Luisa a big smile. "Thank you."

"We'll do it again," Luisa promised, hoping she'd be here to keep it. "So you get the hang of it."

Then, when both the others had cleared her office and she could hear the bustle out front and had faith that she wasn't needed, she reached down into her purse and hit the screen to see that she did have a message from Helen.

CHAPTER FORTY-FOUR

Devin walked toward where Su and Beck were doing a training exercise, seeing he'd caught her attention. Signing carefully and clearly, he asked, "Do you want to go get another burger today? I mean . . . *train two of the dogs for public interaction.*"

Su frowned for a moment and then he could see when she put all the pieces together with context. She immediately said, "Yes!" then "Is that okay?"

Devin assured her, "I asked Beck."

Beck added, "You'll be taking Austen and Shelley."

"Right now?" she signed back, though it was clear she would make it work, whatever the timing. Devin appreciated that she signed to Beck, even though the trainer could speak. It helped Devin follow conversations much better. But Beck just signed, "Ask him," toward Devin.

"Thirty minutes. Finish what you're doing here, and I'll meet you at the kennels?" He started to walk away, then turned back as he remembered. But Su was facing away. He stomped the ground, once, then twice before he saw Beck turn and then Su catch on and turn around as well.

Devin added, "Burgers plus go to the library." It was an excellent training space.

She nodded enthusiastically. Burger/public behavior training was going to be one of his favorites. Beck had suggested the library and several other places. Since Devin didn't need a grocery store run today, he asked her, "Do you have errands we can do?"

"I'll think about it," she signed. Today she was just a little smoother and faster than yesterday. She was absorbing words like a toddler and didn't seem bothered by the task at all, though Roz had told him later she was starting each new hire on ASL classes before they even arrived if she could.

For a moment he wondered what it would be like when he had to leave here. He'd not worked a place where everyone knew ASL since the pizza parlor near Gallaudet. Though no one was fluent yet, it was impressive. No one could talk philosophy with him, or even quite the ins and outs of grant proposals, but if he stayed long enough, they would.

It was a heady feeling beckoning him. A different kind of mountains calling.

Beck motioned for him and suggested that he leave Curie behind this time. "These dogs are not as far along in their training."

Devin understood. They were three full weeks behind the first group. Beck and Roz were trying to railroad the onboarding—just a few dogs at a time, getting more attention, before the next batch came in. It spaced out Ash's veterinary work as well.

Once they got the system working, they could hand out as many dogs as they had rooms for every three or four weeks. Still, Devin didn't quite think it was just the rooms for the people who matched that was going to limit them, but he understood the idea.

It did mean that Curie would be a distraction. Austen and Shelley would need a little more attention. He headed back to his cabin and quickly hopped in the shower.

He'd been out in the yard today training the first batch—the composers—with Ash. He hadn't done any work on the current grant proposals. One needed a second round and was due soon. That should have his attention, but it would have to wait until tomorrow. Devin knew the attention he would give it today wouldn't be what it deserved.

His thoughts constantly pulled to Luisa and to his mother suggesting that it couldn't be anything so bad for him to completely break up with her.

His mother had pushed him hard last night. Though he'd had dinner here at the Sanctuary, he'd driven down the mountain immediately after and watched a few TV shows with her. But his mother wanted to talk.

"Did she cheat on you?" she asked, not even looking at the TV, though he guessed maybe hearing it was enough.

"No."

"Did she try to kill you?"

He laughed. The idea was preposterous.

"Fine." His mother nodded, pleased with herself. "I'm assuming she lied to you, then."

He nodded. As much as he wanted to spill the whole thing to the person he trusted most, it wasn't his to share. He was realizing now, too, that part of the reason he didn't want to tell her was because if—a big *if* that he couldn't really see beyond— Luisa came back into his life he would want his mother to like her.

His mother had waved her hand in front of his face, trying to grab his attention back from the imaginary world it had drifted to. "Did she tell you why she did it? Did she have a good reason for the lie?"

His mother was starting to really irritate him. He was mad and he had a right to be mad. He missed Luisa, but he wanted to hold on to his anger.

"Did she have a good reason?" His mother pressed. When his response was only clenched teeth, she added, "I'm assuming *yes*, because you won't even answer me."

He admitted to himself then that the fears Luisa had were legitimate. He didn't ever think they weren't, he'd just avoided thinking about it, unable to reason through the haze of red he saw.

It wasn't stupid. It wasn't some irrational hangup. She was genuinely afraid and with good cause. So he'd nodded *yes* to his mother.

"Then maybe understand that it was never about you."

How did she know that? He wondered, maybe it was about him. But he couldn't tell her she was wrong.

Grabbing the remote, she finally paused the TV—getting serious. She turned to face him and held still until he looked at her. "You really love her."

Devin kept his expression flat, neither confirming nor denying anything. Because to admit it was true would have cut him deeply all over again.

She seemed to understand, "You're probably right to be mad."

At least she recognized that!

"But you still have to choose." She paused. "Stay mad and not have Gabi or forgive and be with her." But she held her fingers up near her face and signed the name for Gabi—not Luisa.

That was the problem, wasn't it?

"Thank you, mom. I'll consider it," he told her. It was probably the best he could do. He'd been unable to think about anything else all day. His mother's words hung in the air around him.

As he stood in the shower, getting ready to go to town and have a burger with the other trainer, he wondered if maybe he shouldn't swing by and get some coffee.

CHAPTER FORTY-FIVE

They'd buckled the dogs in, working well together since this wasn't their first time. Devin was looking forward to a burger. He could feel his stomach rumbling and wondered if Su could hear it. He understood sometimes people could . . . but he couldn't tell the difference by feel.

As soon as they were in the car, Su tapped him on the arm. When he turned slightly to look at her, she asked, "Are Brandy and Ash a thing?"

He laughed. "Very much so."

"I thought so, but then it seemed like they were trying to keep things professional."

He laughed again. "They try. It doesn't always work."

Happy to have a smile on his face again, Devin headed down the mountain and changed the subject. "I saw that your light was on at three last night. Everything okay?"

She turned her head and quirked one eyebrow at him, the purple ponytail falling to the side. "That means you were awake in the middle of the night, too."

He was nodding to say yes. He wasn't sleeping well. He

would say it was Luisa's fault, his mother would say it was his own.

Suddenly, Su looked surprised and worried. "I didn't wake you, did I?"

"How?" he asked, wondering what she was referring to.

"I don't sleep well, a lot of times. Sometimes I have really bad dreams and I cry out—"

His laughter cut her off. But he quickly tried to rein it in. He didn't want her to think that he was laughing at what was clearly a concern. Trying to be diplomatic about it, he offered, "I'm really sorry you have that. But the good news is I'm Deaf. You can't wake me up that way."

This time it was Su who laughed. At least she had the fortitude to laugh at herself—huge belly laughs where she tipped her head back. "Oh, that was dumb of me." It took her a minute to get herself together.

"I asked Roz . . ." She signed the name that Devin had given to their boss, "to put my cabin away from everyone else, so I wouldn't wake anyone if . . . *when* it happened. She told me not to worry."

"Well, yeah, she put you next to the Deaf guy."

"One worry off of my checklist!" Su declared, almost happy about it. Then she added, "I'm so excited about this burger. I'm so hungry *all the time.*"

Devin understood. "You're doing the work full time. I'm only part time but before this, I was used to being at a desk all day. I used to go to the gym."

"Me, too!" Su said. "Almost every day! I was worried I'd have to drive down the mountain to find a gym."

Devin laughed at her again. "You don't need a gym with this job."

"No, I do not." He could see her sigh about it. "And I've got the trails to run if I want to go do actual exercise. The trails are amazing!"

He told her about the snake that he and Luisa had seen. He almost signed Luisa's name but quickly covered it up. At least, Su wasn't likely to catch the gaff. But Lynzee might if he made it in front of her. Soon enough, any of them would.

But he thought about her as *Luisa*. It was hard to say *Gabi* when he was talking.

"Did you see the snake coming at you?"

"No." Devin didn't bother to mention what he was doing at the time. "Curie saw or heard it and alerted me."

"Good dog!" She grinned. "That's been an interesting thing to watch the training for. I'm glad everyone's willing to teach me how to do it."

"You like the work? You like the dogs?" he asked. With one hand on the wheel, the other signed the best he could. But she was getting it.

"I do. I have always loved dogs and wanted one. I just worked in the office so much. Sometime things would get on . . . take too much time. I would stay late, sometimes until eight or nine or ten at night. And what if I had a dog?"

Then she continued, "I did get to work at home for a while and that made me think I could get a dog, but what if they wanted us back in the office?"

He saw something in her expression, something troubling, but she seemed ready to tell. "I found that working from home meant I was alone with the data. That was hard."

Devin frowned as he took the turn onto the main road. The tall trees opened up on fields and rolling hills with a few farm houses, letting him know they were closer. He looked in the rearview mirror, checking that the dogs were still sitting upright, and that they still seemed happy to be wearing their little service vests.

"Can I ask?" He started. "You said data gives you nightmares?"

"No." She thought for a moment, seeming to find the signs. "We gather . . ." she tried again to figure out how to explain it and started over. "We gather the data from a bunch of different places, and it doesn't match. It's not all the same information. So, I have to read the cases and figure out how to put it as matching data."

Devin nodded, hoping she meant to sign what she was signing, but it made sense.

"So I was reading case file after case file that needed to get entered into spreadsheets about whatever bad system it is that we're trying to fix." She looked out the window briefly then turned back. "For three years it was missed diagnoses for kids with cancer. I would read over and over about tests that I now *know* the doctors should have ordered. They just missed it. Sometimes, the notes said the doctors told the patients it was all in their heads. Or that they just needed a vitamin."

Devin felt his eyes go wide. That was horrifying.

"Then the kid died. They all died because that was the data set."

"But that was rare . . ." he watched as she didn't catch it and he spelled out R A R E and signed it again. "Right?"

"No. Way too common. The last project I was on was maternal . . ." she actually signed *shit!* making him laugh again in the middle of a tough conversation.

Reaching over, he tapped her wrist and motioned for her to move around, to put her hand in front of the window, then he told her to fingerspell.

"Maternal mortality." She spelled slowly and carefully, making it easy to read. And again, he felt his eyes go wide.

He could have demonstrated the signs but one hand was on the steering wheel and she could learn them later. "Oh shit. You're reading stories about women dying?"

She nodded.

"I'm guessing from the look on your face that it's bad."

"It's *really* bad," she told him. If she burst into tears, he wouldn't have been surprised, but she turned more stoic. "We're supposed to be the best in the world, yet we're letting these women die and we know how to stop it."

"But we don't? Why?"

"Sometimes because they are—" She held her hand up in front of the window again. "R U R A L. And we closed their hospital. Sometimes because they are black, and the doctors don't believe when they say they have pain."

He had to admit it was something he'd not considered. It wasn't the kind of thing that crossed his desk. As much as he hated the idea that the information was enough to give Su nightmares, he wondered if it might be something he would take up after he was through here with the dogs.

His thoughts took a sharp turn with that. Leaving here would likely mean that his mother was no longer in Charlottesville. And that would mean . . .

He didn't want to think about it. He told himself she was doing well, and reminded himself that the job here was fantastic. As Su said, he didn't even have to buy a gym membership.

Right then, he wished fervently that he could stay here in perpetuity.

"Okay," Su started as they pulled into the burger place. She changed the subject fast enough to give him whiplash. "I thought you had a girlfriend here and that she worked at a coffee shop."

Devin didn't quite answer.

"She came for dinner one night and . . ." she paused. "I was not sure I understood correctly."

"You understood right," he signed. "We had a fight." As if that would simplify the whole thing down to four little words.

"Well, if you're ready, we can go get a coffee after this."

It was nice of her to volunteer, and he cursed his mother for planting the idea, because he didn't want to forgive. He wasn't ready. But for the first time he actually considered it.

CHAPTER FORTY-SIX

S he was standing in the front of the store, making coffee for a customer during a rush, when she felt it.

Luisa was facing the espresso machines, her back to the door, and still it hit her: the electric charge that ran up her spine and made her suck in a breath. Suddenly, happily, she realized *Devin is here.*

She almost forgot the hot coffee coming out of the machine. She started to turn to say hello or just grin like a fool, but then she reminded herself that she was a professional. Also, it looked like she was just a barista and not the manager. She had on that apron that she'd worked so hard to graduate out of. It seemed to take an eternity for the super fast machine to spit out its fresh brew. And for Luisa to remember that a wide smile might not be the best greeting for a man who hated her.

When the machine sputtered and quit, she turned with her cup in hand and scanned the sea of faces. It was that busy. But she found him in an instant, as if he had a magnetic pull she couldn't refuse.

He saw her too, but his expression somehow only seemed neutral.

Had she ever even seen Devin James with a neutral look? Not about her, certainly. Laughing, excited, red hot passionate, or red hot angry, yes. But never neutral.

Not until now.

Using her one free hand, she signed to him, "Devin, hi."

There was absolutely no way for her to keep the hope out of her eyes.

He was Deaf. By nature, he was observant. He stayed alive by what he saw. And if he wanted to use it against her, he could be vicious. In that moment, she suddenly became very afraid of what Devin James might say.

Not that he would try to hurt her. But what if he accidentally called her Luisa? More and more, her employees had been learning sign.

She'd shared whatever she could when they had a few moments. So had Paul, so shy and withdrawn the first time he'd come in with Fred, he now had a smile on his face. She'd learned more about him, too, in the moments when the shop wasn't busy. Happily she'd signed with him, as though that alone might replace the loss of Devin in her life.

Obviously, it wasn't even close, but she'd learned three new signs—or maybe old ones. Paul was over seventy and on a fixed income. He was also in desperate need of interaction beyond riding the bus to the Deaf Community Center. She was going to have to figure out how to get him paid to teach a class to her employees.

Because while she could absolutely show them intro signs, she was still a hearing person, and the best way to learn was from a Deaf person. Also, she didn't really have the time.

So now as she looked at Devin, she wondered what he might say that her staff could understand. But all he said was, "Hello."

He didn't use her name or say anything else.

Only then did Luisa notice that a woman stood beside him.

Her even features were clearly curious but Luisa couldn't quite tell how much she knew.

"Gabi," Craig said, and for half a second the name didn't even register as hers.

Jerking, she whirled around almost spilling the coffee, but not quite. She had been doing this for far too long to spill because of a fast motion. She got back to work.

Maybe that was the problem. This had been too much of her adult life. Too many draining customer service jobs. Too many promotions she'd turned down because she wasn't sure her papers would hold up. After talking to Helen, she had brief flashes of moments she couldn't control, in which she had begun to dream of a radically different life. Of a job that she wanted to have, not just one that she *could*.

Forcefully pulling herself back to the present, she stepped out of Craig's way and smiled a little at Devin and the woman as they stepped into the short line. He was neutral to her, she could be neutral back. Maybe.

Was this woman his new girlfriend? She was pretty with blue eyes and purple hair that somehow seemed to compliment high cheekbones and a mouth that was more expressive than friendly.

Luisa ignored the sharp stab at her heart. *Surely, Devin wouldn't.*

Her brain snapped into place for the fiftieth time since he walked in and she pumped flavoring into the coffee, added foam and a lid and offered her best version of a genuine smile to the man who stood at the counter. She remembered his name as she'd taken his order a few very long minutes ago.

She'd only come out to help as the place had gotten busy. It was starting to die down now, but she was not going to duck into the back, even though she could. Not when she could stay here and stare at Devin James just a little. Maybe get him to talk.

She knew his coffee order by heart, of course. She watched

as the cup was passed hand to hand down the row, each person reading the markings on the side and doing their part as they shifted back to a more normal assembly line.

Next to his cup, she saw the name Su. An iced latte. She seemed like an iced latte kind of woman. Luisa watched as the two of them signed to each other, Su's signs a little bit choppy, some vocabulary missing as she finger spelled a few words.

Even as she stared like a jealous ex-girlfriend, Luisa heard the bell ring as Paul walked in. Motioning to Luisa with a smile, he signed, "I finished outside but I'll wait until the customers die down."

As she watched, he caught sight of Devin and Su.

They had occasional Deaf customers in here and her goal was to get more. People would come if the staff could actually speak their language. Still, she kept her idea to herself, she couldn't offer a teaching job to Paul until she cleared it through Greg.

There were too many moving pieces. Too much Devin James standing right in front of her. But she was grateful to have something to say other than a weak *Hello*.

Devin saw her signing to someone else and his head turned. *Perfect opportunity.* Luisa motioned to Devin and Su and said, "This is our new employee, Paul."

Paul happily said hello. Devin turned and simply began speaking to the man.

It wasn't always the case that they knew each other. Deaf people didn't know each other the same way hearing people didn't. People would ask her, "Oh, you're from Texas. Do you know the Rodriguez family?" She never did. Being Latina and from Texas didn't mean she knew every other family with a Spanish or Latin surname.

But Devin—having attended a school were only his interpreter and Gabi and Luisa could actually speak to him— had gotten friendly whenever anyone clearly spoke ASL. There were only a few others who knew even a handful of signs at school. A couple of teachers tried for one period each day, but didn't get very far. She wasn't surprised that today he was happy to start a conversation with the new guy.

Luisa watched as Paul's face lit up and they spoke rapidly, some of it even getting away from her.

But then the coffees were made. And Devin and Su took them, heading out the door and the time ticked by slowly, too slowly. All she'd really gotten to say was *Hello* and *this is Paul*. And she had a horribly late shift tonight. Marietta had asked for the time off and, with nothing better to do, Luisa had traded her for the day off tomorrow. She'd sleep in, something.

Heading into the back, she wondered how she would make it through the rest of the shift without thinking of him, without replaying every little moment, gesture, expression.

She wouldn't.

It was well past dark when Luisa walked herself out to the small parking lot, feeling alone and dejected. She drove home on relatively empty streets, as her mind wandered to what it might mean that he'd come in with Su.

But as she climbed the stairs to her apartment, she saw someone waiting, leaning against the door. Luisa sucked in a breath.

CHAPTER FORTY-SEVEN

"Oh my god!" Su seemed to be unable to sit still despite being buckled into the passenger seat. She did, however, seem to have gotten the hang of sipping her coffee with one hand and signing with the other.

"That was . . ." She leaned forward, swiveling, putting her hand almost in his face. "T E N S E."

Devin nodded. He was driving and didn't even try to demonstrate the sign.

"You definitely need to talk to her," Su told him.

"Thank you for your advice, Dr. Love."

Beautifully, she caught the nickname and laughed at him. "Okay, fine. Don't take advice from me, but seriously, she's beautiful." Su paused, "Normally, I would not say something like that, because that's clearly not anybody's best quality. But that's all I could tell about her because I didn't really get to meet her!"

She managed to lace that last part with blame. Devin laughed at that too.

Still, he shook his head. "No, it was just awkward."

He caught her expression even before it was a full frown. "A W K W A R D."

She nodded, "No, not awkward. T E N S E. It's different." In her excitement, she seemed to forget that she was speaking a different language. For the first time he watched her actually *talk*.

He would have been really excited about it if his brain wasn't completely caught up, reliving memories of every movement of Luisa's face as they had stared at each other like complete total fucking Junior High idiots.

"I think she thinks that I'm your girlfriend."

His head snapped around at that comment. "Why would she think that?"

Su laughed at him as though he were a fool. "Because I was there with you, and you didn't say I wasn't."

"Fine," he agreed, not sure he believed her.

The coffee shop had been the last stop. They'd eaten their burgers, making sure the dogs had stayed on "lay" at their feet. They were only allowed to move and bump a leg until they had their person's attention if they heard a noise that needed alert. Austen and Shelley had taken a good deal more corrections than Vivaldi and Brahms had the other week.

But then they'd gone to the library where he'd gotten a library card and checked out several books. Partly because he wanted one, but also partly because it would take longer and the dogs needed training on that.

Now, they sat in the backseat, worn out. He and Su had decided to let them go to sleep. It was a long day with a lot of focus required. It would get easier for everyone in the future.

"You should definitely talk to her," Su told him, but he didn't quite know how to reply.

Maybe he should. His mother sure seemed to think so, but there wasn't much time to stew on it. Su—who'd been a little reticent when she started and had focused on the work and hadn't been able to sign much—was now smiling and interacting with everyone a lot more often.

Between the dogs doing something ridiculous and Su trying to keep a stern face or simply coming along and talking to her coworkers during non-working hours, she was coming out of her shell. For whatever reason, she seemed to think Devin was the one with all the information.

Yeah, he was absolutely not. Or maybe she asked everyone, but she asked him anyway. "So Brandy and Ash are a couple?"

Yes, he nodded, wondering. She'd asked that before.

She signed again, still turned to face him, no longer frightened about him both signing and driving at the same time. "Roz and Beck?"

She put a question mark at the end of it.

Oh, that was interesting.

"I don't know," he replied. She didn't seem to be asking it to spread gossip, but more to simply know how the world around her functioned. He'd never seen her tell anyone else or heard anyone complain.

Su looked at him and asked, "You see that too, right?"

Again, he tried to be diplomatic. He had to admit, "I've wondered, but I don't know."

"Interesting." Then she stopped for a moment before signing, "Okay, if you don't want to answer, it's fine. I'm just curious. No J U D G M E N T."

He nodded, now very curious what her next question might be.

"Beck was in prison?"

"Yes." Devin told her, he at least knew the answer to that one. Sooner or later, Beck would say something about his time inside and she would know. It was rare, the comments few and far between, but Beck never hid it. "It's not a secret. But he doesn't talk about it much at all."

Su nodded. "Thank you. That's good to know. I don't want to say anything to hurt anyone's feelings."

As Devin thought about it, that did seem to be the place she was coming from. He'd never seen her say anything negative or gossipy about anyone else. She simply asked questions and seemed to tuck it away into her files, as if maybe she were making one of her data spreadsheets on all of them.

When he noticed motion in the rearview mirror and saw Su react quickly, he realized the dogs were barking at something. But he was driving, so he let her handle calming them down and letting them know that this wasn't appropriate.

"What were they barking at?" he asked when he got her attention again.

"Nothing I could see or hear." She shrugged.

That was the point. He actually didn't get to train the dogs to alert like that because he couldn't hear things to let them know if they had alerted correctly or incorrectly. Once she was facing him again, she said, "You really need to go talk to her. And not just order a coffee."

It was one thing for his mother to tell him that and yet another for Su to say it. Maybe the universe was giving him a sign.

CHAPTER FORTY-EIGHT

Beck sat on the log at the backside of the campfire, the mountain behind him, his view was the trail where they'd all made their way out here. The weather had turned enough that they no longer had to rotate to the fire periodically because their fronts were hot and their backs were cold.

The flames were lower tonight because they'd built the base wider. The fire was now more about light and being able to roast things on sticks than providing heat for the group.

Around him, everyone talked, some in English, some in ASL. Across the fire from him he saw Roz take in the group as she drank a bottle of that high-end soda she liked. Another reminder that she had not grown up around campfires and budgets.

Though Su had often joked about her dinner being hotdogs roasted over an open flame, this was the first time she'd come through on the threat. Truth be told, they'd all had a brilliant time doing it. Everyone laughed as they roasted or burned their dinner. And, despite the threats that she couldn't cook anything, she'd managed to bring hot dog buns in regular and whole wheat, and even some that she'd toasted in the oven to near perfection.

Beck had pointed that out. Su had grinned in response, "I can toast like nobody's business!"

He'd had to laugh at her, even as he'd thought about doing a roast chicken with lemon and greek yogurt and stone ground mustard for tomorrow night when it was his turn. Around him the conversation turned this way and that, with words and chuckles and hands moving as they spoke whatever worked for the conversation.

He found his own mind wandering. The feel of the wood log through the cargo pants that he wore was somehow becoming ordinary rather than miraculous. He'd spent so much of his life in concrete and cinderblock that simply getting to the halfway house and having a bedroom with a door that he was allowed to open on his own and a real mattress, had been almost too much. He hadn't quite realized until he arrived at the Sanctuary that there was more that he could want. But he found he needed the trees and the grass and the dirt. He needed the open sky. The clouds. The log he was sitting on and the fire crackling before him. And only very very recently had he learned that he needed Hallie.

He looked at the blue peep marshmallow on the end of his stick and decided to stop contemplating life as he stuck it directly into the fire. The brightly colored sugars bubbled and burned onto the surface as the marshmallow puffed up. Across the way, he got the stink eye from Brandy, and shrugged at her. She was trying to perfectly toast a yellow peep which of course was a painstaking process.

Su had provided the bright marshmallows along with hot dogs, baked beans and even a salad. He could admit that they'd all eaten well around the fire. Then, she'd made them all laugh and exclaim with surprise that she'd upgraded their usual s'mores to include candy. She'd even run a masterclass on how to caramelize the sugar on the outside of the chicks and bunnies.

Beck and Ash, of course, had followed the lesson carefully then immediately stuck theirs directly into the flames. He was watching his third one burn and trying to figure out when to yank it and blow the flames out when a bump came at his hip. Roz, of course.

She'd picked up and moved over to sit next to him. "Are you still mad about the search and rescue contract?"

Her voice was soft and he fought the urge to turn closer. Instead, he almost laughed. It would figure that that was what she would think it was. "No. I'm not confident it will work. I'd rather have better odds. But you explained your reasoning and I understand it."

"Then what?" she asked, leaning in close, her voice low. Across the way Devin and Su laughed together, as Lynzee wailed while her so-close-to-perfectly-toasted peep accidentally caught an ear on fire.

Brandy and Ash were having their own conversation, no one was paying attention to him and Roz, and it wasn't a conversation for the masses anyway. He didn't sign his answer and he kept his voice low like hers. "Just things going on in my life."

Not that that would make her feel any better as she understood he was holding back. Her next words, as she leaned in even closer, came with a caress of her breath against his ear. "I don't like when you're mad at me."

He shivered, the soft sound tracing down his spine like a lover's touch. As he turned to look her in those large hazel eyes he saw that their faces were so close that he could lean in and simply taste her. But he'd never kissed her before, despite the fact that he'd wanted to.

She'd never quite shown him that it was what she wanted.

And there were people here. Anyone—*everyone*—would see. Then there was Hallie to consider.

Still, they lingered that way, too close, for a long moment. Enough for him to see the need pass through her eyes, too. And he couldn't even tell her why he wouldn't do it.

CHAPTER FORTY-NINE

L uisa scrambled for her key. She'd probably hugged her friend for a good five minutes and woken the neighbors with her excited greetings.

Only after stubbing her toe on it, did she see the suitcase at Helen's feet.

"How long are you staying?" Luisa had asked excitedly.

"A week, maybe," Helen offered, then changed her mind. "I don't know."

"Are you just taking a vacation?" Luisa calculated the number of shifts she had in that time as she pushed the door open and led her friend through. She thought about her apartment. She only had the one bed but it was a queen. She could take the couch.

"I figured I'd get a hotel and not put you out."

"There's absolutely no need for that!" Luisa protested. She would love to have Helen stay here. "If you're comfortable in my bed, I will change the sheets and—"

But Helen, having followed her through the door, simply hugged her hard one more time. "I wish I could say it was a vacation."

Luisa watched as Helen's whole demeanor shifted from excited to sad. She leaned back against the door, clicking it softly behind her. Luisa turned as Helen pushed herself away, into the middle of the room, not quite able to get her words together.

That was a first for Helen.

Stepping over, Luisa turned the bolt, another click and a constant in her life, making her feel safe in the apartment. It was a feeling she cherished, one she hadn't always had growing up. She hoped she could share that, but mostly she felt concern for her friend.

This time she was the one who leaned back against the door as Helen stood in the open. She wasn't in a business suit, just jeans and a classic white button down blouse. Looking between them, everything about them would tell anyone with eyes who was the lawyer and who was the shop manager. Luisa fought the pain that her life hadn't been able to go any further.

It occurred to her then that Helen was checking on her. She'd texted the lawyer's name to her two days ago. "Oh Helen! I'm going to call the lawyer tomorrow. I simply had so much going on these past few days."

Had she, though? The lawyer was supposed to be her number one priority. But once the message had come through, she'd frozen, afraid that if she started with the call it would end with a lawyer telling her there was nothing that could actually be done. Or worse, that they would start the process and ultimately it would fail.

"It's not that. It's fine." Helen waved her concern away. "Honestly, it's been this long, a day isn't going to make much difference. It's . . ." her words trailed off.

Luisa's first instinct kicked back in. *This wasn't about her.* "What's wrong?"

Helen's eyes grew wide and almost watered, "Everything!"

Her friend plopped down onto the couch, her brown hair

bob swishing at her shoulders with class, even as the tears started to fall. "I guess I just held it together until I got here."

Sitting down next to her, Luisa wrapped one arm around Helen's shoulders and pulled her close, waiting until her friend's head fell against her shoulder. Then waiting a little longer for the words to start.

Reaching out, Helen grabbed for Luisa's hand, and only then did Luisa notice her ring was missing.

Oh shit.

She lifted Helen's hand the same way she had years ago to inspect the new, shining diamond engagement ring. Only now, she inspected an empty finger which—when looked at closely— bore the mark where her wedding band had been.

Helen nodded. "Josh and I are getting divorced."

"Oh no, what happened?" Luisa asked just out of sheer curiosity and not realizing until the words were out that she shouldn't have. "You don't have to tell me. It's okay."

"No. It's fine," Helen said again, though clearly it wasn't. "The worst part is neither of us cheated. Nobody's mad. We just . . ." she sighed, then added, "I don't even know how to admit this. I spent so long building everything. You know." She looked at Luisa, "*You know* how driven I always was."

Was. Luisa heard the past tense.

"About six months ago, I had a breakdown at work." Helen breaking down was something Luisa would have thought wasn't even possible. "My boss assigned me this client and it was this huge thing. I needed to crush it. This case was going to put me on track for junior partner."

Luisa remembered. They'd all been following Helen in the chat, checking the boxes as she climbed her way up at the firm. "The one with the awful contact person?"

"Yes!"

She hadn't told them about the breakdown.

"He was awful. Then, when I made all the changes to the

contract that he wanted, and I handed it back in, *perfect,* he told me everything was wrong. And I just lost it. I yelled at him. I told him he was an idiot, and I wasn't changing anything back, even the things I had tried to talk him out of because they were bad for his company." Helen shrank back, her words having grown angry with the memory. She sighed, a thick heavy sound of regret and despair. "Luisa, I called him a *fucking idiot.*"

"To his face?"

"On the phone."

Just about as bad, Luisa thought. She'd been there—the tough days when she was told conflicting things and expected to simply manage them. When she'd had to act as if it was okay to be given all the tasks—even things well outside of her duties or the hours she was getting paid for. She'd always sucked it up because she needed the job. Rent was due, or she needed groceries, and probably her bosses had taken advantage of that.

She'd been angry and felt powerless. She'd never imagined Helen in that position.

"They put me on probation at work. Took me off partner track and told me that I could try again next year." Something changed in Helen then. She turned, sitting more upright and looking at Luisa. Her hands outstretched, fingers resting on Luisa's arms, as if she simply needed the human contact. "I've never felt more relieved. Since then, I've slowly been undoing every single thing I worked for.

CHAPTER FIFTY

"**A**re you okay?" Roz asked him, her expression worried. Devin could easily ask the same of her. She'd seemed a little *off* lately, but he wasn't in any space to take care of anyone else's problems.

Instead of responding with a rote *I'm fine,* he said, "Just thinking a lot."

"About Gabi?"

Well, that answered one of his questions: Everyone *had* been following along.

He nodded his head, but he wasn't thinking about Gabi. He was thinking about Luisa. And—as much as they had been following along—no one else knew the difference.

"You're finished for the day, right?" she asked him.

It was early afternoon still. He'd made it through the whole weekend without running to Luisa and telling her that he didn't know how to fix things, that he was so mad, but that he missed her so much. That he wanted her back but he never wanted to deal with her betrayal again. He didn't know how to make any of that work. So he hadn't said any of it.

Devin nodded at Roz. He'd trained the dogs in the morning

with Beck and Lynzee. His job had been to be the Deaf person that each dog got to alert to a loud noise. Beck said it was the perfect training, because Devin didn't have any subtle reactions. He couldn't hear anything and maybe subconsciously react and alert the dogs. Though Devin understood that was good, he also understood he was mostly just the dummy standing in place as a training tool.

"Did you finish the two second-round grant proposals?" Roz asked.

"I just sent the second one." He smiled. He'd done the job he was hired for, now he needed to win a few more of them. Grant proposal writing was a never-ending cycle of hurry up and wait and his job depending on other people's opinions.

"Then go," she told him.

"It's barely three."

"What does it matter? You were hired to do certain work. You finished the work."

"Thank you."

"It's not your night to cook dinner anyway."

Another question answered: Not only was everyone following along, Roz was keeping score.

He didn't even have to ask, she told him, "My opinion is not important, but I think you should talk to her."

Something clicked inside him. He'd thought of it before, but he felt it now. It was in the way Roz referred to everybody at the Sanctuary as *family*. He'd been the new kid for quite a while. Maybe Su coming in and being the *new* new kid had made him feel like he fit better. Now there was someone asking *him* questions. Someone who saw him as more established.

Whatever it was, it felt like *family*. It couldn't have come at a better time. Finding Gabi and then losing Luisa all in one stroke, had been too much to handle. Though he had his mother and though she was doing very well, there was an impending sense of a piano about to drop on his head, with her health.

The Sanctuary felt stable, despite Roz being a little *off* this week. Something settled into his bones right then, and Jade River Sanctuary began to feel like *home*.

Looking up at Roz he agreed, "You're right. I should. I don't know what it will do or if it will solve anything, but . . ." *He should talk to her.*

It felt good that Roz understood him. She literally spoke his language now, all of them having come such a long way since he'd first arrived. He realized that—though it shouldn't be—it was a monumental thing to be in a group of people who were willing to immerse themselves in a new language for him.

"Go!" Roz grinned as she encouraged him, "I hope it all works out however you need."

He smiled, saluted her, and turned to head out the back door, not even calling for Curie, knowing that his faithful companion was right at his heels.

Roz didn't wish that he and Luisa got back together, just that it turned out in a way that was *good for him*. He would remember that, he thought as he headed towards his cabin.

His feet squished into the dirt, the ground damp and muddy from the torrential rains yesterday. They hadn't been able to train outside, hence the makeup session this morning.

In the distance, he saw Su, who turned to look at him as if she were concerned.

Shoulders up, hands out, he asked, "What is it?" Then he watched as realization crossed her face.

She signed. "I can hear Ash and Brandy fighting."

Fighting? he thought. That was beyond his scope of reasoning. Not the two of them.

Su looked worried, so he asked, "What about?"

He watched as Su struggled, then said, "I don't like to share gossip."

But he'd already figured that out about her.

"But I can hear them easily!" She began to interpret.

That was interesting. Su Abbott serving as an interpreter.

He felt his own eyebrows rise. Okay, Su's interpreting wasn't the best, but he was getting the gist of it.

"Brandy said she didn't want to move off the mountain but that she would need to in order to get to work in Charlottesville. Then Ash argued back that he needs to stay for several years." Su looked over her shoulder, not moving from side to side to show different speakers the way a trained interpreter would, but Devin followed. "It's not in his contract. He doesn't have to stay. She said, I'm leaving for a new job after this batch of dogs, after this C O H O R T."

"Whoa," Devin signed. That was not something he'd expected to deal with. If Ash and Brandy had previous fights, he hadn't seen them, and he certainly didn't hear it. But he hadn't felt any tension between them, either.

He motioned a hand for Su to stop and then said, "Roz told me they fought all the time when they first met. Hopefully, they'll figure it out."

"Do they know everyone can hear them?" Su leaned in, clearly worried.

Devin shrugged. "Not *everyone.*"

He was glad as her face lit up and she laughed.

Beck walked into the middle of the courtyard just then. He started to ask what was going on, but then he clearly heard something. Motioning with one finger to Devin, he sucked in an obviously deep breath and yelled.

From what Devin could see on his lips, Beck had called out, "Hey, we can all hear you!"

Devin signed again at the same time Su did, "Not *all.*"

The three of them laughed together and Devin felt the warm comfort worm its way deeper into his bones. Still, he told the two of them, "I'm off."

Though she didn't ask what he was doing, Su signed a very intuitive, "Good luck."

He walked away happy with the idea of a family waiting for him at the top of the mountain when he returned. They would be there for him, no matter how it turned out.

He wasn't even sure what he wanted from Luisa, he just knew that he had to go find out.

CHAPTER FIFTY-ONE

A knock came at the door, Luisa's head lifting at the same time her phone pinged.

Helen had a key. So who would come to her apartment door? Unless someone was trying to sell her girl scout cookies. With her phone in her hands, she headed toward the front door and only absently looked at the screen in time to see Devin's name.

— I'm at your door.

She froze mid step, heart clenching. Then, almost as quickly, hope bloomed. *Was he here because he wanted to forgive her?* She wasn't sure she deserved it, but she knew she needed it. *Was he here to yell at her again?* She was pretty sure she deserved that.

She tamped down the false hope with the weight of an anvil before she forced her feet to move and her hand to reach for the doorknob. Some crazy part of her thought it would actually be a girl scout on the other side. But when she opened the door, there he stood, somehow looking exactly as he had the first day she'd seen him in her coffee shop.

Throughout the years, she'd wondered about the man he'd

grown into. She'd imagined him so many different ways, but none of her imaginings had been as good as the real man. Nothing in her fantasies had accounted for the way she could smell him and breathe him in when he was close. Not for the softness of his shirt over the hard planes of his chest. Or that she could see him in the flesh, right in front of her, living and breathing and looking at her.

His body didn't move other than his hands saying, "I was hoping we could talk."

Without thinking, she stepped back and waved him into the apartment. But it took only a second for him to spot the blankets and pillows folded and stacked at the end of her couch.

"Someone's here?" he asked. No jealously or anger or even real curiosity. *Damn*, she needed something from him. She'd take blazing hot anger over this *nothing*.

Shaking her head, she said, "That's for me. My friend Helen came to stay."

"If it's a bad time—"

She reached out, wrapping her fingers around his, shrinking his hand into a fist with her grip. Her other hand motioned, "This is fine. It's good." Then, letting go of the hot lightning she felt just from touching him, she added solemnly, "We do need to talk."

He looked around the apartment almost as if he were taking it in for the first time, almost as if he were reliving every memory there. But what he said was, "Is your friend here?"

"No. But she should be back any minute."

Devin's gaze darted away, and she knew what he was going to say before he said it. "We should talk in private. Maybe another day."

But Helen was here for maybe as much as four more days. She was on indefinite leave. In fact, Helen had started saying things about looking for an apartment, maybe for just a few months. She might stay in town as she tried to recover from her burnout and the realization that she hated her job and that she and her husband made the perfect logical equation, but nothing else. She'd loved the idea of being the wife and a lawyer on track to partner. She'd once thought two lawyers were the perfect power couple, but then when their tracks had diverged, he'd simply not supported her. Offered only platitudes and didn't even try to make her feel better.

Helen had confessed she wasn't certain she'd ever loved the man at all. So here she was, in Luisa's apartment, just when Luisa needed her most. Helen's divorce papers were signed and waiting to be officially filed. Only the other night, with the two of them side by side on the sofa, had Helen found the courage to announce it into the chat.

While Luisa had the friend she needed, she didn't have a place to talk to Devin. For a moment, she had the brief thought of messaging Helen and asking her to stay away for a little while. But she had no idea how long a little while could be. "There's a trail into the mountains not far from here. We should be able to find something private. It's the middle of the day on a weekday."

He nodded to her, and she reacted quickly. Maybe too quickly, not even thinking about what she was wearing. Grabbing her purse and keys, she motioned for him to come along. He was out the door and she was locking it behind her, her heart pounding that they were actually going to do this.

She had no idea how she found the courage to have this conversation, because her heart had already broken a thousand different ways. But she was leading him down the steps as if she couldn't stop moving, couldn't trust that her feet would keep going if she paused even for a second.

Devin didn't follow her. He headed to his own car instead, telling her, "Give me the address," as if he wanted to be sure he could get away at any time.

It only occurred to her then that maybe she would want to get away too. She messaged it to him then watched as he climbed into his car. Starting her own engine, she followed him out of the lot, trying to drive carefully as well as update Helen.

— Devin came by. We're heading out somewhere to talk. Let yourself in. Help yourself to anything.

The drive made her nervous. Luisa's heart lodged in her throat and wouldn't budge. She only realized then that she hadn't eaten. Digging in her purse, she found a cracker pack and then the tiny hand sanitizer and bug spray that she carried with her. As she ate, she lost track of Devin's car in front of her.

When she pulled into the lot, she stepped out of the car and sprayed herself down with the little bug spray. Then she turned, her tongue hitting the roof of her mouth as she realized he wasn't there. *Had he abandoned her? Changed his mind about wanting to talk?*

The parking lot had only two other cars and—as she'd hoped—no one else was in sight. Then she heard the faint sound of tires on gravel, and she watched as the car she knew headed toward the tiny lot and pulled up next to her.

Stepping out, he closed the door behind him, still looking like everything she'd ever wanted, and still stoic as hell. He managed to stand solidly in front of her as she searched for something—*anything*—to say.

But they were here. She had to do something. "I thought we could take one of these trails. There'll be no people around. If we take that one, there's a picnic bench maybe a quarter of a mile in."

Devin only motioned for her to lead the way.

Looking down at her feet for the first time, Luisa was glad to see she'd worn decent sneakers if not good hiking boots. The trails weren't difficult here. Trying to think anything reasonable amidst the swirling thoughts in her brain and the petrified churn in her gut, she was glad that she at least remembered to lock her purse into the trunk while Devin still stood there without saying anything.

Then she headed up the trail, her heart clogging her throat until she almost couldn't breathe. Closing her eyes, she carefully put one foot in front of the other, wondering if he was even following.

CHAPTER FIFTY-TWO

When at last she turned around and looked at him, Devin was there right behind her.

Luckily, he didn't make her wait. "Why did you lie to me?"

She had told him this before, but he had a right to ask anything and he had a right to her honest answer. "I lied to you because I lied to everyone. Mama told me to—"

"She's not your mother." He interrupted.

"Yes and no. I lost my birth mother about a year before you and I met."

"Still, you called her *Tia.*"

Some little part of her sparked happy, pleased that he remembered that. Then it sparked angry. "Once Gabi died, she gave me very strict instructions to call her mama. And she was my *mother* for all real purposes. She was the woman who raised me, fed me, sacrificed to keep me safe!"

"Fine. I understand why you started the lie. But why did you continue it?"

Maybe he didn't really understand, Luisa thought. "Because while I could have told someone when I turned eighteen, what would have happened to me?"

"You could have applied for DACA!"

Another interesting moment. He'd been doing some research. But maybe he hadn't done enough. "What do you think would happen if I applied for it?"

"You'd get to stay! You'd have all the rights of a citizen."

She nodded, but . . . "Nope, not all the rights. It hadn't been around for long when I was eighteen. I looked into it, and it was only working for some people. I didn't think it would work for a girl who had been lying to everyone for seven years."

Taking a breath, Devin seemed to absorb that but not well. She could see it butting up against his moral code.

Luisa had her own moral code, but it had been bent to the point of cracking more than once. Reaching out, she touched him, hoping to get his attention, not remembering that it would send fire up her arm. Or maybe she did remember and that's why she'd done it.

She wondered if he felt it, too. It was tempting to snatch her hand back as though she had been burned. "I need you to imagine what it was like."

Whatever he was imagining it didn't show on his face, but he looked at her, eyes open and seemingly willing.

"I was scared. Petrified. Only eighteen. What if I explained and they deported me? Where would I go? My mother was dead, and I didn't know where my father was."

"I thought you said he died," he interrupted again.

"I only found that out later. My brother never survived. My grandmother is gone. I *think* I know the name of the tiny town in Peru that I came from, but I'm not certain." She watched as the color of his eyes changed, thoughts swam past, changing him as he imagined it. "How would you handle that *today*? If you were suddenly pulled out of your life and sent to a foreign country where you didn't speak the language?"

He started to move his hands, but she spoke over him. "Crime is high. There are no jobs to be had—at least, that's what

I've been told. I don't know if they let you take your money with you. Not that I have any."

She saw it starting to shift on his features. This time, with soft gestures, smaller than his usual, he signed, "Okay. I understand that. But then you were twenty and then twenty-five . . ."

"And thirty!" *She knew this! She'd lived it for fuck's sake. Why didn't he trust that she'd made the only decision she felt she could?*

Her eyes darted to the dirt at her feet. They were standing in the middle of the trail, not even having made it to the picnic table. The conversation was flying hands in the middle of nowhere. She could hear the rustling of the wind at the tops of the trees, the twittering of birds, and the chirping of frogs or crickets or some other animal she'd never learned to identify.

"When I was twenty, I had been an adult criminal for two years. At twenty five the number was seven years."

"But the crime wasn't your fault," he pushed as though she should have done something more. "Your Tia made you do it. You were a child!" He was arguing now, the words coming hard and heavy as his hands moved with more force.

Luisa felt her emotion slip. She'd come here prepared to apologize and beg forgiveness. He'd asked instead for explanations and her calm need to answer him was sliding away as the anger bubbled up. "Yes, I could have done that. I could have gone to the authorities and told them what had been *done to me.*"

She signed the last three words like an accusation. "What you are suggesting is that I would save myself from a good life. I have my own apartment that I can afford with my own money. You think I should throw all of that away for a chance to become a citizen. But *at the same time* my attempt to get myself saved would send my aunt to jail for the crime that she committed by doing that to me."

Sucking in a breath as though she were yelling it with her

voice, Luisa gestured to him with bold, angry strokes. "She was an *adult*. She was not a child. You are asking me why I did not sacrifice the woman who gave up everything for me? She did it for *me*, not her real daughter! When her real daughter died, she told everyone that the dead child *wasn't her daughter*. I cannot imagine what that must have taken. But in that moment, that horrible loss—"

Luisa felt the tears welling behind her eyes, starting to spill over, tears of relived pain and anger. Anger now at Devin for not understanding, for not thinking it all the way through, when he was so smart. He should have figured it out! "In the middle of all of that, somehow, my tia realized that she could take that terrible thing and give me her own dead daughter's identity, so I could have a better life. She was an adult, *you're right*. She *knew* she was risking jail, deportation, and I don't even know! So how can you stand there and suggest that I try for a program that doesn't even give me citizenship, by hurting the *only person* who ever loved me and took care of me that way?"

His expression didn't change as Luisa stood there, her eyes and heart burning at his arrogant assumptions about her. So she waited.

CHAPTER FIFTY-THREE

Devin couldn't process all the emotions assaulting him. He watched as Luisa went from timid and regretful about the things she'd done, to an angry vengeful angel defending her heart.

She was right, he hadn't put the pieces together. He'd seen from the outside, through apparently a much smaller window than he believed he had. A window he was only now realizing was narrowed even further by his own anger, anger he'd always carried at Luisa for leaving him.

Sure, they'd been eleven, and he'd heard that awful rumor that one of the girls had died. But no one had contacted him, they'd simply disappeared. Through the years, as he'd tried occasionally to find her, he'd looked up *Luisa Montalvo*. He'd checked various social media platforms, then, when more had sprung up, every once in a while he would put her name in. He realized now it was his own fault for not also checking for Gabi Montalvo.

He'd had little sparks of anger, adding up along the way, that no one had reached out to him. If Luisa had been the one who had died, why hadn't Gabi thought to just reach out, say *hey*

Devin, I wanted to let you know . . . Why had Mrs. Montalvo—an adult—never thought to reach out to the child left behind? No one had.

Though he understood now that they had cut all ties on purpose—a clear attempt to let Luisa live a full life as Gabi, Devin was only just now realizing how deeply that had burrowed in. Somehow, when he'd been there, falling in love with a woman he believed was Gabi, the anger had still been in there. *Maybe it was time to let it go.*

He didn't know how to say, *I didn't think through all of that.* But what he did know was the other question that he had been ready to ask. He asked it now, wondering if he would get the timid, regretful woman ready to apologize or the angry brown-haired, brown-eyed spitfire who was ready to put him in his place. "But why did you lie to *me*? I understand. The first day I walked into the coffee shop, you recognized me, but you didn't know me *now*. But you *kept lying* to me."

He watched as her hands moved, ready to form a sign, but then drifted away. Her shoulders heaved, tears were running down her face in earnest now. She looked around the forest, as if she were searching for the right words somewhere in the trees. She didn't seem to find them. Luisa tried, once again lifting her hands and starting to form signs only to have it all drift away. She sighed. "I don't know. I decided to tell you, so many times. Because the truth is, I did trust you. I *do* trust you. I trust you not to hurt me. I trust you to know my secret."

"Then *why?*" he pushed, his anger once again bubbling to the surface. If he'd managed to let go of the little hollow point that sat inside him, mad that no one had ever reached out, this anger remained, still bubbling just beneath the surface. "Why did you not tell me?"

It was a deep cut that wasn't healing. Time was supposed to make him miss her less, but he only missed her more each day. He felt righteous. Though he understood now why she'd never attempted to right the record—and what she said made sense, he wasn't sure he would do anything different—why hadn't she told *him*? Her lack of faith and trust in him was the part he couldn't move beyond no matter how much he wanted to.

"What was the right time to tell you something that was obviously going to make you walk away from me for lying to you?"

"Wouldn't that have been better than letting me figure it out for myself?"

"When though?" she protested. "When were you going to figure it out for yourself? Was I supposed to know that it was going to happen right then? Honestly, I think Gabi has the same scar you and I do!" Her words were getting angry again. Her signs got bigger and her eyes flared at him. "When would *you* have told *me* something that you knew would make me walk away?"

He felt her accusation through his entire body. He loved her so thoroughly that the idea of saying something that he knew would drive her away was unthinkable. How would he have told her that thing? *Would* he have done it? Even if it was something that simply *could* make her leave? Would he have taken the chance?

Devin desperately wanted to believe that the answer was *yes*. That his moral compass pointed in the right direction, and that his drive was strong enough to push him to do it. But he knew he would have always put it off just one more day.

Exactly the same as she had done.

He was breathing heavily, looking away as her hands started to move. He read her words in his peripheral vision as she said, "I'm glad that you know. I'm glad that this isn't hanging between us anymore. Glad that I have a chance to tell you why. And also..."

This time she waited until he looked at her. "I'm glad because it got me started. Things are moving. It's been a year since my aunt died, since she doesn't have to go to jail for what she did for me. Even if I'm forgiven completely for the crime, I don't know how to get citizenship. There's every possibility that they will load me out of that courtroom and directly back to Peru without stopping to pass go, because I have been committing a crime."

He sucked in a breath. There were no good options here, and he hated that he'd pushed her so hard to do something that would hurt her—and him—so deeply. Maybe even get her killed.

What would he have done had he known before now? Could he have gone with her back to whatever-the-tiny-town's-name-was? Where the ground was hard and the jobs were scarce and the gangs were always present.

She was talking again, soft and small, not angry and large, but his heart almost couldn't hear it. "My friend Helen is a lawyer and last week I talked to her."

"She's helping you." Hope sprung up through the concrete setting in his lungs.

"She found me the right kind of lawyer—an immigration lawyer—who can help me."

"Do they think it can work?" He watched as she cried more, the smile spreading across her wide lush mouth.

"Yes. Probably. No guarantees. I might still wind up back in Peru. I have to learn Portuguese," she said, "just as a backup."

He felt his chest spasm almost like a cross between a sob and a laugh.

"She's going to put together a case that pleads for sympathy. She's going to argue that my crime was committed as a minor and that I didn't have control over it. That I didn't turn myself in as an adult, because I would have had to send my aunt to jail to do so. Almost like pleading the fifth, not that I would incriminate myself, but that I would incriminate my only family member."

The thought passed through him right then: her Tia was *not* Luisa's only family member. *He was.* He had been there since they were eight years old. Though they had been apart for more time than they were together, they were as close as any two people could be. It had always been that way.

"She's going to wait and try to get a sympathetic judge."

He fought the pressure at the back of his eyes. Hell, he'd been mad and pushing her, but not prepared for the consequences of what he was pushing. "And you'll get citizenship?"

Luisa shook her head. "I don't know that I can. The standard system now is a holding pattern. It's not a path to citizenship. It would just mean I could be Luisa again."

It occurred to him then—for the very first time—how much she would be giving up just to set the record straight. The fear that she still might be sent away gripped him. The anger had either dissolved or slid so far beneath the other, that he couldn't feel it anymore.

He reached out to wipe the tears from her cheeks.

CHAPTER FIFTY-FOUR

He couldn't help himself. The feel of her skin, even just the briefest contact under his fingertips was too much.

She pulled him in like a flame attracts a moth. He imagined the little creatures knew they could get burned, but getting close was worth the chance. And here he was, putting himself in the burn zone, touching her, acting as if he were wiping away tears that he had caused, when in fact he was just touching her because he finally could.

He was a stupid fool, thinking her selfish. Thinking she was unwilling to set the record straight. He hadn't understood the consequences at all. Now he wanted to tell her not to do it, that he would gladly call her Gabi for the rest of their lives just so they could have a lifetime together.

His fingers cupped the underside of her jaw. She fit so perfectly in his touch. The forest swirled around him, the greens blending together at the top, the browns letting him know the world still resided at his feet, holding him upright, even if he felt as if he were floating. His thumb passed along her cheekbone, coming to rest near her temple, near the mole that Gabi never had.

She was Luisa. She always had been, and he'd seen that the very first moment when their eyes had locked at the coffee shop and they'd recognized each other. That had been true. Making love to her had been real.

Devin didn't even realize he'd moved closer, stepped in, putting himself firmly into her space, until she moved, too. Luisa leaned just a little forward, lifted just a little up, and he could breathe her in as she breathed out.

If anyone was here, he wouldn't know. He'd left Curie behind, not wanting to expose his precious friend to a fight, not wanting to confuse a dog that had only been good to him. That meant now, as the world washed completely away, Devin had nothing to warn him of danger except Luisa. As her lips touched his, he was confident that the danger was her, this.

Heat flooded him and he moved without thought. He was instantly back to that night they'd made love. Before midnight, when things had been right and he'd thought the world had finally handed him a pearl.

It had.

He'd just not seen beyond the flaws. Everyone had them. Hell, he did, too. He might not be hiding anything that big, but he was imperfect at best. Her tongue swept his, and he stepped closer. He wasn't hiding anything from her now.

Some part of him was aware he was standing on a public hiking trail, the bigger part of him didn't care. The part that pushed his hips against hers, that felt her breath rush across his cheek as he did.

His hands still touched her face, as if to be sure she was really there, still with him. He tasted her lips, then planted small, sweet kisses along her cheekbone, though the lower half of him felt anything but sweet. He kissed her closed eyes, tasting the tears that life had given her, but he had made her cry.

As he sucked in a breath of his own, he found that the anger was gone—all of it. The old hard kernel of rage that no one had told him what happened to the Montalvos. The frustration with the universe that no search had ever yielded a Luisa Montalvo who was *his* Luisa Montalvo. The newer, deeper, sharper pain of her lying to him . . . *All forgiven*, the wound had simply closed and didn't even ache anymore.

He breathed in, his ribs only struggling with the need to get enough breath to make love to her. She opened her eyes then, her gaze searching his face and he hoped—desperately—that she found what she needed. He'd thought she was the one who would beg his forgiveness, but he prayed now that she could see the repentance in his own eyes.

When she'd swept all his features and landed on his gaze, he saw her mouth move.

"I love you."

That made his chest constrict. He still held her with one arm wrapped around her back, the dent of her spine the perfect place for his fingers. With the other hand he brushed the curls that had fallen into her eyes away and signed, "I love you, too."

And he did.

For the first time in his life, he felt it and he could say it. This wasn't the young woman down the hall at Gallaudet—he'd liked her a lot. This wasn't the fictional woman he'd created from the girl he'd known. She was here, in front of him—real and ready to say it, ready to hear it from him.

She could have him, all of him. If she was willing.

He moved his hand to say so when her eyes darted away.

What? He stopped moving, except for his heavy breathing, she'd worked him up and he couldn't just turn it off.

Luisa tapped at his shoulder and pointed somewhere behind him. Then signed "Someone's there."

He turned his head, the only thing he could turn—his pants would tell anyone how invested he was. Luisa's shirt seemed to have unbuttoned itself an unseemly amount. They were, after all, standing in the middle of a hiking trail.

Sure enough, a woman stood there, her eyebrows almost up to her hairline as she seemed to say she would *just take another trail.*

CHAPTER FIFTY-FIVE

Luisa laughed at him, pulling the sheet up over her naked breasts. Devin was confused for a moment until she pointed at the door.

With a grin of his own, he stepped off the bed and searched for his pants. There wasn't time for any of the rest of it.

Something soft pinged off his back as he leaned over and he saw the sock hit the floor near him. Confused, he turned to find Luisa grinning at him and motioning that she was looking him up and down.

"Wait for one minute!" he chided her, though he wasn't sure he could wait himself. It would be bad though to leave the food sitting outside the hotel door.

Though he could . . . He'd paid and tipped on the app and . . .

She motioned to him though, with another laugh, "Get the food!"

He opened the door only a crack, saw the bag, folded and stapled at his feet and no one in the hall. Picking it up, he realized they'd really over-ordered, but he didn't care. Maybe they would need all of it. They'd already made love once, the room bearing the faint scent of their pairing.

Locking the door behind him, he turned and set the bag on the table before the bottled drinks sweated through the paper and everything fell. He turned to her and motioned for her to join him, knowing she had no clothes on. Hell, he only had the pants because he was getting the door.

With a flourish, Luisa stood boldly from the bed, yanking and dragging the sheet with her like a regal Roman goddess. He would have gladly taken her naked, but this would do.

They'd fled the trail earlier, Luisa embarrassed that the woman had seen them.

"You'll never see her again," Devin had promised, but Luisa corrected him.

"I work in a coffee shop, chances are I will see her again. She might very well remember the couple she saw making out and *peeling each other's clothing* on a *state park hiking trail!*"

He couldn't argue with her other than that he didn't really care. He hoped Luisa didn't. "Maybe she'll just be jealous."

Now he set out the drinks and crispy wontons and watched as Luisa grabbed for one of the containers and found chicken with vegetables. In seconds, she had chopsticks perfectly held and was somehow managing to be sexy as she slurped up noodles.

He, on the other hand, had to peel the plastic from a fork before he could eat. He remembered his mother introducing Luisa to take-out Chinese food and chopsticks. She'd been in his house the night she'd learned to wield them like a pro. He'd never gotten the hang of it.

A pang hit him, just how far back they went. Fear gripped. *What if it didn't work? How far forward could they go?*

But he pushed it aside, there was nothing he could do about it now, and she was here and naked and dipping crispy wontons into red sauce that lingered on her lips. Leaning over, he licked it off and then accepted as she fed him the other half.

He didn't let her finish her food. Just leaned over and kissed her and let the kiss turn into more. Pulling her to her feet, he plucked at the sheet until he found an end and let it all fall away. By the time it hit the floor, her fingers were working the button and zipper on the work pants he still wore.

It seemed ages ago that he'd walked out of the lodge and fed Curie at the cabin. He'd messaged Su a while ago, asking her to take the dog up to the main building and to Roz, but Su had asked if she could babysit herself. So Curie was having her own fun tonight.

Devin felt the touch of Luisa's fingers, then her palm, then her whole hand riding along his already at-full-attention cock. His head fell back as she managed to control every thought and feeling he had. This was the universe finally, fully, righting itself.

His eyes were closed, his hands reaching out blindly, but surely. He found the soft skin at her waist. He knew the curve intimately. He knew the exact color, lighter than the rich hue of her face. He knew how her deep eyes would go wide and her mouth would fall open as he slid his hands up, cupping her heavy breasts.

Barely able to move, he stepped one foot at a time, feeling as she moved in sync, her hand still stroking him until the urge to be inside her was the only thing driving him. He felt rather than saw the bed behind her. He barely managed to step out of the pants pooled at his ankles before she tumbled backwards onto the sheets.

The comforter had been tossed to the ground some time ago. From the corner of his eye, he saw a pillow under the window. He didn't care. She scooted back, making him follow. And he did. He would follow her anywhere, but right now he didn't examine the depths of that thought or what it might mean in the future.

He chased her up the bed, catching her easily, kissing her until she arched over his arm. Until his fingers found her already wet and wanting. She writhed as he touched her, loving that he could make her lose control so easily. Her mouth opened and her chest heaved as he stroked her. She moved her hips in rhythm to his fingers, pressing into his touch and begging for more.

Her fingers dug into his arms, creating marks that would match from the first night they'd been together. Those, he had ignored until they healed. These, he would take pride in.

She bucked against him until he felt the wetness on his fingers and the pulse inside her as she quieted in his arms. They stayed there for a moment as he didn't move, trying to take in the sight and smell of her, the taste of her that lingered on his lips, the softness of her against his skin.

Then, when she moved, she twisted oddly and he was unsure of what she wanted or needed until she smacked at the small side table built into the headboard and held up a condom.

Hell, yes.

He covered himself quickly and slid into her, feeling her arc like a live wire again.

Once again he ignored the fears biting at the back of his thoughts, warning him this wouldn't last, that she'd be ripped away from him, and there would be nothing he could do about it.

CHAPTER FIFTY-SIX

"I found an apartment!" Helen announced with a smile.

Luisa smiled at her friend though she was sure she'd already been smiling. Her own grin was permanently etched on her lips these days. "You don't have to move out."

"Oh," Helen replied, "I want to."

That was hard to argue with, though. Luisa and Devin were almost worse than high school sweethearts. Despite the fact that she'd given Helen the bedroom, setting out the sheets, the blanket and the pillows on the couch each night for herself, Helen must feel like a third wheel.

Still, Luisa was grateful that she'd decided a few quality items were better than many low quality things. The couch was relatively comfortable, though she was certain staying here was relatively uncomfortable for Helen. When Devin dropped her off and kissed her, their lips lingered—every time. More than once, Helen had stepped into the kitchen to pour herself a drink just to get out of the way.

Luisa tried to be sympathetic. She didn't want to rub anything in her friend's face. Because here she was making out with her boyfriend like a newlywed in front of her friend who was simply waiting for her divorce papers to come through.

Helen had decided that she was going to have to start over from scratch. Luisa guessed that getting her own apartment was the first step to that.

"It doesn't matter what you think, anyway," Helen told her. "I already signed the lease."

"Where are you going? Somewhere else or staying in Charlottesville?" Luisa held her breath hoping her friend would stay. Helen had mentioned the possibility, but she'd mentioned so many possibilities—LA, Baton Rouge, Denver.

"I'm going to stay here, at least for a while."

"How long is that?" Luisa found herself desperately needing to know. As much as she had Devin again, there were too many things up in the air. She'd always counted on Helen to be an anchor. It occurred to her then that maybe Helen needed someone else to be an anchor for a while.

"It's a six month lease." Helen paused, then asked, "Remember, I asked if you'd be okay if I stayed here?" She made a circling motion to the floor.

Luisa did remember, and her nerves flared with happiness. "Are you staying here in the complex?"

"I'm in the building." Helen replied.

"What? Which unit? When are you moving?" Helen was not only going to stay in town, at least for a while, but right here in the same building?

"Tomorrow! I went to the front office and checked to see what they had. The unit was open and they offered me a discount if I moved tomorrow." She shrugged not understanding why.

"Which unit?"

"Four-oh-three. One flight up and two units over."

Of course Helen had a living room view of the pond in the back. Luisa's main view was of the parking lot. But her friend would be a single flight of stairs away. She could run up in her pajamas and slippers, take a bottle of wine, hang out and watch movies, and duck back to her own bed at two in the morning.

She hadn't thought her smile could get any bigger, but Luisa felt it grow wide as she jumped up and squealed and hugged her friend. "I think it's marvelous!"

Helen hugged her back and they danced around for a moment like they had when they closed the coffee shop sometimes. Then Helen stepped back. "I signed for six months but I don't know what I'll be doing after that."

Luisa understood. Helen would get job offers, and they could take her anywhere in the world. Also, Helen and Josh had moved to New York after getting hired right out of law school by big corporate law firms. They'd rented a unit in a skyscraper with a doorman—the kind of life Helen had already dreamed of. Luisa had seen pictures.

It was full of expensive furniture, and boasted a cityscape view, but it wasn't what Luisa would call roomy. To the point where now her friend said, "I can't believe I'm going to have this kind of space to myself. And it's so cheap!"

Compared to New York maybe, but Luisa had never thought of the place as cheap. She counted every penny and was proud that she was able to afford this. Now, with the legal fees and everything, she was just as grateful for the money she'd hoarded.

The lawyer that Helen found her wasn't cheap. Though Helen had even offered to loan her money to help pay for it, Luisa had initially refused. She'd wound up saying, "Not right now. I can cover everything it looks like I might need initially." She didn't admit that the cost would wipe out her savings. She did tell her friend later, though, "If it goes sideways, if it gets bigger, of course, I may take you up on that."

Helen had only said, "Don't worry about that. I've got your

back." And she'd even offered to let Luisa pay it back however and whenever she could.

If she had to borrow anything, Luisa was determined to pay it back. But if she borrowed money, it would also mean that things were going bad. That she might wind up somewhere unknown.

Her brain tripped then. As Helen made plans for four-oh-three, Luisa continued to plan out contingencies for every option. If she could stay in the US as Luisa, she would like to go to college. If she got sent back to Peru, well, she already had that app on her phone teaching her basic Portuguese. She was surprised that it was coming back so well.

Though she hadn't spoken it in decades it was, after all, her native tongue. She remembered her parents speaking it to her, even though she'd never asked either of them for *directions to the library*.

"Are we moving you tomorrow?" she asked Helen now.

"Yes. Please. We can do it, there's not much to move. Do you want to go shopping with me for a bedroom set?" Helen had mentioned that she'd put things in storage in New York, and that she could have a truck bring them to her once she figured out where she was headed. Apparently, she and Josh had divided things already. Helen had kept the dresser from the bedroom—Josh hadn't liked it.

She also had their dining room table, an antique that had belonged to her great grandmother. Helen said she would have fought Josh in court if he even thought about taking it and the matching chairs. Though he'd kept the TV and Helen her car, there had been no children or even pets. Apparently, they'd been as logical about this as everything else.

Luisa could see her friend ticking off things on her list even now. "The unit has a microwave, and all the kitchen appliances. But I'll need a toaster, I think. I'll go grocery shopping once I'm in. But my things are going to take a little while to get here from New York and I don't have a bed anyway."

Of course, she didn't. She'd shared it with Josh and Josh had kept it along with their apartment. Helen had confided to Luisa that paying the rent on his own was going to hurt him. But he'd been so arrogant about being able to do it without her that she figured she'd let him hurt himself. Luisa had laughed at the idea of arrogant and foolish men. Then she had to consider her own hubris.

"Of course, I'll go with you. When?"

"Can we go now? Is there any decent sushi around here? My treat and then we'll go find something."

"Is there anything else you need? Besides a toaster?" she laughed.

"So many things. A sofa. A TV." She shook her head as if the list were escaping her.

"Are we shopping for those too?"

"No." Helen's answer was quick and decisive. "I don't like being forced into decisions, but I definitely need a place to sleep. So I will buy that one thing quickly and everything else I will get as I see the thing that I love."

What a wonderful way to operate, Luisa thought. What a wonderful way to *be able* to operate. She'd had secondhand furniture in her first apartment. Mostly donations from Mama's friends. Even her mattress was one that someone else had slept on until finally she made manager and was able to replace it with a brand new one. Her splurge had only gotten her to a mid level version, too.

Jealousy reared its ugly little head, though it quickly pulled back. She had Devin and that would make up for a lot of it. She changed out of her sweatpants and T shirt, grateful she had the day off. For a moment she was grateful that Devin didn't, that she was home now when Helen announced that she would simply be a few doors away.

As they sat at the counter, eating the sushi handed over the display to them and talking about which store would suit Helen's taste, Luisa's phone pinged.

Grinning, she grabbed it and checked the screen, ready to reply to Devin. But her smile quickly fell away, and she held the phone up to Helen. "It's the lawyer. She's ready."

CHAPTER FIFTY-SEVEN

"It's been a week!" Luisa wailed from where she sat on the end of his bed. Though Devin was trying to stay still, Curie had no such compunction and was pacing a trail on the hardwood floor behind him.

He loved the cabin and was about to tell the dog to stop, lest she actually damage the floor. The little places were actually beautiful . . . once they were restored.

When the repairman had opened one of the unfinished ones up, Devin had peeked in and was horrified. Filthy flooring, cracked countertops, more spider webs than he could count, even a broken window. The repair guy had jumped back, suggesting that something had scurried past.

Roz was investing, getting the last of the cabins fixed up. They all had their fingers crossed that the search and rescue people would show up in droves—or at least enough to break even. Hopefully enough to cover the cost of renovating the cabins and hopefully enough to put money in their pockets.

Roz said in her wildest dreams, the Sanctuary could become a place where they could run an annual search and rescue retreat. The Blue Ridge Mountains were unique in all the world, providing a landscape and surrounding scents that were perfect for trainings. If she could pack the place, they could bring more money into the Sanctuary.

None of it would ever be a real moneymaker—nothing that would put Roz back into the mansion that Devin had only recently learned she had once spent her life in. But it could absolutely keep them in the black. They all worried about how this first one would go.

That was a distant worry, and it warped in his thought. None of it compared to Luisa sitting in front of him, wringing her hands, worry etched into every feature. He wished he could kiss it away. "The lawyer told you it would be a while."

"It's been a week," Luisa repeated, and he understood.

"She called you in for a deposition. You did that last Monday. You said she told you that you did great."

Luisa nodded. She'd said she felt good about the deposition. But it wasn't enough, not now. With a deep breath, her eyes darted upward, and he could see her thoughts straying.

She had told him how the lawyer had coached her on what to say and what not to say. That she was not to drone on or give any unnecessary information. The deposition was good practice if they ever had to put her on the witness stand. She was petrified of that, he knew.

Reaching out, he took her hands and untangled her fingers. The first step was scary. He would have been having sleepless nights himself if he wasn't simply holding it together for her.

But Luisa had given her statements, and the case had been filed. Now it was a crapshoot.

They were hoping they could draw a sympathetic judge. If they could, they would go forward. Then they would hope that they would catch the sympathetic judge on a good day in a good mood. If they didn't catch a sympathetic judge, then they would hope that they could find a legitimate reason to move the trial date, hopefully until they could catch someone who would understand.

He hated how much the plan depended on hope. Nothing was guaranteed. While the odds were reasonable, none of them were good enough to bet his own life on, let alone Luisa's. But there was nothing he could do to change any of it.

"It will be okay," he told her. Even though he knew that was entirely false and he couldn't guarantee anything, it was what he wanted to believe, and what he wanted her to believe. When he saw the doubt in her eyes, he shook his head and rescinded. Once again, he let go with one hand to say, "That's what we hope."

More hope, he thought. He hated that. "It's what we *need* to believe right now. Because there's nothing left for us to do. We played all our cards, and you did the best job that you could."

Pressing her lips together, fighting nervous tears at the edge of her eyes, Luisa nodded again.

"The better we wait calmly, the better we'll be ready to hear whatever the news is." He hoped he was helping. He wasn't calming himself.

She nodded again.

"Come on." He stood up, held out one hand to her. "Let's take Curie. We'll go out on one of the trails, try to shake off some of the stress." He was done for the day and so was she.

She'd simply hopped in her car and come up to see him. He'd gotten a text when she was halfway there. The errors in it had let him know she was recording her own voice telling him, "Oh shit. I'm already halfway to your place. And I should have told you I was coming. I hope that you're not halfway to mine."

He'd laughed. It could have happened. He'd been planning on seeing his mother tonight, but since he hadn't said anything to her about the idea, he would wait. Luisa would probably do better staying here with the group. She could use a big jumble of people, conversations everywhere, to take her mind off the case.

He hoped the family would embrace her the same as they had before.

"There was a snake on that trail the last time we went," she protested.

"I know. That's why we need to go again. To show the snake that he doesn't own it."

She laughed at him. He couldn't take it all away, but he could do that. He managed to get her out the door, his own smile firmly in place. He did his best to make it feel real, because he, too, wanted to wring his hands and fight the pressure at the back of his eyes.

There was no telling how this would all go.

CHAPTER FIFTY-EIGHT

Devin lifted the grocery bags into the trunk of his car then turned to Luisa, surprised at how quickly they'd settled into a normal routine.

"You don't have to help cook," he told her. "It's my mother's house."

"No, but it feels like a family thing to do." She didn't have to say that it had been a while since she'd had a family to cook for.

In the last week, little things had been hitting him here and there. Realizing the ways her life had been different from his had been astounding. He'd always thought they came from such similar backgrounds: single mothers, Texas public schools, just the fact that they both loved movies and hiking and math class.

But his mother had been there from the moment he was born, and she'd given everything for him. For Luisa, her parents had disappeared one at a time in dramatic ways. After losing her beloved cousin—Gabi and Luisa had been much more like sisters—her tia had been the longest standing family member she had, and the only one left since she was eleven.

Devin was more than happy to have her join him to help

cook for his mother. He just didn't want her to feel obligated. He was glad that she'd told him she couldn't see him a few nights ago so she could spend the evening with Helen.

It was good to see her excited about having her friend so nearby. Apparently, they'd had wine and watched Hallmark movies on more than one occasion already.

Pulling up in front of the little house, he opened the door and let Curie excitedly run inside where his mother greeted the little dog like a grandchild. She offered praise and head scratches and treats. It all felt very normal, even with Luisa in tow.

Luisa and his mother signed quick but deep hellos. His mother had forgiven instantly. Then, later, she'd almost chided Devin for holding onto his own anger so long. "It sounds like what she did was actually very reasonable. I don't know if I ever would have told someone." So now, any barriers he'd been afraid of seemed to exist only in his imagination.

"We're making lasagna," he announced with one hand, the other was loaded with bags. He watched as his mother's smile lit up her face. It was her own recipe, adjusted exactly the way she liked it, and she didn't have to do the work. As usual, he'd leave her the leftovers.

He hugged her at the doorway as she waited for him. Then he headed directly to the kitchen while she went into the living room where she reached into the basket of toys that she kept for Curie. It was the same basket that Devin insisted on picking up at the end of the evening and stashing in the corner before they left. The memory of her tripping over the books was still a little too fresh.

"You relax," he told his mother, "Play with Curie. Luisa and I have this."

They hadn't cooked together much as kids—not unless he counted making peanut butter and jelly sandwiches or raiding the pantry for snacks—but they already moved well in tandem in the small space.

It was much too early to be thinking the way he was. There had already been way too many ups and downs, but as he set out food and watched as Luisa reached for a cutting board and knife and washed her hands, he realized she was at home here. With him. With his family. Just like with the family on the mountain.

He was starting to see a future where the two of them grew old together, maybe had kids. But he didn't say it, instead he broke pasta noodles to put into boiling water and reminded himself to keep that thought quiet as Luisa diced green peppers and onions.

Through the pass-through window, he could see Curie in the living room, running back and forth. His mother had to be on the couch. Though Devin couldn't see her, Curie stopped and bowed low, butt in the air, clearly saying it was time to toss the next toy. It made Devin smile. It was all easy right now. And good.

He told himself to hold onto that as Luisa's trial date approached.

Devin was getting the sauce ready when the dog bumped against his leg. He looked down wondering what she wanted—a snack? A new toy?—but Curie bumped him again and again. Then sat looking straight up at Devin, before darting into the other room.

The alert was unmistakable.

Devin followed, not even processing that Curie was alerting to something in the house until he saw his mother on the couch, slumped back, tipped to one side, eyes closed.

He was hovering over her before he realized he'd crossed the room, tapping her on the shoulder and trying to rouse her. Luisa was right behind him.

"Let me try." Luisa motioned him to move, and he could see her mouth move even as she leaned down close to his mother. She must be making noise, calling out, trying to wake his mother that way.

But nothing seemed to work.

Luisa tapped at his mother's shoulder, just as he had, then she patted at her face. Only then did he notice the grayish tone of her skin, the ashy look that extended to her lips. Lifting her hand, he saw the same loss of color in the beds of her nails.

Gesturing sharply to Luisa, he pushed her away and said, "Call 9-1-1!"

As a hearing person, she'd be able to get through faster. She nodded and ran, coming right back with her phone already at her ear, her mouth moving as she was already talking.

It should have made him feel better, but it didn't. Devin continued to tap at his mother. He shook her harder but got no results. He was feeling along her neck for a pulse and trying to watch her chest to see if she was breathing at the same time.

She was. And he found the pulse but not easily.

"What do I tell them?" Luisa asked with one hand, the other still clutching the phone to the side of her head. Her mouth was moving but, with his focus on his mother, his lip reading was for shit right now.

Still, he caught a little and thought she was rattling off his mother's information as well as the address.

"Pulse is slow, too slow!" he told her. "She's breathing."

Then he listed off all the things that Luisa needed to let the EMTs know. Though he was frantic with worry, he told Luisa that his mother would be okay as a way of reminding himself. This had happened before, and she had pulled through.

Luisa nodded and stayed on the phone for what seemed like forever. Devin tried and tried to get his mother to wake up, move of her own accord, or react to anything. Nothing worked.

His heart beating faster and faster as fear gripped him, he didn't respond the first time Luisa tapped him. But the second time he watched as she signed, "I can hear the sirens, they're almost here."

CHAPTER FIFTY-NINE

B eck slid the now empty glass across the surface of the bar toward Liam.

"Last one," he told his friend. It was number three, though he'd been nursing them slowly and wasn't feeling a buzz. Tipsy would have felt good.

"What do you want?" Liam tipped his head up from where he was washing something with a bar towel.

"Give me your best." Beck had left prison with the skills to train and rehab dogs. He knew there were TV shows about it. He'd even watched a couple. A few of them were too ridiculous to merit the time or the attention of his eyeballs even on a bad day. One simply hit a little too close to home.

Liam had left prison with carpentry skills. But, after several roofing jobs and new construction gigs, he'd talked their halfway house manager into his ability to handle working in a bar. Beck knew for a fact that his friend mixed a mean sex on the beach and a killer cosmopolitan, though almost no one here ever asked for that.

Somehow, Liam managed to convince the owner of the bar to stock a variety of local and high-end draft beers. The drinks were upper level, but Liam's prison tattoos kept the place more suited to the locals. And Liam was constantly telling the patrons what they wanted to drink and giving them disappointed looks when they wanted the cheap stuff. He tested the new beers on Beck whenever he came in.

Liam's eyes narrowed at Beck's request, and he thought for a moment, then turned around and picked a draft that Beck couldn't see as his friend's body was blocking the pulls. When he set the glass down it had a perfect head of foam and a slight orangey color. Liam's expression had a slight question. "I don't see you in here on Saturdays much anymore."

"I have a standing arrangement every other Saturday with Hallie. Since I know everyone else likes their Saturday's off, I'm pretty much working all the other Saturdays now."

"How'd you swing it tonight?" Liam asked over the growing noise of the busy bar.

A handful were like Beck, people who'd stopped in to drink, unwind by themselves, and maybe shoot the breeze with the bartender just a little. Others were couples passing through on their way to some other part of their evening, or even ending the night here.

When Liam glanced up and looked over his shoulder, Beck only vaguely realized he'd heard the door open again, a faint sound in the mix of all the other noise inside. But it was Liam's words that startled him. "Your friend's here."

Wondering who on earth Liam could be talking about, he turned to find Ash walking toward him. Ash motioned hello to Liam as he quickly claimed the empty stool next to Beck.

He'd brought Ash here a few times when they had a chance to get out or simply needed an evening away. He wasn't surprised that Ash opened with, "I was hoping I would find you here."

With a motion of one finger, Beck asked Liam to pour one for his friend. "What's going on?" In fact, what was *possibly* going on that they couldn't talk about during the day when they lived on the same patch of land at the top of a mountain?

Ash accepted the beer, sniffed at it, tasted it, and then held the glass up to Liam. "Once again, an excellent decision."

Liam smiled and nodded, and then turned away to help someone else further down the bar.

Ash looked at Beck. "I'm sorry. I shouldn't bring work stuff here on a Saturday night. But if not here, then we need to talk soon, somewhere where we can't be overheard."

Back had to admit that that piqued his curiosity, though he tried to look casual. Taking another sip of the beer, he once again nursed it. He just needed time to himself, and that was in shorter and shorter supply with Hallie, though he wouldn't change that for the world.

He'd thought no one really knew him here except for Liam, that it was a place where he could drink with his thoughts and get lost in the noise around him. Ash burst that bubble. "Is this about the search and rescue thing?"

"Don't get me started on that," Ash replied, and Beck felt himself set up a little straighter.

If not that, then . . .?

Ash sighed, shrugged, took another sip of the beer, and did everything he could to postpone answering. Beck was beyond curious, though he tried not to push.

Sure enough, Ash only needed a moment before he said, "It's too much of a gamble."

"That's what I told her, too!" It was a relief not to be the only one on this side of the fence and Beck realized he'd fallen into old patterns: Keeping everything to himself and showing nothing. He would have felt a lot better if he had been talking to Ash all along.

Hell, had the two of them joined forces together, they might have talked her out of it. Too late now. The contract was signed. But if they survived it . . .

Beck mentioned the idea to Ash, who agreed. "I hate to gang up on her. I love her. I really do. And I can't fault her for the job that she's given me."

"Same." Beck nodded, absolutely not wanting to throw Roz under the bus.

"But . . . But . . ." Ash said.

Understanding fully, Beck clinked their glasses together in solidarity.

"Also," Ash added between sips, "Apologies if you've been hearing Brandy and me fighting about where we're going to live."

"Oh," Beck replied with a grin. "Everyone's heard that. Even Devin."

"Fuuuuuuhhhhck," Ash replied, drawing the word out. "I love living on the mountain."

"Oh, we all know that now," Beck told him, still grinning.

"Thanks, dude."

"You'll work it out." Beck wasn't lying. They'd all been privy to the arguments. But no one doubted that the two belonged together, just that they didn't know where that place should be. "That's what this is about?"

"No." Ash told him and once again he looked away, his eyes drifting down into his hands at the bar. Into the distance, through the people milling around the tall tables beyond them. "It's about whatever this standing Saturday date you have is. It's driving Roz crazy."

Beck blinked. He knew Roz didn't like him having a specific day of the week off, that she'd hoped they would all be more flexible, but he simply couldn't manage it. This was about Hallie, he thought.

Ash held his hands up in surrender. "I do not know what's going on between you and Roz, or between you and the new girlfriend. And I'm not judging, but I just thought you should know."

CHAPTER SIXTY

Devin leaned back in the hard chair, his eyes falling closed. Then his head jerked as he came awake suddenly.

He'd been far enough asleep to be disoriented for a minute before he remembered: He'd ridden here in the ambulance with his mother. The whole ride, he'd crushed himself into a corner where he could watch out of the way. His medical knowledge was limited, and he could answer questions, but lip reading was next to impossible in that situation. Neither of the EMTs signed so all he knew was what he saw on the monitors. It wasn't good, but his mother was alive.

Again, he reminded himself that they had been here before and she'd come through. He just kept repeating that until one of the EMTs turned to him, phone in hand, the screen asking if she was on any blood thinners.

Luisa had stayed behind at the house. She'd messaged him letting him know that she'd turned off the burners and put away all the food and cleaned up the kitchen quickly before hopping into his car to come meet him. She was only a few minutes behind him—already waiting for him in the curved orange chairs that lined the ER waiting room after he plodded through the long check in process.

He'd entered everything he could onto the tablet—everything she was being treated for, all the medical trials she'd been on, even copying the list of her current medications from his phone. Every time he did this it hit him again: how much they had been through. There were so many boxes he had to check on the symptoms she experienced on a regular day: irregular heart rate, chest pain, kidney disease, digestive issues, COPD, and on and on. His mother was being kept alive by science and he had to believe that science and medicine could save the day one more time.

He shuffled around in the orange plastic chair, trying to rest against Luisa. She'd waited patiently until he was finally allowed back to the bed his mother was in. He'd stepped behind the curtain and been offered a different, but slightly less uncomfortable chair here.

She still hadn't woken up, not enough to do more than roll her eyes. She had said nothing; not with her voice according to the nurses and not with her hands. After two hours in which nothing changed, she'd been admitted and moved to a room.

Though it was temporary, there was finally a nurse who signed enough to communicate without him having to text or write everything back and forth. One in the ER had tried to use a tiny whiteboard. Devin had refused, getting her phone number and starting a text chain. It was a hard lesson he'd learned. This gave him a record of what he'd been told about his mother's condition.

Now, he looked around the room. Though the night was well under way, the room was only half dark. Shades blocked the parking lot beyond the wide, industrial windows, but not the yellow glow of the lights. Fluorescents on the wall behind his mother's bed and the TV on the wall offered more light. The screen had a list of the hospital's food and times of day each was offered.

Devin blinked himself fully awake, feeling gummy and raw. Checking his phone for the time he saw another message from Luisa. — They won't let me come back.

Hell, he'd completely forgotten about her!

The message was already two hours old. He was so ragged he'd missed the phone buzz. Swearing to himself, he texted her back. — If you haven't already please go home.

Her return came quickly. Shit, she'd just been sitting there waiting for him!

— I have your car. I'll take it home and come get you when you need.

— I'll catch a ride.

It occurred to Devin then, despite the fact that it was the middle of the night that he should message Roz. That way, if he fell asleep again, she wouldn't be left wondering where her grant writer was.

He was midway through letting her know where he was and that he wouldn't be in for the morning when he jolted yet again. Switching over, he messaged Luisa frantically.

— Do you have Curie?

— She's at your mother's I'll pick her up and take her to my place with me.

Devin let out a heavy breath. He loved the dog, loved having a companion. He hadn't thought he needed a service dog, but Curie had proved herself and it turned out Devin was definitely a dog person. But it had been an adjustment that he was responsible for the creature twenty-four-seven. Curie needed to be walked multiple times daily, and fed and played with.

While she absolutely was well enough trained to be left alone in various places, no one had put any food out for her at his mother's house since they hadn't finished dinner yet. Devin checked the time again. Shit, Curie likely needed to be walked.

He was messaging all of this, typing out instructions with his fuzzy mind and tired, clumsy fingers when Luisa's message popped back to him.

— I'll take care of her. I'll walk her and get her food and take her home with me.

He was a fool for giving her instructions. Luisa knew well what to do. She loved Curie as much as he did.

In the morning, he would find a way to get to Luisa's apartment and get his car and the dog and head back up the mountain.

He wasn't yet willing to admit the sheer wishfulness of that thinking. Looking over at his mother, Devin scanned the tower of machines behind her. This time the lights were green and white. Some of the numbers were red—her oxygen was low. But apparently not low enough to make the nurses do anything other than put the mask over her face.

Standing and realizing he needed to stretch, he headed over to read the machines. His mother didn't stir, and he told himself that was okay. The number for her oxygen mask said "2L"—two liters. Not great, he knew. Something he'd learned on previous visits. It also wasn't the worst she'd been on.

If a doctor had come in to check on her tonight, no one had woken him to tell him what was happening. Flexing again, Devin tried to shake the cramps that had taken over while he slept in the awkward chair. He stepped out into the hallway and caught a nurse's attention and signed, "Debbie?"

The nurse sitting at the desk shook her head, showing she didn't understand. But he signed it one more time. It didn't matter if she understood that he was looking for Debbie, but she would understand that she needed to get the nurse who knew ASL.

Catching on, she stood up and walked over with a small whiteboard and a marker, writing furiously. By the time she arrived at the door, she held it up. "Debbie's shift ended two hours ago. We're moving your mother upstairs."

He understood now: Not only was she admitted but they expected her to stay for several days. Motioning to take the board, he jotted his question at the bottom.

"Are any of the tests back yet?"

The nurse shook her head and added, "The doctor will see her, and you'll get the results upstairs. They're already coming to move her."

As Devin watched the nurse's head turn to the left, he saw the team heading down the hallway with the bed. He wasn't going home in the morning.

CHAPTER SIXTY-ONE

Devin woke again to a hand on his shoulder, pushing him slightly. He blinked as sunlight streamed into the room jarring him into remembering where he was.

He twisted a little, waking and feeling a bit better rested. At least this time, the room had a hospital recliner to sleep in. His head rolled to the side, ignoring the doctor standing in front of him waking him. Devin looked first at his mother.

No obvious change.

His heart sank. Around her the machines still blinked, the lines moving in sometimes unsteady waves across the screen. A nurse stood next to Dr. Tedecki, looking a little uncomfortable. Devin had learned to ignore that, but he looked to his mother's doctor, here in the hospital now.

That the nurse didn't sign wasn't a surprise. Neither did the doctor, but Devin already knew that. He looked up and signed "Hi, Dr. T."

"Hi, Devin." That exhausted the only two signs the doctor had learned. Still, Devin liked the man.

Pulling his phone out of his pocket, he motioned it toward Devin and began typing. Devin waited for the message to appear. Dr. Tedecki was very good about keeping him up to speed, explaining what was going on when Devin or his mother didn't understand. He also took whatever time was needed to accommodate the fact that he was writing or texting most of it.

The slight buzz in his hand was unnecessary as Devin was watching the message pop up. He looked up at the doctor then back at the message.

— Her blood pressure is precariously low.

The doctor added some of the results from the blood count, knowing that Devin would understand her white cells were high and that wasn't good. Devin had already seen the fever on the monitors.

After reading through the message, he quickly tapped his own back. — What do we do to treat her? IV antibiotics? Oxygen? What else?

— Just her usual medications and what we are already doing.

That was a long list, but Dr. T was up to date on it and would make sure that she got the right mix in the hospital.

— So we'll adjust them?

Dr. T moved, taking a step forward to stand directly in front of Devin as he shook his head. No.

— Why not?

This wasn't okay. They had to change something to fix this.

The reply popped up quickly. — We hope the antibiotics work on the infection and then we wait.

The vice in his chest, already far too tight, ratcheted down another notch.

— Then what?

— There's nothing more that we can do. She's already on medications that contradict each other.

Devin understood. They'd talked about it a year ago. The balance was delicate. The medications that helped her heart would slowly destroy her kidneys. The medications that controlled her pain would degrade her liver. One medication gave her gall stones and another stopped that, but it gave her digestive issues, reducing her overall health. All of them would throw her systems out of whack, making her body over time become unable to regulate things like temperature, breathing rate and blood pressure.

— She'll come through okay, though, right?

Devin tapped out quickly, his heart hammering as he wanted a reassuring reply quickly, or a bad one not at all.

Only a few words came back. — I don't know.

CHAPTER SIXTY-TWO

"I don't know!" Luisa wailed and shoved popcorn into her face. She was sitting next to Helen, who'd come down to her apartment because Helen still did not have a TV or a couch. They were in their pajamas with a romance movie on. Helen had, however, brought a very nice bottle of wine and, as she proclaimed it, the best microwave popcorn.

"That sucks. I'm so sorry."

The movie played on in the background but the two of them had continued talking, barely paying attention. She hadn't heard from Devin in three days. She didn't say it out loud, but she didn't know if Ms. James was alive or dead.

Luisa had gone to work the morning after the ambulance had come. With no word from Devin, the best thing to do was cover her shift. She was going to need a lot of time off with the court case coming up.

Still, she hadn't made it home with Curie until close to two a.m. She'd kept the worried dog overnight. Then, in the morning, she'd woken up realizing she needed to get to work and that Curie needed to go to the Sanctuary. She couldn't stay here all day without her.

Though she'd visited plenty before, this wasn't her home. This wasn't where she would feel most comfortable, as if she could feel comfortable anywhere without Devin by her side. It was too late to get it all done and still be on time. She called in late to work, glad she'd almost never done it before. Then she headed up the mountain, showing up at the lodge unannounced and realizing she didn't have phone numbers for anyone.

Luckily, Roz was up. It was six in the morning and Luisa should have been at the coffee shop by five-thirty. She wasn't scheduled to open—thank God—but she was certainly supposed to be there to cover the rush.

The Sanctuary could not have been more out of her way, but Roz had helped by opening the door even before Luisa was out of her car. "I just saw Devin's message! Do you have any further news on his mother?"

"No," Luisa had said. Then she had to add, "I was hoping I could leave Curie with you. She can't stay in my apartment while I'm at work all day."

"Of course!" Roz was like an aunt, hugging Luisa and adding, "She's used to it here. We have everything for her."

With a flick of her wrist, Luisa released Curie from where she sat perfectly by her feet. It was the same as she did for Devin. The dog seemed to understand that if Devin wasn't here to protect then Luisa must be her charge. But now, off duty, she bounded happily into the room, greeting Shadow and Astra and making Luisa wonder what the dogs were talking about.

It was Roz who'd quickly said, "I don't have your number." They'd traded, agreeing to keep each other posted with what they heard. That had been three days ago. All they'd traded were random daily messages that his mother was still in the hospital and that she wasn't yet improving.

Roz had Curie, but Luisa kept her vigil by herself. She had no experience with this. No one in her family had lingered, not even Gabi. Her mother had taken the longest at two days—she'd gone into the hospital, feeling sick, and never come out.

"What do I do?" Luisa asked Helen now, trying not to cry about it.

"Do you know the room number? Do you want to send flowers?"

"That's a good idea." *Why hadn't she thought of it?* "I want to go sit with him. Take over sitting with his mother for a while so he can shower or visit Curie."

"Why haven't you?" Helen asked, also not paying any attention to the movie.

"Every time I suggest something he says *no.* He says he's okay, that he's used to it." She'd even messaged *I love you* and gotten no response.

He'd told her before that he'd grown used to sitting in hospital rooms and waiting for results. She knew, given the language barrier, that he was more alone in that than most, and it wasn't an easy task even without the issues.

"Then there's nothing else you can do," Helen said. "You can't force help on him. He probably can't even process it right now, so it's not help."

Luisa sucked in a breath. That was likely true.

"But . . ." Helen pulled out her phone and started tapping on the screen. "Let's order the flowers now."

Once they picked a nice bouquet that was friendly, colorful and nothing too ostentatious for when Ms. James woke up, Helen hit the button.

"You don't have to do that," Luisa protested, noticing that her friend had paid for it.

"You've got so much on your plate right now, even before this. I'm happy to do it. *You* need to save your money."

She'd learned in the past that arguing with Helen was pointless, so she said, "Thank you, but so do you." That seemed to be the end of the conversation, still Luisa tucked the memory away for later.

With her phone pushed to the side of the couch again, Helen's attention shifted back to her. She reached out with a hug, reminding Luisa once again of how very good it was to have her friend here—even if the thing that had driven her into town was awful. "If he says there's nothing more for you to do, there's nothing more for you to do. As an adult you have to respect his decision."

Helen was right, even if Luisa hated it.

"He may very well be forgetting that he has you here and that he can take advantage of you offering relief and sitting with his mother. He may not understand just how willing you are to do this. But he's in a horrible space right now. It's not the time to force your way in. All you can do is wait and offer again next time."

But Luisa had learned enough about Ms. James's health to know there might not be a next time.

CHAPTER SIXTY-THREE

Devin sat with his laptop in the hospital room next to his mother's bed.

Though the hospital offered large recliners with trays and cupholders for visitors, he hadn't slept a comfortable night in over ten days. When his mother wasn't awake, he tapped away on his keyboard, glad his laptop and his job were relatively portable.

Not that he'd shown up for any of the dog trainings. Roz had assured him not to worry about it—as well as not to worry about the days Devin wanted to leave Curie at the Sanctuary with her. Knowing Roz, he shouldn't have been surprised that his last paycheck had been the usual size though he'd been doing only half the work.

"Go home." His mother's hand movement caught his attention out of the corner of his eye.

Devin looked up. "It's fine, Mom. I'm good here. I'm working."

"No." She shook her head softly at him. "Go home. Sleep in your own bed."

"Maybe tonight."

They'd had this conversation several times before. As of yet, he had not gone home. He did go back and forth, today he had Curie with him. They'd walked around the hospital grounds several times already. The nurses knew the adorable dog better than they knew Devin. For the first rotation of shifts, someone had complained, but Curie was a highly trained service dog and allowed to stay. Devin thanked Roz and his fellow trainers who'd made that happen.

Still, he knew the hospital wasn't the best place for the dog. His mother used that against him now. "Spend the day tomorrow with your puppy."

Devin tipped his head at her knowing what she was talking about. The doctor had discussed sending her home. They expected another two or three more days to stabilize her blood work. It had taken them this long to balance her medication out. Everything they gave her had some unwanted side effect that then needed to be adjusted or dealt with via another medication.

"Okay, Mom," he said, though he wasn't counting that as agreement.

Dr. T came into the office then, the nurse on shift was at his side and Devin was glad to see it was Wendy. He liked her. A few of the nurses simply ignored him, probably because they didn't speak his language.

The doctor put his hand on Devin's mother's shoulder and spoke directly to her. He leaned in close as if he struggled to hear her replies. *Not a good sign.* But Devin ignored it.

His mother was only awake a handful of hours a day, and Devin hated that a chunk of that time was spent talking with the doctors. She slept more than Devin thought was good, but the doctors were in charge here.

The nurse signed in halting individual words. Devin

watched, grateful that she was working to convey information directly to him, rather than let him dig for it after the fact. "Home. Two days. If no problems."

"Thank you," he replied, the single sign was as clear as he could make it.

She'd been practicing. But then she pulled out her phone, more information coming than she had the ability to convey.

The message popped up on Devin's phone. — You'll need a home health care nurse.

Devin looked between the message and the doctor talking directly to his mother. Devin's lip reading skills were passable at best, but with the doctor speaking medical terms and looking sideways, he wasn't getting it.

His mother nodded. But Devin didn't. He sent a message back to the nurse.

— I can do it.

He watched as all three people turned and told him *no*.

His mother signed, "I don't want you to." The doctor replied and Wendy added another message. — She needs a skilled caregiver.

Devin started to say he could learn, but even as he started to say it, he realized he was behind the conversation and the doctor turned to him, his lips already moving. Devin had missed the first part.

As he realized that he hadn't been looking at the right time, the nurse held up her phone and a moment later a message came through. — She needs a trained nurse.

His eyes glanced between the three others until another message came through. — or a hospice facility.

Every cell in his body railed against the idea. He'd known this was coming but it should have been much further away! He wasn't ready. He'd never be ready.

Fingerspelling, he asked his mother, "Hospice?"

He wished then he'd learned better how to create the sounds for words. But he tried over and over as a kid, spending hours in speech therapy. He never did quite get the hang of it. It turned out lip reading and vocalizing were talents that some people had and others didn't.

The nurse seemed to catch on and she was typing again. All he could do was wait. But his mother nodded to him.

He didn't even let her reply. "No," he said. "There's more to try."

Without looking up, he typed that same message to the nurse and motioned her to show it to Dr. T.

They didn't need time to think about it. The doctor spoke to the nurse and the nurse wrote her message back to Devin, as his mother replied, "No."

"Ask the doctor," Devin insisted.

"No," his mother replied again, and he ignored the message popping up on his phone. He watched his mother's hands move. "I don't want to."

It felt like running, full body, into a brick wall. "Why not? I'm sure—"

The sharp movement of her hand cut him off, stilled his own words midair.

It was the tic at the corner of his eye that let him know that even her just cutting him off hurt, though he was ignoring it.

She waited until she had his attention, an old trick from when he was a child. "I'm done with treatments. They'll only make me feel worse. We have to admit that it's time."

It couldn't be time. She was barely in her fifties, far too young. She should have had years—decades—before her. Hell, he should have had years and decades *with* her.

He hated to be selfish, but there were so few people in his world who spoke his language, that losing her was catastrophic. Pushing that aside, he watched as his mother spoke to the doctor again. This time she signed at the same time so Devin could follow along. "Thank you. I'm okay with this decision."

He squeezed his eyes shut, so he wouldn't have to see any more. He couldn't swallow, couldn't breathe, his joints ached. His mother might be able to make this decision, but he couldn't. He wasn't ready to accept it.

CHAPTER SIXTY-FOUR

L uisa stopped dead on the courthouse steps. Her hand shot out to the side, grabbing Helen's arm for stability.

Ahead of them, not seeing what was happening, Maria Salvadora, her lawyer, kept moving solemnly upward.

"Are you okay?" Helen leaned in close.

Luisa stupidly nodded. She wasn't okay. She couldn't breathe. Her fingers wanted to clench into fists. Her muscles were locking.

If she just leaned over, maybe she could breathe better, or she could sit down and put her head between her knees. *Not possible in this suit with its slim skirt.* And it would not be good to do that here on the stone steps leading up to the courthouse. What if someone involved in her case saw her? What if they saw this wildly public panic attack? Could everyone tell?

By sheer force of will, she stood upright.

"You've done harder things than this," Helen reminded her even as Luisa reminded herself of the same thing.

It was something she had told her friend before. How she was talking herself through all of this. *I've done harder things than this.* Luisa started listing them in her head. She'd buried her mother, then buried her cousin with her own name on the certificate. She'd buried her tia—the mother she had for most of her life. No matter the outcome, this wouldn't be as difficult as any of that.

She took a breath.

Her phone pinged in her pocket, and normally she would have ignored it. This was their third day in court, but they'd started almost a week ago. Mostly she'd sat through other people's cases, listened to the crimes they'd committed. She'd already seen a few get sentenced to harsh jail time and a few more getting sentenced to deportation.

It was all adding up in her mind, stacking the odds against her, despite Maria Salvadora's reassurances and her belief that everything would go Luisa's way.

There was absolutely no guarantee of that.

She could wind up in jail. She could get deported. She knew all of this because Helen kept reminding her that America did not have a justice system, it had a legal system. Helen had said this for why Salvadora was arguing things certain ways that Luisa thought they would just be better off saying she was protecting Mama. But it was about laws, laws Luisa had broken for decades.

Though there was generally leniency for children who hadn't committed the crime of their own accord, her adult life had been hers. Being punished for it was certainly an option.

Forcing her lungs to expand, she took a breath but still felt as though she was breathing through a straw. She could not have a full-blown panic attack now. Her hand reached out for something that wasn't there: Devin.

She wanted him desperately. She needed his support. But, aside from a few texts here or there, she'd not heard from him at all. He had wished her good luck but hadn't shown up.

His mother was not doing well. He was basically living at the hospital, driving back and forth to the Sanctuary to take care of

Curie. But part of her panic attack was that, while she understood all of that, while she knew he was dealing with ongoing issues and grief of his own, she was having her own crisis.

And he wasn't here.

She had given him all the information, but he often didn't reply. Often, she'd turned and looked into the back rows of the courtroom, but not once had she spotted his blond hair and green eyes. Her throat closed again.

She was being sentenced today. Her case was done. Maria Salvadora had made very clear arguments as to why Luisa should not face deportation or jail time, but they played on the sympathy of the judge. Maria was banking on "any of us would have done the same in her situation."

But Luisa wasn't even first on the docket. Though all she could do was wait, she had to show up at eight and sit through everyone else's cases. Maybe she should just be glad it wasn't some grand jury trial, because certainly they would not like a woman who had used her cousin's identity for over twenty years.

Her eyes blurred with fear. The judge had already made her decision. There was nothing else any of them could do, just breathe and wait until it was time for Luisa's sentencing to be read.

Helen pulled her forward. They had to go. Maria was already at the top of the wide marble steps. If Luisa didn't show up, or if she was late, it would only make things worse for her.

"Can you do this?" Helen asked.

Luisa nodded that she could. Though she'd barely eaten, she was finding that having no food in her stomach was making it worse. She was grateful right now that Helen had left Josh—that her friend was staying here. That Helen didn't have a job other than to help Luisa relay information back and forth to Maria Salvadora. She was always on call to talk Luisa through navigating systems to find all her old paperwork, certificates, and more that Salvadora had requested along the way. The lawyer had even asked for her high school transcript. Jesus.

Pulling her phone out, Luisa checked again to see if it was Devin. But it was Chandler and Jenna, chiming in. — Good luck today. — We're behind you, no matter what.

This time she actually took a full breath. *She'd been through worse than this.*

She thought about it for a moment. Devin knew what today was. And she knew that tomorrow his mother would be heading home. That Devin had lined up a nurse to care for her at the little blue and white house.

She messaged as best she could, picking her words carefully as Helen and the lawyer motioned her toward the large heavy doors and into the cool air of the courthouse. — I hope your mother is feeling okay today.

She'd considered saying, "I hope your mother is doing okay," and immediately realized it wasn't the right thing. Ms. James was absolutely *not* doing okay if she was going home with a care nurse. This had to be end stage care.

But there was nothing else she could do right now. With the message sent, she stared at her phone until Helen tugged on her arm. She moved one step down to be even with Luisa and said firmly, "We cannot be late."

One more time, Luisa pulled herself together. If she was sentenced, it could very well be for deportation. Helen and Maria Salvadora had warned her, the bailiffs would likely cuff her and remove her directly from the courtroom. Though she was assured by the lawyer that outcome was very unlikely, it remained a possibility.

It all depended on the judge's decision. And if it was bad, she would never see Devin again.

CHAPTER SIXTY-FIVE

Devin sat at his mother's dining room table, laptop in front of him, notes and phone beside him. Periodically he looked up at the bedroom door. Karen, the day nurse was in with her now.

His mother had always been a smart woman and she had sprung for the good health insurance. Still, Devin was emailing back and forth to the hospital, requesting itemized listings, paying the bills that had already come in, and working with the pharmacy to get medications.

The medications had to be picked up during certain windows of time. At least some number of days since her last refill—or the insurance wouldn't cover them—and definitely before she ran out. There were too many to keep reasonable track of and many were contraindicated with each other, which meant he had to talk to a pharmacist directly—a pharmacist who didn't speak his language or have an interpreter on hand. Some were "schedule three"—meaning they required duplicate prescriptions, doctor permissions and more. When he added in that he could not pick up the phone and simply call the hospital or pharmacy it was one more layer of crap he had to tread through.

Having paid the last bill and written down the confirmation number on the paper, he then clicked over to a pop up from one of the tabs he had open. His eyes flew wide, and his mouth dropped open. *A congratulatory letter.* They had gotten the grant!

His breathing sped up, his lungs opening fully for the first time in days. Good news.

He'd been so worried. He was half-assing his job at best and Roz kept saying she could understand. That he shouldn't worry. Devin had warned her when he hired on that his mother was not in great health, that he might have to leave suddenly for doctor's visits. But he had not explicitly said *I might be gone for months. Because eventually, my mother will require hospice care.*

He hadn't been willing to admit it then and somehow, even with it right in front of him, he was still hardly willing to admit it now. So this, this was good. It was the second grant he'd gotten, and it meant he was doing his job for the Sanctuary. At least part of it.

Luisa's messages had all but stopped and he understood he'd been terrible to her, but he didn't know what else to do. He understood her better now though. He'd been mad about her protecting her aunt, but he was feeling that bone deep need himself now. He wished he'd understood then and not been so mad at Luisa about it.

His own mother had been the one steady factor in his whole life. Devin knew in his heart that he was not dealing with what that would mean when she was gone. Each time he tried to think about it, his brain—and his body—just rejected it as 'not a possibility' even though the inevitable loomed in front of him daily.

Looking over, he saw Curie's bed was empty. Though Sylvia, the night nurse, had protested, his mother had insisted that Curie could sleep in her room and even on her bed. Devin was proud of the pup for watching over her so well. That's probably where she was now.

With a deep breath he tried again to admit that she would be gone soon. He owed her everything: his education, his ability to do the job he had now, how she'd moved from place to place for him and for his school, even when he was an adult and off on his own. His mother was apparently always a regular at the local Deaf community center, even when he didn't live with her. She volunteered, helping with others—particularly hearing parents who discovered their child was Deaf. She'd always been there for him, too, ready to lend a hand whenever he needed it.

If these moments were coming to an end—and this was no longer a case of *if*—he didn't want to miss any of them. How would he ever forgive himself if he did?

Some nagging part of his brain told him he would never forgive himself for not being there for Luisa either. And that was true. He loved her. In any other circumstance, he would have been there right by her side. But there were two incredibly difficult decisions in front of him. In the end, his mother had always chosen him above everything else. So now, he needed to choose her.

Karen came out of the room, motioning her hand at him to get his attention. Not interpreter certified but fluent enough to communicate what medical information she needed, she was as good to him as she was to his mother.

The look on her face now told him that something else had gone wrong. His mother's blood pressure medication wasn't working as well as it should. That had started a handful of days ago. Her oxygen levels had been declining despite the fact that they'd been turning up the oxygen on the nasal cannula.

Ms. James had made it out to the table for meals only twice in the whole time that they'd been home. Devin had catered to her in the meantime, eating every meal with her, often almost forcing her to eat as her requests for food got fewer and further between.

Now, he looked up at Karen, noting that Karen wasn't quite willing to start the conversation. "What is it?"

"Her last bloodwork came in. Her kidneys are not doing well." It was exactly what Karen had suspected. The nurse continued, "I've talked with Dr. T. Your mother will need dialysis now."

That, too, had been discussed. In fact, Devin was familiar with it. She'd been on dialysis for a handful of weeks at one point when one of her chemo therapies had harmed her kidneys.

"Okay," he said, wondering why that was even a question. They would simply set it up.

But Karen shook her head. "You should go talk to her. She's awake."

CHAPTER SIXTY-SIX

"No," his mother said.

Was it her favorite word now? She was breaking his heart.

"You need dialysis." So many times Devin felt like he'd run headlong into a brick wall, but right now he felt as if he were the brick wall. Unable to comprehend the things coming at him, he recognized the words, but couldn't put the pieces together.

"No, I don't *need* dialysis," she replied. "It's so much effort and it doesn't get me anything."

It would get her *everything*. He knew. She would perk up if her kidneys were working better. He told her that. "You'll feel better afterwards."

"I won't feel better enough. It's three times a week," she argued as if it were simply too much effort.

There was nothing that was too much effort for him. "We'll make it happen."

His hands moved with the words, his fists hitting together in the signs harder than normal. Not enough to leave bruises, but enough to feel the determination in what he said.

His mother barely raised her hand and signed again. "No."

"If you don't do this . . ." He couldn't finish the sentence, knowing that kidney failure would leave her with two weeks at the most.

His mother finished the sentence for him. "I will die from it."

Tears pushed to the back of his eyes. He'd been standing beside the bed, but now his knees buckled and he sank into the comfy armchair. He and Karen had brought it in from the living room, so that someone could sit next to his mother at all times, hold her hand as needed, and let her feel someone else's pulse against her skin.

Now he grabbed her hand in his own as he hovered over her and he simply told her *no*. He wasn't going to let her just waste away. Her hand looked as fragile as it felt. He'd grown afraid he would grind her bones to dust because she offered no resistance. Her will was resistance enough.

"It's time." She was looking him square in the eyes.

"No," he replied again, though it had no force this time. His throat was closing, the joints in his elbows and wrists stiffening as though not to let him tell her she couldn't just leave without fighting.

When she didn't say anything more, he said, "Let me do this." He had to let go of her hand to say the words clearly. "You did everything for me and now it's my chance to do for you."

"Yes. That's exactly what I want."

The relief flooded through him, but it was so short lived.

"How I want you to do that for me is to let me make these choices. I want you to live your own life not in a chair by my bed but on your own terms. I want you to bring Luisa to see me." She didn't have to add, *to say goodbye*. But he knew that's what she meant.

She paused as though saying so much took a lot out of her and he didn't want to admit that maybe she was right—that whatever dialysis bought her, it still wouldn't be enough.

When she was ready, she spoke again. "I want you to live a

long and happy life with friends who speak your language. And I want you to find your great love—"

He shook his head, moving his hand at her, making a sharp cut through the air the way she always did to him.

"No," he replied, his tone now softer than the cut. "I know you gave up everything for me. I know that you . . ." He paused as he thought about George, and how she hadn't followed the man she loved. Devin thought about how the other men she dated sometimes lasted for five, maybe six, years. In the end, they always wanted something, and she always chose Devin. So he said that now.

"I know that you never found the great love of your life. That you always chose me instead. Even when I was an adult . . ." His eyes were watering, her face before him blurring and he felt her hand on his, simply weighing his motions down to stop him.

"That's not true," she said.

Devin caught the signs. Though blurred, his vision was just clear enough to understand.

"It's not true," she repeated. "When I was a teenager, I was a mess."

He wished she wouldn't waste her energy. He had heard this before. But she kept going.

"Having you straightened me out."

He smiled. She seemed determined to tell him all these same things. Maybe it would be a gift to let her tell it again. Though he feared for a moment that she didn't remember that he already knew this. He'd heard how she partied as a teenager. That the man who was his father wasn't the first one she'd even slept with. That she knew he was too old for her and that she was stupid—her own words—when she later found out that he was married.

She reached up to touch Devin. Her fingers soft, the skin now crepey and far older looking. The disease had eaten at her, little by little, until it left only this. Touching the side of his face, she turned him toward her, letting him blink a few times to clear his vision.

Then she said, "You were the great love of my life. That's why I always chose you."

CHAPTER SIXTY-SEVEN

L uisa stood over Ms. James. Though her throat constricted, she laughed. She was an adult now and Ms. James had insisted several times to call her Jacinda. But Luisa had never been able to bring herself to do it.

"It was awful," she replied, and she was sure it was clear that she was just relieved it was over.

His mother had asked about the court case and seemed to want to hear every detail. Devin hadn't even come in with her, though Curie had followed her right into the room. The dog had a readymade step up onto the bed, so Luisa didn't question it when she curled up at the woman's feet and went right to sleep.

"We sat there for five hours waiting for my sentencing." She saw Devin's mother's hand move, as if to bring it up to cover her mouth. But it didn't quite make it.

So many things struck her about how weak and frail the once robust woman had been. She'd gone downhill so fast that Luisa still struggled to process it and she understood how Devin struggled too.

"They deported two people before me," Luisa added, grateful

that the memory carried less and less of the lingering terror each time she told someone.

"That's terrible." This was all she signed, mostly with one hand. Luisa suspected it was either too much effort to lift the other or that her left hand just wasn't working as well now.

"They weren't charged with the same thing as me," Luisa said, "but it made me so scared. They handcuffed the men and walked them out of the courtroom. Then they're held, and they're put on a plane. They don't get to say goodbye to their families."

Ms. James didn't sign an answer, but Luisa saw the sadness and disappointment in the woman's eyes.

It was difficult to understand unless someone had been there, but Luisa was painting a picture. "I stood up when it was my turn. They called me to the front of the courtroom with my lawyer."

"Your friend, too?" The words were short, the connecting signs all but gone now.

"Yes, Helen was there in the rows waiting. But she could not come to the front of the courtroom with us. I was so nervous. My knees were shaking. I thought everybody could see it."

She could see Devin's mother's expression turn almost comically sad for her, and Luisa agreed. "I almost threw up right there!"

"But you didn't?" She asked it just to reassure herself it seemed, so Luisa reassured her.

"No, but everybody *could* see how bad it was. The judge even told me 'honey, you look so nervous.' All I could do was nod and she said, 'Don't be.'" This part stopped her each time she thought about it. Luisa pulled herself together and went back to the story.

"I almost cried!" She signed tears bursting from her eyes almost cartoonishly.

Devin's mother laughed a little though the whole story was

truly terribly stressful. Ms. James moved her one hand in a sign that it took Luisa a moment to recognize as "of course."

"I was still stressed. That didn't mean she wasn't going to deport me, but I hoped it meant that she wasn't."

The older woman pointed out, "You're still here."

Luisa, every time she thought about that moment, could feel it all again. Relief like a tsunami washing through her. "She gave me four-hundred hours of community service."

There was no set path for a case like Luisa's. But the judge commented that Luisa had been a stellar student in high school and an excellent worker who never remained unemployed. "Then the judge asked me, what was I going to do if I stayed in America? Well, I almost threw up again, thinking that maybe her decision about me would change if I said something wrong."

"What . . . tell her?"

"That I wanted to go to college. That my friend Helen is a lawyer and that Maria helped me with this case. And that I think I want to go to law school to be a civil rights lawyer." Luisa watched as Ms. James's mouth fell open with pride and happiness.

With one hand, the woman signed, "Wonderful. So smart. You great at that."

Again, she was missing pieces and Luisa almost wanted to tell her not to speak.

But school was a possibility now, Luisa knew. Thanks to Helen, Maria Salvadora, and the judge who'd placed her on a path to citizenship. It would take years but Luisa didn't mind the wait or the work. Ironically, she would only get that path to citizenship—as she told Ms. James—because she'd been tried and it was part of her "rehabilitation."

She explained how she had a probation officer now. That her record would get expunged when her case workers signed off on all her community service. How she planned to complete it in half the required time. When it was done, and her record was clear, she could begin applying to schools. Then she could try to become a citizen, too.

Her heart was bursting and Ms. James seemed to get a second wind. "You're truly Luisa now." Then her shoulders slumped at the end of the long sentence. Even that little bit seemed to wear her out.

"Yes." Luisa couldn't fight the wide smile. "My name tag at my job says Luisa. I told my staff and they were wonderful. Well, my direct boss was a bit of a dick. But his boss was wonderful to me. She told me she understood and asked if that was why I had refused promotions in the past."

Luisa felt all of that again, too—the embarrassment and shame of having to admit what she had done and not knowing if they would fire her.

"I am so happy for you," Devin's mother told her as she reached out slowly, grabbing one of Luisa's hands. Only then did Luisa realize that they held the entire conversation in sign even though they were both perfectly capable of speaking English. ASL was the language in this house. This was where Devin was even when he wasn't in the room with them.

Ms. James's words now were the ones Luisa had expected all along.

"I know my son loves you." The change in topic made Luisa feel the terror in her spine that the woman would ask for something that couldn't be answered. "I know you love him, too. And I am hoping that you will have a long and happy life together."

Devin had warned her that sometimes the medicine made his mother a little loopy. But he'd messaged and said his mother wanted to speak to her. Luisa had driven herself over immediately but wasn't able to bring herself to speak to him more than just in passing in the main room.

So now, she smiled at Ms. James and held her hand, squeezing just enough to let the woman know she was here. She hoped no one could see the lie in her eyes when she replied, "That would be wonderful."

CHAPTER SIXTY-EIGHT

Devin sat beside his mother's bed in the same position he'd been in for the last twenty-four hours.

He was scared to get up to go to the kitchen, or even use the bathroom. What if she passed while he was gone?

What if she still knew that he was here? She hadn't opened her eyes other than the briefest of gestures for two days. Her skin had changed color. Her failing kidneys and her rebellious liver had left her a sickly yellow-gray. Her lungs were filling with fluid. Karen had told him Dr. T had come by for a home visit a few days ago when Devin had been out.

Devin couldn't help but be mad about it. In reality, he understood that the doctor had come by when he could. Devin had just been out running Curie up to the Sanctuary so she could play and be a dog for a while. No one was trying to keep him out of the loop, but he was automatically somewhat out because of his deafness. So he hated that he'd missed the chance to demand the doctor do something, even though he knew they were simply carrying out his mother's wishes at this point.

Dr. T hadn't changed any medication or done anything except say that Karen had taken care of everything. It was clear to Devin it was their job now to make her passing as comfortable as possible. And he hated it.

His mother's chest rose and fell now in an uneasy pattern. Her breathing looked as if it stuttered, and Karen told him that that was because of the fluid. Sometimes his mom squeezed his hand in return when he held hers. Sometimes her fingers would go slack and he would be petrified that she was gone. But each time the flashing numbers on the monitors stayed on.

They were all red now—letting him know that she was still here but not for long.

Karen stepped into the room, checked a few things without bothering either of them then motioned for him to look up.

"I can hear the rattle in her breathing," she signed.

Devin only nodded.

"I don't think it will be long."

Then Karen left as unobtrusively as she came.

Somehow, this was all normal for her. While it shredded Devin to his very soul, Karen did this over and over. When his mother was gone, she would pick up her next assignment and hopefully help the next person die in peace.

Devin was not providing any peace to the room. If his emotion was coming off him in waves, it was terror and grief. It was constant vigilant prayer for a miracle.

But, in the end, there were no miracles.

As he sat and held his mother's hand, he felt her fingers—already slack under his—somehow relax just a little more. Looking up at the monitor, he saw the last two heartbeats were already spaced too far apart in their little yellow blips. Then the number dropped.

Her heart rate was getting slower and slower. Until at last there was nothing but a line.

Tears poured down his face. He felt Karen's presence in the room. She had told him before that the machines beeped regularly. From the look of them now, alarms were going off, left and right.

Because the world was blurred and he couldn't breathe and his muscles clenched, he barely caught the movement of Karen stepping around the bed. She checked the digital watch she wore on her wrist—something fancy that was probably logging her own heartbeat right now. She noted his mother's time of death and began the tasks at hand, the ones Devin wouldn't have been able to bring himself to do even if he could.

One by one, the machines went blank.

He didn't ask if she was gone. Karen didn't tell him that his mother was dead, or if she did, he didn't see it.

Instead, he folded his hands on the old chenille cover his mother loved, one that she had inherited from her own grandmother. He hated it. Always thought it was horribly old fashioned, but now he put his forehead down on the edge of the bed and finally cried.

CHAPTER SIXTY-NINE

Luisa showed up for the funeral. How could she not? Though Ms. James had only been there for a small portion of her life, Devin and his mother had played a huge role in the person she had become afterward.

She saw the entire staff from Jade River Sanctuary, including the four dogs who were about to graduate. They were well enough trained by now—their people would be showing up in a few weeks—that it wasn't a concern. Luisa thought it was possible that Ms. James had requested their presence. The thought made her smile, at least a little.

Brandy came up and hugged her and said, "I'm so sorry." Though whether that meant because Luisa's boyfriend had lost his mother or because Luisa had lost a brief shining light from her own life, she didn't know. She didn't know if anyone here—besides Devin, of course—truly understood how his mother had provided a haven for her when she'd needed it so much.

Su came up to her and signed her condolences. In fact, most of them spoke to her in ASL. Only Beck and Roz used English words to express their sympathies. Roz hugged her but held on a little longer than she should.

After a moment, Luisa understood why she chose to speak. There had been an interpreter throughout the service and now at the gravesite. A handful of Jacinda's friends from the local Deaf Community Center had showed up. Also, it was for Devin.

Ms. James's sister Laura, whom Luisa had never met, gave her eulogy in spoken English. She talked to Devin afterward using the interpreter and Luisa hated the woman just a little bit for not learning the language her nephew spoke. Her own tia had given everything to her when her mother died. It wasn't as if Devin lived several states away. But this woman offered nothing even though he'd been in her life for multiple decades, a good portion of that as a child. She'd simply never bothered to learn to communicate with him.

Luisa had stepped to the side, out of the main circle, not sure she belonged there anyway, but hoping not to interact with the woman. Now Roz nearly cornered her, hugged her, and whispered in her ear.

"If he has another mother, I don't know of it."

It would have been her own tia who would have been Devin's other mother, Luisa thought. She wished she had found Devin before the horrific car accident and the moment that had changed everything. Mama would have loved to have seen him again.

"So I'm his mother now," Roz continued, "Until someone better steps up."

Luisa grinned, tears forming in her eyes, happy that he had people who loved him that much.

It had been a tough day. It had been a tough week, and a tough couple of months. The path before her wasn't easy, but it was workable. Devin's path she wasn't so sure about. She didn't know if he would stay at the Sanctuary now that his mother was gone. That was what had brought him to Charlottesville and the Blue Ridge Mountains in the first place. He might have nothing tying him here now . . .

But Roz still held on, saying to her, "I hope you can find it in your heart to forgive him, because he needs you more than ever."

Luisa tried to give the same reaction she had with Ms. James. *Was this just how Devin's mothers worked?* She offered only a tight smile and a nod, refusing to give full agreement. Devin had abandoned her. She understood that he'd had an impossible choice, but it wasn't one that Luisa had pushed on him. She would have never made him abandon his mother to be there for her.

But he'd made his choice and it hadn't been her.

CHAPTER SEVENTY

It was almost a month later when Roz called him into the office and asked him the question he'd been waiting for.

"I need to know." She leaned forward, waiting. "Are you staying?"

He was glad she'd waited and not asked him right after the funeral. It was something he thought fully through. Roz had afforded him that option, not demanding more, not asking point blank until now.

He'd thought about nothing at all in the weeks after his mother had died. Devin had thrown himself back into training the dogs in the hopes that having something to do would take his mind off it.

But in the evening, when there was nothing else, he felt broken and adrift. He'd left Curie without her human for so long and when he'd come back, he'd been despondent, doing only the bare minimum. He felt guilty for the way he'd left Luisa hanging.

He'd been checking in with her in texts and short, friendly conversations, but nothing more. Something about the way she answered seem to put him in his place. It took him several weeks before he realized that she wasn't reaching out to him. Aside from a few rote, *are you okay?* questions she only answered what he asked and only with short, direct replies. She volunteered nothing.

Though she wasn't *not speaking to him*, he'd lost her. And that broke his heart almost as much as losing his mother did. Maybe more because she was still here, and he couldn't seem to fix it.

Devin stood before Roz now as she sat behind her desk, the large monitor blocking part of his view of her, which she didn't seem to notice. When she signed to him, he saw enough. "If it's okay with you, I'd like to stay."

Her face lit up instantly, smile beaming wide. "I'm so glad that's what you want! You've done wonders for the Sanctuary. If you left, I would have to hire another grant writer and hope that they're as good as you are."

It was good to feel that kind of praise. His mother had always talked him up, told him he was smart when school teachers were often frustrated with his poor English grammar or struggled to give an oral quiz through his interpreter, or just got frustrated by their own failure to communicate.

"It was smart," he told her now, "to have me do half of my work training the dogs."

Before she could ask why, he added, "Because I understand now the way the place works and what the outcomes are. Because of Curie," he motioned to the dog waiting patiently beside him, "I'm able to explain exactly why grants should choose us for their money."

She grinned and laughed. "Honestly, I hadn't thought of that. I just didn't need a full time grant writer, and I definitely needed another dog trainer."

Devin laughed too. It felt good, the humor pushing its way through his system, even as the grief fought back and told him he didn't deserve to be happy. But he tried right now to let the laugh stand.

He'd been in this war for a while. It had been Su who pulled him aside and said, almost out of the blue, "It's okay to be happy and it's okay to have fun. I know you feel guilty about it."

He'd looked at her oddly, as if she were wrong. But she stared him down. "I can see it."

When at last he admitted she was right, and asked how she knew that he needed to hear it, she shook her head softly. Her eyes fell closed, as if remembering something that she wasn't going to share with him. She said only, "Because I know."

He tried to remember that now as his guilt ate at him while he laughed with Roz. "I'm sorry I left you without a trainer for so long."

But she was holding one hand up, palm out, motioning his concern away. It was not the sharp cut his mother liked to give him. "It's okay. I knew when I hired you that losing you for a while was a possibility."

Had she? Devin didn't think he'd told her the full extent of what was happening with his mother. Apparently, she'd figured it out somewhere along the line on her own. So now all he could say was, "Thank you."

She said again, "I am *so glad* that you are staying!" and her relief felt genuine.

He turned with Curie right beside him as he headed out. He was working with the hearing ear dogs now. There was already one person—an adult—who had moved into the first room in the lodge. She had met Vivaldi, who would help her manage her type one diabetes.

Having been out of the loop for a while *and* not speaking the language of the people coming in, Devin continued training the second round of dogs as the others rotated out. It was the first time the Sanctuary was training the people who were meeting their new dogs with another training running in the background.

Only four dogs were in each cohort. They could have

brought more funds in if they had tried more, but Roz said often that she didn't like to stress them all out or maybe fail. Now that he was staying, he wondered how that philosophy was extending to her gamble with hosting the Search and Rescue team.

But it wasn't his to solve, not that he could.

He had several hours of work to do this afternoon. He started to tap out a message to Luisa as he headed to the other side of the compound. Then, halfway through, he erased it.

There was a better way.

CHAPTER SEVENTY-ONE

Luisa looked up as the bell chimed over the door. She expected to see Paul come in, ready for his coffee. But instead, she stopped cold.

They'd had a rush and Craig was out today. She was working the counter alongside her employees. It was the only reason that she locked eyes with Devin James as he came through the door. Just beyond the counter she caught the gray ears of Curie, staying right where her person needed her.

Devin smiled at her as he stepped toward the counter, pulling his phone out. September had to bump into her and apologize, "Sorry, boss!" before Luisa shook herself and went back to her work.

He started to show his phone to Hope, the new worker at the counter. But part of the reason she had hired Hope—what made her application stand out above the others—was that she was already fluent in ASL.

It had taken only a nod from Luisa, and Hope's own experience to recognize that Devin wasn't hearing. Despite him holding out the phone, she fluidly signed, "What can I get you today?"

His smile lit up the whole shop and Luisa tried to ignore it.

She was angry at him, and hurt, and none of that changed that she missed him more than anything.

Helen had started volunteering at a local organization, putting her legal skills to good work. But that meant she wasn't around every afternoon when Luisa got off work or when she needed a friend on the weekend.

Luisa had tried again to make more friends, going out for drinks twice with Mika down the hall. On their first outing, she'd sucked it up and explained that she wasn't actually Gabi Montalvo. Though she was always sick to her stomach with worry before she confessed to someone, Mika seemed to accept the changes with grace and ease. The two had had a wonderful evening together, and Luisa wondered why she'd lived here a whole year and hung out with Mika only a few times. Maybe they could be real friends.

It had to be because she was more open and honest now. She didn't have to hold back, worried that someone would find out and turn her in. That she might have to pick up and disappear. It hadn't happened—her tia had made her theft of Gabi's identification almost air tight. Someone would have had to dig hard to prove she wasn't Gabi Montalvo. But the fear and guilt had always kept a wall between her and everyone else.

Things had shifted.

She knew it in herself and she knew because here was Devin ordering his coffee. He ordered a second one then stepped further along the counter to where she was working one of the machines. She'd chosen to work on the side that faced out into the shop on purpose. It had been to keep an eye on things, to make sure that customers weren't neglected even if the shop was insanely busy.

Now it meant Devin James was right in front of her.

He waited until she looked up from her task and then signed, "Do you get off work soon?"

She'd not been paying attention to the time, so she turned, looking over her shoulder at the clock on the wall. Had he timed it?

"Ten minutes if nothing goes wrong," she said.

He pointed over the counter to where she was making the second cup of coffee. "That one's for you."

She'd noticed it was her usual order. But it wasn't an unusual order in itself, it could have been for someone else. Still, she felt her heart unclench, since she'd been thinking he'd somehow done the asshole move of bringing some new girlfriend here, to her shop.

He hadn't. She was being stupid. So she said, "Thank you," and handed his cup over the counter as she finished it.

With a small nod, he took his one drink and he and the dog headed to a table. He sat inside this time, though she knew he preferred sitting outdoors. Maybe he was keeping an eye on her.

Did he not remember they had a back door? She could easily escape without him knowing. But she didn't.

Fifteen minutes later, back in her tiny office, she hung her apron on the hook on the wall. Her name tag stayed tacked in the corner, the one that Greg had grumbled about having to get reprinted for her. That was ridiculous—they fabricated the tags for workers who stayed only a few weeks or even a few days or hours.

But she loved it. The silly little metal bit that finally said *Luisa*.

But the name tag wasn't the thing making her need a few deep breaths. Opening the desk drawer, she pulled out her purse and checked her phone just to burn a little bit of time. When she headed out the front, he was still there at the table.

Standing, he faced her. "Can we talk?"

It had been mean making him wait. Because now she said, "I have to go to my community service."

He knew she'd been sentenced to four-hundred hours and that she had two years to complete it. "Can I come?"

She frowned at him. It was an odd question. Because community service needed to match the crime committed, she'd been assigned to help out at a juvenile facility. She was specifically working with kids who'd committed identity theft—stolen credit cards and IDs and such. It was her job to help them make restitution to the people they'd stolen from.

She also knew that she would be judged by how well they did when they were released. The counselors had her talking to the kids about legitimate career options and how to prepare for them. She was even considering hiring one of them at the shop.

"I don't think you can come," she told Devin. Surely with a juvenile facility—and all the paperwork she'd signed to get in—the kids' identities were protected. *The irony wasn't lost on her.*

"Okay." He said it with ease, as though he hadn't sat and waited for her.

Curie followed along at his feet as he walked with her to her car. "When do you finish?"

"I have four hours this afternoon," she commented. She expected to get done around seven.

"Can I take you out to dinner afterwards?"

"Yes." The word fell out of her mouth without her permission. She missed him so much that she hadn't even thought about it. Just . . . *yes.*

For the first time in a long time, it felt as if Devin was actually seeing her.

CHAPTER SEVENTY-TWO

I t had been difficult for Devin to wait. He tooled around town, not quite willing to drive back up the mountain. He found a park and threw a tennis ball for Curie while he waited for Luisa to finish with her community service. He didn't want to get in the way of that.

It had been difficult to act normal when he was parked at the restaurant and watched her climb out of her car. And it was difficult to tell himself that her wanting to meet him at the restaurant didn't necessarily mean his little date would go well.

It had been difficult to keep his hands still while they ordered drinks and an appetizer and food. Difficult to make small talk with a woman he knew so intimately. He could see in her eyes that she wondered why he'd asked her out if they were just going to offer trite little conversations.

Then, with the drinks and appetizer now sitting between them, almost untouched, it was just as difficult to lift his hands and say what needed to be said.

But as soon as he signed, "I don't know how to tell you how sorry I am," the weight began to lift from his shoulders.

Luisa paused for a moment. He could see her figuring out

how to respond as she grabbed a piece off the sampler tray and took a thoughtful bite before saying, "For what?" Then she hastily added, "Is this just a general blanket apology or—"

Devin shook his head, cutting her off. He knew. "What you went through was terrifying. I'm sorry I wasn't there when you needed me." He saw the change in her expression. The subtle tensing of her muscles beneath her skin, because his apology only acknowledged what he'd done not why or how or . . .

There were so many things to say that it couldn't all possibly fit into one dinner. And he didn't know if he would have more than one dinner to say them.

She ate another bite, one hand on her food as the other asked him, "Do you regret it?"

What a terrible question. There were no straight answers to any of it. He tried to be honest. "Yes and no. I regret that I wasn't there for you. I regret that so much. I knew you had Helen and knew your lawyer was good—"

"Did you *know* that?" she interrupted him.

That was valid. He'd never met the woman. "That's what you told me. There were a few times I asked, and you said Helen was going with you. You said that you really liked Maria and that she was very supportive."

For a moment, everything stopped. Luisa looked at him and he didn't know if she was thinking or blaming or questioning his choices. Any of those were fair, but had she wanted him to read her mind?

"Am I not supposed to trust what you told me?" he asked.

A small nod was his only concession. "Yes, you are. But having Helen and Maria there wasn't the same as having you. I needed *you.*"

"I know." That part hurt the most, but the hurt was his own doing. "I don't know if you can ever forgive me for that."

She didn't say she could. But he wasn't willing to give up.

Maybe it wasn't the right tactic, but he dove in anyway. "You lied for twenty years. You didn't straighten out the record because it would have hurt your tia. I understand needing to give back to the women who sacrificed for us. So I stayed in the end."

"I know." This time she seemed to concede the point. "There was so much all at once. Two massive crises and I don't blame you for choosing your mother."

Devin saw her flinch as she said it. The next part was just as bad.

"I do understand that no matter what the decision was on my case, I wasn't going to die from it. But you didn't come once!"

He blinked, jerking back almost as if she had slapped him. "But I did." She looked at him disbelieving, so he added. "It was not enough, and I know that, but I did come."

It was difficult to explain because he hadn't been there for any of her case. "The first day, I tried to come. I told myself I could stay and sit for several hours. You told me you weren't the first on the docket. I tried to figure out when would be the right time to show up. I wanted to be there when you were up, but I couldn't stay all day, waiting.

"So a few hours after you started I got in my car and I headed there and . . ." Just the memory shot him with a small part of the adrenaline he'd felt at the time. "Then I got a message from the home nurse that she couldn't balance my mother's oxygen and that she'd taken her to the emergency room. I thought she was going to die. So, I turned around before I even made it to the courthouse."

Luisa blinked at him, and it was his fault that this was the first she was hearing this. He hadn't told her any of it. He'd shut down so completely, pulling up the drawbridge on his castle and leaving his moat to keep everyone away, including Luisa.

He told her, "I didn't want to burden you." She could probably see it on his face—the feeling that had been a stupid choice. But he was learning that it was better not to leave things unsaid. "That was stupid, and I see it now. I didn't then."

When Luisa didn't say anything—not that he wasn't stupid or that she had forgiven him—he continued. "They sent my mother home that night, and your second day in court was just a few days later. I made it that time."

He was proud of that. But she hadn't known he was there—which was also likely his fault for not telling her. "The second day you told me about, I sat in the back for three hours—"

"I didn't see you and I looked!"

Was it an accusation? He didn't know.

CHAPTER SEVENTY-THREE

H e'd come? Luisa hadn't seen him, but it would have meant everything to know he was there.

Her eyes blurred, but she could still make out his words. "There was a crowd, I was in the back. You were wearing a new sage green suit . . . And the pearls your tia gave you from your mother."

Luisa smiled softly at him. It was either that or cry. He was right and he'd remembered when she'd told him offhandedly that the pearls had been something her mother had brought with her when they left Peru.

She was gazing up at the ceiling as she fought the tears, so she wasn't looking at him as she signed, "I wish I had known."

When she finally got herself together enough to look at him, he shook his head and shrugged as if he could brush all their mistakes away like dust. "I didn't say anything because I didn't get to see your case. I got called away again."

He rambled as though telling her the whole story would make it more real. But all it did was convey his frustration to her. "The pharmacy didn't have the morphine my mother needed, and she was about to run out. I had to straighten out the prescription and pick it up."

It hadn't quite hit her until then that they'd missed so much these last hard weeks. He hadn't told her what was really going on. She'd answered his attempts to find out about her with only exactly what he asked. The only things she'd volunteered to him were her court dates.

Fuck. She'd been an idiot, too. She tried to keep her thoughts practical and not be swayed by how good it felt to sit across a table from him again. How her heart swelled that Devin had actually been there, even if she hadn't seen him. *He had come.*

"I thought you spent the whole time sitting beside your mother while she slept."

"I wish I could have," he sighed. "But I paid the bills and I talked back and forth with the hospitals about the bills— through TTY or email or . . . I went there and talked with the billing department with an interpreter. I talked with her doctors about her medication. Every adjustment means a trip to the pharmacy."

Luisa almost blurted out, "You can just call it in!" But suddenly it hit her. He couldn't. She blinked her own stupidity away. Despite the time she spent with him, she was still missing a lot. He couldn't use the voice automated system. Of course not.

"Doesn't the pharmacy have TTY?" she asked, referring to the phone system that allowed typed messages back and forth— it was old school but pharmacies didn't have other ways to have a quick conversation.

He shook his head. "The TTY is a national line, so it doesn't get me to my mom's pharmacy. If I go in, sometimes there's video remote interpreters, but it takes a while to set it up."

Luisa rolled her eyes at the ridiculousness of it all and at her own ignorance. She truly had thought that he was just sitting in a chair with a sleeping woman rather than sitting in the courtroom with her.

"It was a lot?" she asked now as she began to understand all that she had missed.

"It's a full time job," he replied.

"I'm sorry."

"It's not your fault." He waved her away.

"No," Luisa protested, "I'm sorry that I didn't see how much effort it was to take care of your mother. And it was a lot more because you're Deaf."

He nodded looking over her shoulder as if he hated to acknowledge that. "I don't think of myself as disabled. I'm fine. I live a great life. I'm educated. I have friends. I have a great job."

She smiled at him. All those things were true and most of them were because of how much his mother had made sure he wasn't held back by other people's lack of understanding.

"But I know the world sees me that way." He laughed. "I mean, I qualified for a service dog!" He pointed down at Curie who looked up and barked softly. Luisa laughed, too.

Devin thought for a moment. "I don't think of myself as disabled until I have to interact with people who aren't prepared for me. And most aren't."

Luisa thought about it then, maybe truly for the first time. How frustrated she could be dealing with her own tedious life chores. How irritating it could be to wait in line at the pharmacy. Sometimes everything worked, but just the idea that she couldn't call the pharmacy and check to see if her prescription was ready or ask for information about it was something she hadn't considered.

As close as she was to Devin, she hadn't been around him when he experienced that. He wasn't running his errands in front of her or paying his bills.

He was thoughtful for a moment and then told her, "When I got Curie, when I was first at the Sanctuary as a service dog recipient, there was a woman there in a wheelchair. Her name was Talia. She told me that there's a tax on being disabled."

Luisa frowned at the term, but Devin quickly explained.

"She said she has a special car for her wheelchair—which costs more. Because her car costs more, her insurance costs more. She's a baker, but because of her wheelchair, she needs special counters. And because most people don't use them, they're not high demand, so they—"

Luisa caught on. "They cost more." Then she asked, "Do you think you pay more?"

"Not money." Devin was confident in his answer. "My payment is time. The time it takes to type out what I need on my phone and for them to type it back. I *am* incredibly grateful for that. The old timers at the community center talk about carrying whiteboards or the little gray tablets that kids would have so they could write back and forth. This is faster, but it's not like talking.

"I have to go into the pharmacy to talk to the pharmacist. I wait in line, and then I have to wait for the video interpreter to be available."

It hit Luisa again then that caring for his mother would have been a monumental task for anyone. But for Devin in was multiplied.

She wanted to stay mad at him. She wanted to nurture the hard little kernel in her heart that said he'd made a decision for his mother instead of her. She'd been so angry—hurt, really—that he hadn't come to support her on her days in court, and yet he had. Of the three days, he'd made it once, and tried twice.

Her anger hadn't accounted for the mistakes she'd made too. She hadn't given Devin enough credit, but . . . still, there was a wound, and she began to pick at it. "If I had been deported, you never would have heard from me again."

He took a deep breath. His eyes glanced away. But when he spoke, he stunned her all over again.

CHAPTER SEVENTY-FOUR

Luisa's fingers clenched together tightly under the table, but he probably saw it anyway. She knew she shouldn't still be mad at him. She could hear Ms. James and even Roz Binkley telling her that she should forgive him, but the hurt wasn't gone yet.

Then Devin told her, "No. I checked! You probably would have been held for a few days and probably offered a phone call. Even if you hadn't been, I know where Helen lives. I would have found her, and we would have found you."

He'd made a plan? She was so caught up in her own fear at what could happen to her that she'd not thought beyond getting loaded on a plane and dumped in a foreign-to-her country. But he was right. Helen wouldn't have let her disappear, even in South America.

Devin was telling her he wouldn't have either.

"I didn't have a lot of spare time," he told her, "But I found a local lawyer who signs. I was ready to retain her if needed to help with your case to get you back into the country. And I renewed my passport. I haven't used it in forever, so it won't get here for two more weeks." He was rambling, but she didn't care.

He hadn't abandoned her. "I didn't know then how long my mother would hold on, but I promise you I was not going to *never see you again.*"

She felt the tug at the corners of her mouth, then behind her eyes. Her throat sealed shut. She tried not to cry. He'd done so much more than she gave him credit for.

Luisa fought back the tears. She was not going to cry in a restaurant. At least they were a little off to the side. The server said it was so no one would trip over Curie.

She'd been mad and scared. She hadn't liked his choice to not be with her and, because of that, she had basically shut him out. She'd only offered him court dates. Not her restless nights. Not the terror that ate away at her gut. The fear she denied to everyone, but mostly to herself.

With hindsight came clarity. She'd issued her court dates to him as a test to see if he would choose her over his mother. It had been a shitty thing to ask of anyone. She understood what it was to be the only child of a woman who was willing to go to great lengths, to sacrifice so much, to protect that child and give them the best possible future.

But she did not understand what it was to watch that parent die for years. To go through phases of hope and despair and to have to make the terrible decisions that Devin had made.

It was her turn to apologize. Right then, the food arrived. It came with hot plates and instructions from the server. She'd always noticed, but she catalogued it this time. The server spoke to her and expected her to relay instructions to Devin. Devin was only offered a small smile. The server knew he couldn't communicate with her boyfriend and he didn't seem to want to try.

This time she was livid, even if she didn't know what to actually do about it.

When the server left, she looked across the table. Despite all she'd let go of, there was still a space between them, a vibrating wall of anger and hurt and apology.

No longer solid, it finally offered her a glimpse through to the other side.

She motioned to Devin getting his attention before he dug into his food. "I'm sorry, too."

"What for?"

She almost laughed at him. He seemed not to notice that he had thrown her words back at her. "I was angry with you. I was mad that you chose your mother."

He started to frown, but she waved her hand at him, making him wait. "Looking back, it's stupid. You should have chosen your mother. She was dying. She was your mother. As much as I love you—" She hadn't meant to admit it, but there it was. "I was not a guarantee."

Though she felt in her heart that she would always love him, that part of what she felt was unconditional, the relationship they had wasn't. She'd been so mad and he'd been so caught up in grief that they'd taken themselves away from each other. All romantic relationships were—or should be conditional—even if the love wasn't.

"If I didn't tell you things that you needed to know, it was because I was mad."

He nodded. "I was so scared. I just shut down."

"Me, too." It was hard to admit how good it felt to see her own contributions to the problem. Those, she could fix.

The food in front of her smelled fantastic, but she couldn't process her hunger. Her stomach growled, but she couldn't acknowledge it. There were other more important things to take care of first.

"Do you want there to still be an us?" She asked it, looping her fingers together, showing their connectedness in a way that couldn't be said in English but was perfect in ASL.

There was no hesitation as he nodded. "More than anything.

That's why I came to the coffee shop today, so I could ask you out tonight. I want to mend this."

Luisa took a deep breath, the oxygen filling her lungs for the first time in months. But it still wasn't the deepest, freest kind of breath she could take. Not yet.

Relieved and scared at the same time, she was still frightened that everything would fall apart. Ready now, with all the crises out of the way, and open to a future between them, she was still struggling to take the first step. "So how do we get there?"

CHAPTER SEVENTY-FIVE

I t was Saturday again.

Beck still fought against the butterflies he felt each time he left the Sanctuary.

Hallie had been a surprise and a delight he'd not expected. But didn't the philosophers like to say people found things when they weren't looking?

No gift today.

Though he wanted to shower her with everything he could afford and many things he couldn't, he didn't want to be just a gift-giver. He needed to know in the end that she loved him for him.

A puppy. He kept thinking what a wonderful gift that would be. But not today.

Some people couldn't handle the responsibility of a dog, but he didn't think that was Hallie.

The closer he got, the more his stomach fluttered. His nerves flared. The more he feared today would be the day he screwed it up. But he had to remind himself that he'd thought that each time they had plans and so far he hadn't.

He parked on the street and took a deep breath, getting out

with empty hands for once. But the front door flew open and she smiled at him, so happy that he was there. The butterflies dispersed, and he knew that he loved her.

"Beck!" she called out as she threw herself into his hug.

His heart settled into an easy rhythm. But he still wondered, when was he going to be able to tell her to call him something else?

CHAPTER SEVENTY-SIX

D evin rolled over and watched as Luisa slept.

In the corner, he saw the shadow the moonlight cast on Curie, sleeping, curled in a ball on her bed. Assured his furry companion was sleeping well, Devin rolled back to Luisa.

She'd squirmed a little in her sleep when he'd moved away. Now she settled in, naked skin against his, her spine pressed into his front, his arm under her head, her hair streaming across his pillow.

He lifted one finger and traced her shoulder blade until he found the scar there. The same one he had. He couldn't see it in the dim light, but he could sense it against the delicate silk of her dark skin.

Should he tell her it was their one month anniversary? One month since he'd gotten his shit together and gone to the coffee shop. One month since he'd apologized. And so had she.

He'd not expected that.

In his dreams, they simply kissed and made up. In reality, it had been a little wary at first, they had been hard pressed to trust each other again. They'd both failed each other. But they'd promised not to do it again.

Luisa had suggested a code word that would mean they had to think hard and tell the whole truth. He'd been there at the beginning of the week when she'd started work as a regional manager, overseeing the old shop with a brand new manager and a new shop that was opening. A third shop was under construction, and Luisa would be in charge of that too.

She'd been so excited on her first day, smiling at him in the mirror as she'd gotten ready at his place. So he'd said it. "Watermelon."

A stupid word, but her face had transformed. "I'm scared I'll screw it up. I'm in charge of *managers*."

He nodded. "That's reasonable. It's a big promotion, but you're really good at this."

"I've just been winging it!" she complained, and he'd been afraid she would cry and go in on her first day with red eyes.

"And your *winging it* is more than good enough to run three shops. These places make a lot of money, they wouldn't put you in if they didn't have faith in you. So you should, too." He'd watched as she'd calmed down and the smile returned.

Today was Luisa's first day off after the promotion. She needed the downtime, the week had been stressful. He'd asked Roz for the same. While the last week had been crazy for Luisa, the last two had been for Devin.

He'd done no grant writing as the cohort of hearing ear dogs met their people. For two full weeks, he'd been on-call twenty-four/seven. As the only native signer, he helped when the two young teens or even the adults had a question. When the questions got complex, he was the only one who understood without another layer of translation.

Even Roz had exclaimed, "I thought my ASL was good until there was an entire lodge of people having conversations." Devin had grinned at her. That was a normal step in the process of getting fluent, but he couldn't argue when the whole of the Sanctuary was working toward it.

His heart had broken for Shandy, a thirteen year old whose parents' sign skill was passable at best. *How had they not learned more?* He silently thanked his mother, even as he hung out with a kid just so she could be with someone who could have real conversations with her. Lisa, one of the Deaf adults, getting her second hearing ear dog after losing her first a year ago, had told him she'd grown up like Shandy, and offered to be the girl's face-time-pal.

He'd breathed easier as Shandy left with her parents and her new dog Shelley, heading back to the place where no one quite understood everything she wanted and needed to say. But the lodge was empty now—no new cohort coming in since the Search and Rescue team would arrive next week. Beck and Roz still seemed at odds about it, but Devin wasn't letting that get to him.

He was looking forward to spending his day off with Luisa: The woman he'd found again and then again. The one person he trusted above all others now.

Devin didn't know when exactly it had happened, but they were *here*, somehow better than before. He knew now when he was getting tied up in himself, she knew she should push. He knew that if she was afraid, he could press her, and she would answer honestly.

He didn't fall back asleep, but the sun was almost up, and he wasn't surprised that Luisa woke with the first rays through the edges of the curtains. She wouldn't have to be up at four a.m. anymore, but she hadn't adjusted yet.

Rolling over, she looked at him through sleepy lids, then leaned in to kiss him.

He'd been intending to go for a hike, but he knew something she didn't. The kiss seared through him, spiking his nerves and putting a flare in the center of his chest. Letting her seduce him first thing in the morning was easy.

She kissed him, down his neck and across his chest. The heat flooded him, making him hard and she didn't take long before she was riding him, her back arched, his fingers gripping her hips.

He couldn't think as he let himself go, coming hard as she bucked against his touch.

This was better than before. They'd been broken, but fixing it made it better. When had it happened? He couldn't put a finger on when, only knew that it was here now. She fell lazily forward onto him, her breath coming in heavy waves, the feel of her breasts pressed against him as soothing as it was sexy.

He didn't know how long it was before she pushed her hair out of her face and asked, "Are we still going on that hike or was this our exercise?"

Laughing, Devin replied. "Hike. Curie needs to walk, and we should go."

He watched as she got ready, wondering if she had any idea what was to come. She could read him sometimes like an open book, and sometimes he surprised her. When his shoes were tied, and water bottles weighed down his pockets, he snapped Curie's leash into place and headed out.

"I love that we can walk right out your door and onto an amazing trail," Luisa told him, a bit over her shoulder as she moved ahead. He'd said hike and she was now committed.

He loved that too. It was a bit of a distance between her apartment and here, but they were making it work. She was burning through her community service hours as fast as she could, trying to be a model citizen, and knowing she couldn't take her next steps until she finished it.

There was nothing he could do to help with that except support her. He made dinner when he was at her place and she drove up and ate with the family at the Sanctuary a lot of nights so she didn't have to cook. He'd asked Roz about the extra mouth to feed, and his boss had simply declared that all were welcome. *How had he gotten so lucky to find a place like this?*

The answer, of course, was that it was his mother again. Even gone, she'd left him with so much. He hadn't been able to do it while she was alive, but he had to believe she was watching as he tapped Luisa on the shoulder to get her to stop and turn around.

"Another snake?" she was asking it even as she looked frantically into the trees on either side.

"No!" he was laughing, but he hadn't realized that's exactly where they were. He pointed at Curie to show her the dog was calm and not on alert at all.

"Okay." He could see her breathe out in relief.

"So, I know you can apply to become a citizen after you finish your service and your record is expunged, but . . ." he took a deep breath, but nothing changed. He was ready for this, and he hoped she was, too. "How would you like to become a citizen by marrying one?"

He tried for a classic, dropping to one knee, opening the ring box that he'd hidden from her for three days and stuffed in his back pocket this morning. Devin had been grateful when she'd wanted to walk in front of him and hadn't noticed the bulk. But kneeling here like this tied his hands. He couldn't talk, only wait.

She looked at him, eyes wide, expression concerned, not happy.

Well, fuck.

"I— I—" She paced a tight circle. Not a good sign.

Devin tried to keep his dignity intact as he stood up and had to brush dirt off his knee. This was not going the way he planned.

When she looked at him again, she was almost frantic. Her expression struck terror into his heart though he tried to tell himself surely he hadn't just fucked up royally.

"Thank you." She said it with a tight smile.

Not good.

"But I want to earn my own citizenship. I don't need . . ."

"Shit, no!" He closed the box at the last minute, afraid he'd fling the very expensive ring into the underbrush as he frantically tried to explain. "That's not . . . I *want* to marry you. Will you marry me?"

He *had* fucked that up royally.

She stood with her hands on her hips, worry in her eyes. Then, lifting her hand, she said one word, "Watermelon."

Oh thank God. She would believe him. "I guess I thought maybe you would marry me for citizenship even if not for the real thing. But I want to marry you. I want to spend my life with you. I had to find you three times, and I never want to lose you again." Then he said what he knew he had to. "Watermelon."

A stupid word, but it put a question on her face.

"Can you wait until I get my own citizenship?"

"If that's what you want." It would be a long time. Would she want to wait to get engaged, too? He could keep the ring . . . somewhere safe . . . somewhere—

"Then yes." She smiled at him, her eyes wide and wet. She held out her left hand and he had to scramble to open the box again. For a split second he was afraid the ring was already gone, tossed away with his petrified signs. But no, it was right where it should be. And he was right where he should be as he slid it onto her finger.

"No date yet," she signed, the stone winking in the morning sunlight.

"That's fine," he signed back, a smile on his face that he thought nothing would wipe away . . . until she threw her arms around him and kissed him.

His world had shifted. He wouldn't get pulled under his own grief again, because he wouldn't be alone in it again. She'd said yes.

He wanted to tell his mother that he'd found the great love of his life, that he was home. But he would tell Luisa.

Thank you for reading! I love romances with real love and believable characters, and I hope you found all that in these pages. I want to fall in love right along with the characters, and I do, while I'm writing it.

About Savannah

I started writing when I was eight--I hand wrote an 80-page novella that I believed to be (adult) romantic suspense. I'm proud to say, I've gotten a lot better since then. I've grown up to be a nerd at heart! I love neuroscience and people watching, and if you look, you'll find some of that in each Savannah Kade book. Most days you'll find me in my office, looking out my window at a handful of the neighbor's cows, or watching my dogs or my cat roam the backyard.

Follow me, find me, ask me questions! I would love to hear from you.
www.SavannahKade.com
Savannah@SavannahKade.com

.